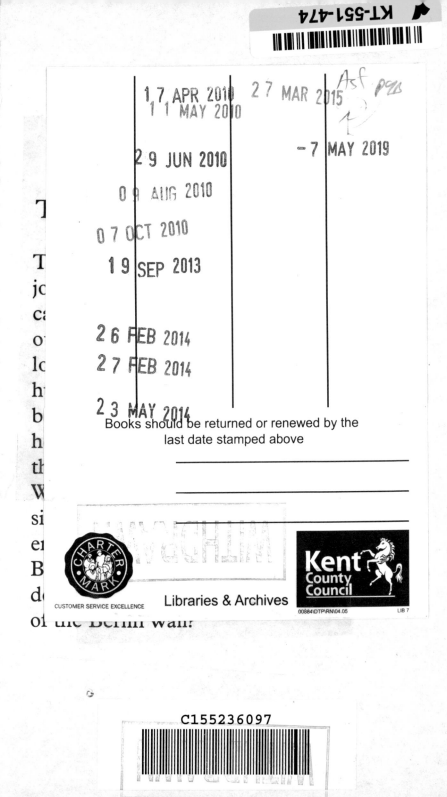

THE MAN ON THE LANDING

Tony, a journalist who has left his wife and job, becomes infatuated with the mysterious calls made by Peter Kraslo over the phone beside his bedroom in a Marylebone lodging-house. When Kraslo makes a hurried escape from the police, Tony takes beautiful refugee Nina under his wing, but he can never entirely fathom the hold that the sinister Mr Winton has over her. Was it Winton who lured the French night-club singer Louise to lure Tony to a nightmare encounter at the British Grand Prix at Brands Hatch? How has Tony become so deeply enmeshed in violence on both sides of the Berlin Wall?

THE MAN ON THE LANDING

THE MAN ON THE LANDING

by

Fred Jones

Dales Large Print Books
Long Preston, North Yorkshire,
BD23 4ND, England.

British Library Cataloguing in Publication Data.

Jones, Fred
    The man on the landing.

    A catalogue record of this book is
    available from the British Library

    ISBN   978-1-84262-735-8 pbk

First published in Great Britain in 1984 by Jonathan Cape Ltd.

Copyright © 1984 by Fred Jones

Cover illustration © Valentino Sani by arrangement with
Arcangel Images

The moral right of the author has been asserted

Published in Large Print 2010 by arrangement with
Fred Jones, care of Watson, Little Ltd.

Dales Large Print is an imprint of Library Magna Books Ltd.

Printed and bound in Great Britain by
T.J. (International) Ltd., Cornwall, PL28 8RW

For Jean and Chris and to the memory
of Anton and Martin

I

Every time he picked up the phone on the landing outside my door I would stay very quiet to listen. His accent was from somewhere east of Vienna, or north or south of it, his voice was soft and sympathetic, and he was infinitely patient. I suppose I would have listened anyway – who doesn't? But my listening was an anti-social habit cultivated when I was a newspaper reporter, trying to catch something I needed to hear but was not meant to hear, or just listening anyway, even when I didn't need to hear: to people on underground trains, on railway stations, in airport terminals, in pubs, in the street, anywhere.

But the man outside my door had me hooked for more particular reasons. There was the time he spoke, anxiously and with great urgency, about the travel arrangements they still hadn't made. For whom? It was something to do with Nina, I gathered, after listening through half-a-dozen conversations that followed. He talked about Nina very often, but not just about Nina – there were all these other women. If it wasn't a woman, or women, he was talking about it, was a woman he was talking to.

One of them I had spoken to myself when I'd answered the coin-operated phone that the landlady had installed on the landing in this grubby and rather seedy terraced house that I lived in, in Marylebone. Could it have been Nina, or was Nina, as I imagined, still beyond the Iron Curtain? Was Mr Krasko in? she had asked, in a voice as sympathetic and patient as his, and even softer. And I had run up the stairs to knock on his door and fetch him down.

So that was Mr Krasko. I had seen him shopping in the High Street in slightly choosey bachelor fashion, picking out two or three tomatoes, a jar of sweet and sour gherkins, a round of Camembert, to put into his battered briefcase, or carrying an unwrapped French loaf under his arm. Not quite intense but always preoccupied, pale and, as they say, sensitive-looking, with thinning hair, he should have been a poet or someone equally unworldly.

After I answered the phone for him he would greet me when we passed on the stairs, and of course he knew now where my room was. But it didn't seem to inhibit him on the phone, talking just outside someone's door, as it would have inhibited me. Nina and the travel arrangements still came up from time to time, and there were almost endless patient unravellings of misunderstandings that had developed on Saturday night or Wednesday, at dinner or after dinner, or on the way home from the movies or the pub. Strange, though, that after several weeks of it I still hadn't any real idea of what Mr Krasko did. His was not only one-way telephone talk. From all that I could make of it, it might also be in code.

I was a new boy at the terrace house, almost a hiding place for me among small streets and mews, yet not far from the High Street with The Keeler and The Old Rising Sun, The Baker and Oven and The Prince Regent, The King's Head and The Queen's Head, The Golden Eagle and The Prince Alfred and a few other pubs all close enough to be my local. It made my kind of life agreeably varied. We called The Devonshire Arms The Keeler, of course, because it was where Christine used to drink with the Russian, across the street from her flat.

Call me Philby, if you like, though Alf Prufrock might be better – for, like Prufrock, 'I am not Prince Hamlet, nor was meant to be.' Besides, I'm not a spy, double or single, and if I was hiding from anyone it was only from my wife, and I didn't think she would come looking for me. But wasn't it Philby they told that story about, how he walked out of his office one lunchtime and never came back? That's the little bit of Philby in me. I used to think of it every day, going unwillingly back to my office from the pints and round of cheese in the pub and coming back home at night.

There was nothing I wanted to do more than get right away, and now, cowardly, while Jill was away in Dublin, I'd done it. I'd split the three thousand quid that we had saved towards a country cottage – half for her, half for me – and left a note propped against the coffee pot in our Maida Vale flat, just like suicides do in the movies. And with more money in my wallet than I'd ever had before to spend as I liked, I had walked across to Marylebone, a mile and a half away, and from among the cards in a shop window for Swedish massage and lost and strayed cats I had picked out the seedy bedsitter.

Unless I believed what I wanted to believe about Mr Krasko, my new life wasn't, after a month, turning out to be very romantic. I had thought I wouldn't bother to tell my office that I would not be back, but I did. I rang the first morning with a story about having to take a long rest. Then I went back to the double bed I had all to myself and enjoyed the incredible luxury of going to sleep in it lying diagonally, with, all around me, unoccupied space that I could roll into if I wanted to. I woke and wondered where I would go to abroad after I got tired of drinking before lunch, walking in Regent's Park and feeding the ducks, and eating and sleeping whenever I felt like it – which was all I planned to do for a week or two.

Perhaps I'd have another look at Berlin, which for a man brought up in a political household was still the most exciting place I had been to. After that I would make, in reverse, the journey I'd made last time – across East Germany to Warnemünde, over the Baltic, and up to Copenhagen and those beautiful Danish women. Alone, staying at the cheap kind of hotels I liked best, and eating self-service, I could last quite a while on fifteen hundred quid – if I didn't drink too much.

The phone on the landing began to ring. It couldn't be for me. Even the office didn't know my number. But as it went on ringing I had begun to think I should answer it when a door opened somewhere above and someone ran down the stairs. I heard the receiver come off the hook and a man's voice, and as I listened I knew that he must be talking to a woman. That was the moment, on my very first morning of freedom, when I began to get interested in Mr Krasko.

The walkout on my wife wasn't altogether unpremeditated, and I had a feeling that she wouldn't greatly regret it so long as I kept the promises that I'd made in that letter propped against the coffee pot. Our time together had eaten up the years from late youth to early middle age – which was what thirty-eight was beginning to feel like. At the start we'd been obsessively fond of each other, counting in agonising minutes the agonising hours that we were apart. We shared quite a few interests. We liked much of the same kind of reading: Chekhov plays, Thurber, early Eliot – things like that. It all sounds a bit old-fashioned. We liked movies and took them seriously. We specially liked to travel abroad together. Some weekends we went climbing. We'd both grown up with left-wing politics.

Jill had been a very good secretary: that was how I had come to meet her, when I was a reporter and she looked after my news editor. We shared a few friends around the office, but I should have taken more notice of her liking for some people I detested: trendies whom I thought shallow and pretentious. I used to see and, yes, hear them in the pub, think how welcome they were to each other's company, feel glad that I didn't have to know them. Still, I go around feeling glad that I don't have to know most people.

None of the cracks in the foundations of our enormous liking for one another showed up badly enough to stop us getting married, though we both realised afterwards that we'd seen them. What Jill hated most about me was this distaste for most people, though she recognized my devotion to those I did like, as I recognised hers.

When we got married I began to see how hard it was never to have a really private life, but I got used to that, too. We enjoyed it in bed together, and fulfilled one another in that physical sense. Jill wanted a child more than I did, but I learned to want one and was tender about it. Even so, after it was born and before she brought it home, I'd lie awake at night more scared of the physical business of caring for it than I had ever been of any other responsibility.

I still think the first weeks of being a father can be rather alarming. But is anything else so satisfying as being a father or a mother? I still think it's the greatest thing that life, that skinflint, offers you. When I remember Peter waking us before we wanted to be woken in the morning and crawling in between us, or going off with us on expeditions, I think I was happy then, if I have ever been happy.

Then, just before he was three, he was killed by a car. He had been taken for a walk by one of the neighbours' children and had run on to the road after a ball. I was sure the car driver was going too fast, but then I'm sure that nearly all car drivers go too fast all the time. This one, though, was going too fast to stop quickly in a busy street where many children went. That was unforgivable.

What does it convey if I say that Jill and I were numb for months? It seems now that we didn't think about anything else and seemed hardly to talk about anything else. What does it convey if I say that we were a great comfort to one another? Then how could I have walked out on Jill, who had gone through all that with me?

For a start, she found that she couldn't have another child: no one's fault. For quite a while that held us together. We both liked music, and at home, and even at concerts, it was a great comfort. In the summer there was the sea and the sand; and we would always have our Continental holiday. It was on one of those that we'd gone to Copenhagen and come back through Berlin.

Of course my roving eye didn't help. I've always noticed every pretty girl and nice figure, and she noticed that I noticed. Sometimes she mentioned it. It wasn't that I slept around. What I missed most was Jill's affection. After the early passionate days we were more like very good friends who got along well in bed. So if affection was on offer elsewhere I couldn't say no, which didn't help what was left of our marriage after Peter was killed.

Another fault, on my side, was my drinking. After the early, foolish years I seldom got drunk, but there was never a day when I didn't drink to make life bearable, or a bit more dramatic than it would otherwise have been, or, sometimes, just because I enjoyed it.

16

Then, for Jill, my unsociability became harder and harder to take. She thought of my office life as a gay social whirl and wanted us to have people in at nights so that she could have her share. I always said that she had her days to do what she liked with. In the end she took a job and started her own gay social whirl, with the shallow kind of people she had never been able to see through, as I reckoned I could. They had interests that went along with their shallowness – all the modern fashions in music and the other arts – and these became Jill's interests. She didn't, so far as I could see, have any interest in bedding down with any of her new friends, and I don't think she did. She'd always been the kind of person who would have had to tell me. Or so I believed.

But what is a marriage without children? What is there, without children, to stop you growing apart – so far apart that the things that brought you together in the first place seem only a nostalgic memory? If I hadn't done anything about it, perhaps Jill would have. Living together had become not much more than a habit, and not a very good one.

Our values, I thought, a bit smugly, had become more materialistic than mine would ever have been if I'd been alone. The bank balance and the modern furniture and the holiday cottage in the future were all part of it. Thinking about it while Jill was in Dublin, enjoying having the bed to myself and the luxury of guilt-free nights at the pub, I decided to do what, probably, we both wanted to do.

II

It was the end of June, hot, thirsty weather, and I was spending more money on liquor than on anything else. I was back to my easy Continental habits: rolls and cheese and coffee in my room for breakfast, a cheap, solid meal out in the middle of the day, generally in a pub, a sandwich in the evening at the start of two or three hours of leisurely drinking. It was pleasant at first but became less and less satisfying.

Lying in the sun in Regent's Park after I'd given the last of my stale bread to the ducks, I would watch the vapour trail of a big jet running up the sky. Then, listening to the changed engine note of a low-flying plane as it dropped its flaps for the descent into Heathrow, I would envy the lucky ones among the passengers who, from a window, were seeing London for the first time, and were just about to discover it. I'd wonder whether I would fly to Amsterdam for a few days' stopover on my way to Berlin, but I knew that I wouldn't. I had never yet bought an air ticket out of my own pocket, and that was a habit I'd find hard to break.

On the other hand, the hours that I would have to spend on the ferry between Harwich and The Hook put me off when I thought about going my usual way. Another jet would come in sight just as the hee-hawing of a police car began, away in the distance above the dull roar of the London traffic, and the two together – the plane and the police car – would start me thinking about Mr Krasko, and about Nina. Sometimes I wondered whether I was hanging around in London waiting for dramatic developments in their story.

Three times in the last days of June I had seen him in The Old Rising Sun around ten o'clock, sitting up at the bar with a drink. Each time, it seemed to me, he was watching both doors of the bar with a mild anxiety. He would say 'Hello' and still be sitting there with the same drink half-an-hour later.

In the mornings I was dry tongued and dehydrated. I never got drunk, but I knew from the things I was hazy about when I tried to recall the last hour before I came home that I'd had too much. The forgotten bits of conversation with women were specially worrying.

It had become a great waste of time. With a kind of New Year's Day resolve I got up on the first day of July earlier than usual, rang the office, and asked for Jane, the girl who did my typing. Was there, by any chance, any mail? There wasn't, she said, and how was I? I said I was so-so, and that I was going abroad in a day or two.

She waited for a bit and then said, in a voice that touched me, that she missed me. That was kind of her, I said, and took my turn to wait a bit. Then I said that I was going down to Cook's to make some travel inquiries. Would she like to meet me for a lunchtime drink and a sandwich at a pub we knew – was it still called The Marlborough Head? – not far from Oxford Circus? She'd love that, she said.

I buttered a roll and sliced a tomato to go with the cheese, ate it, and headed for the High Street with a feeling that, with Cook's to go to and a girl to lunch all in one day, my life had become very complicated. I came out into the High Street just as The Old Rising Sun was opening and had a couple of pints because I needed them. I began to feel better.

I only wanted to pick up a copy of Cook's International Timetable, because that was the do-it-yourself way I planned my travel. I saved myself the cost of the timetable by getting, free, a month-old copy from a man I sometimes did business with in Cook's postal order department.

I looked in to say hello to a sweet Jamaican

girl I knew at J. Walter Thompson's. She was having lunch and half-way through a bottle of white wine. I couldn't help thinking that her taste had gone up-market since I'd first met her. That was when she'd worked for a disenchanted editorial man at *Radio Times,* and they had spent their late afternoons with paper cups of cider hidden, between sips, under manila envelopes that they called tea cosies.

I got to my meeting with Jane early and had started on my pint when she came in. She surprised me a little, and pleased me a lot, with a short kiss and a rather long hug. Usually, she was more restrained. This was what I might have expected after, rather than before, drinks.

I found a couple of seats in a corner by a window and asked, was it Campari and soda? I could see she was pleased that I remembered, which I'd been trying to do for the past few minutes, but she looked at my drink and said no, she'd have a half of bitter, and, on second thoughts, a pint. When I brought her drink I said, 'You're lashing out a bit?'

Jane smiled and said, 'It's a special occasion.' Then she tasted her drink and gave me a long, almost sorrowful look.

Jane was not quite beautiful, but she had very big, very dark eyes, a generous mouth, and the kind of figure that in any woman would have fed my fantasies.

'Why so sad?' I asked.

She didn't answer but started to talk about the things that had been happening at the office since I'd last been there – not that anything had happened that was worth talking about. I supposed she thought so, too, because we had both gone to the small motor sport journal as professionals – she as a secretary, I as a sub-editor looking for a quiet life away from Fleet Street – rather than as enthusiasts for a new way of life. In fact, I quite disliked the car club matiness and adolescent humour of most of the younger people who did the writing, though I had got quite interested in Formula 1. I had even once travelled away as far as Cheshire for a race that I didn't have to go to.

Jane's gossip suddenly stopped when she noticed my Cook's timetable. She reached over and took it from under my *Guardian*.

'Where are you going, Tony?' she asked.

I said that I hadn't quite decided. I thought it would be Amsterdam for a few days, then Berlin. She looked surprised.

'It's not all frontier excitement,' I said, guessing she was thinking that I needed something restful. 'I don't mind that, anyway, and I'll certainly go through to the East for a bit. In Berlin I know a quiet place in Dahlem, not all that far from the Grunewald. When I think about it' – I gave what I supposed was a pleased look – 'I'm in a hurry to go.'

She put the timetable down and looked at her watch.

'Tony, I'm sorry, it's nothing to do with me, but why did you leave your wife?'

It was very unexpected, and untypical of Jane, and I didn't want to talk about it. So, trying to soften it with a smile, I said, 'If it's nothing to do with you...'

'No, no,' Jane said. 'No. I'm sorry. I shouldn't have spoken. But your wife phoned, two, no three times, asking if you'd been in and wanting to know your address. I shouldn't have spoken. But I'm sorry, anyway.'

She really was upset. She looked at her watch again.

'I'll have to go. No, I don't want to eat anything. It'll take me twenty minutes to get back to the office.'

She wouldn't take up my offer of a taxi, but I said I'd see her to the tube at Oxford Circus. She didn't talk as we walked down through the mid-summer crowd to Regent Street. As we passed Little Argyll Street I glanced at the flower and fruit stall and, on a tender impulse, told her to wait, bought her a red rose, and pinned it on her white frock. She took my hand then and held it hard. As we went down the short stairway to the tube station she asked suddenly when I was going away.

23

'Tomorrow, probably,' I said.

'So soon!'

By the ticket office she hugged me again and took both my hands.

'I do wish I could see you again,' she said.

I smiled and said, 'I'm the one who's supposed to say that.'

That upset her again.

'Of course,' I said, 'I'd love to see you. I've got an evening job, you know, feeding the ducks in Regent's Park. It's one of my things. Come and see me there.'

So we settled to meet at Baker Street when she left work that evening.

Walking back north to Marylebone, I remembered again Jane's few, rather hungry kisses after an office party, which her embarrassed silence the next day had cancelled out as mere after-drinks affection. As for her concern to do just as I wanted it done anything that I might ask of her as a secretary, that seemed to me no more than any good secretary would show.

Still, with no wife to go home to, here was something different, for both of us. There'd been so few women in my life that I was still a pushover for the rare one who came along and, liking me, didn't hide her feelings. Yet I wanted so much just now to be both unattached and alone that, along with my perennial hunger for affection and tenderness, went a real fear of finding myself trapped, just as I was about to flee to freedom and safety.

So when I realised, walking along, that already I was impatient to see Jane again that evening I was scared and knew that I must go to Amsterdam next day. Outside the Heart Hospital, not far from my room, I looked at my watch, crossed over to The King's Head, and sat and looked up the London–Amsterdam timetables in Cook's. Twenty-past ten in the morning from Liverpool Street was a bit daunting. Better go at eight in the evening. I'd book a cabin on the night crossing to The Hook. It would be good to get to Amsterdam in the morning sunlight in time for one of those wonderful Dutch breakfasts, sitting in the window of the little hotel I knew so well, looking out on a bridge over Singel.

When I got home I had a quick, speculative look at myself in the mirror, took off my jacket and shoes, loosened my belt, lay down, and went straight off to sleep.

It was six o'clock when I woke. I remembered Jane with a start and, feeling like something that the cat had brought in, jumped up and shaved. It was something I hadn't done in the evening for a long time. I knew I'd be late, and Jane was nervously walking up and down outside the station when I arrived. She didn't say much until we'd walked up Baker Street and got inside the park gates. Then she took my arm, patted the air travel bag she had over her shoulder, and said, 'I bought bread for the ducks.'

'Just as well,' I said. 'I didn't.'

By the pond, already busy with boating parties and an oarsman so energetic that he might have been training for the Olympics, she took out a bag of bread rolls so fresh that I felt hungry as I remembered that I hadn't eaten since breakfast. Jane handed me a couple and broke one up herself, but she tossed only a few crumbs on the water. The ducks and a solitary goose gathered, and one duck was bold enough to feed from my hand. Jane watched with a smile whose tenderness touched and troubled me. When the goose, too, came near, waded ashore, and reached out for the bread in my palm, she said, 'You're so gentle.' I laughed at that, tossed the last of the bread among the ducks, and quickly stood up.

We walked north across the park, looked at the boats in Cumberland Basin and wished we were living on one, crossed over to Primrose Hill, and, taking our time, climbed to the top and lay down on the grassy slope that looked down to the city. I took Jane's hand, and we turned to look at one another.

She gave me a happy smile. I wondered if she was feeling as I had so often sixteen, seventeen, eighteen years before, when I had been as young as she was, at the start of an

26

evening with someone I badly wanted to be with. Was she feeling safe and untroubled because there were still two or three hours till parting? Only as we went back towards Marylebone, I suspected, would she become unhappy. Remembering my own old panic in the last half-hour before a long separation from someone I couldn't bear to be apart from, I felt a little afraid. I had never known what to do about tears, except tell the tender lies that later I'd regret.

Jane said suddenly, 'Are you really ill or just tired?'

I laughed and said, 'That's direct, anyway. Fed up is nearer the truth.' I almost added, 'And wanting to be alone,' but remembered just in time that it would hurt her.

'Will you ever come back to the office?' she said.

'Oh, I guess so,' I said, with a grin. 'In a year or two.'

'Don't say that,' she said unhappily. 'I told the boss I'd, well, run into you. Was that all right?'

'It doesn't matter one way or the other.'

'I told him you were going to Germany. He remembered the bit you wrote – for fun, he said – about the girls at the British Grand Prix. He wondered if you might feel like doing a colour story about the Nürburgring. The crowd at the Karussel – something like that.'

I frowned. 'I'm not planning to go to the 'Ring,' I said, 'though I'd like to go to the Eifel. It's a wonderful place to get away from' – I could feel the ice split under me – 'from it all.'

'From people like me,' Jane said.

'I didn't say that,' I said, 'or mean it.' I got up and stretched and reached down to help her up.

'Let's walk some more.'

It was around ten o'clock when we got back into Marylebone. We'd walked up through the Stringalong country beyond the park, and east to Camden High Street. Jane had been a bit nervous when I'd taken her into a noisy working-class pub north of the canal.

I was an idiot to take her there – she looked out of place and got too much attention. But, stimulated by several brandies, she was animated and talked in a cheerful, extrovert way. When she told me that she'd moved to a flat in St Mary's Mansions, not far from Little Venice, I said I would walk her home. She liked that.

As we came back along Marylebone Road there was a warning roll of thunder and a few spots of rain, and I decided that I'd go to my room for a coat or an umbrella. Perhaps it was the thunder and the forbidding clouds that did it, but suddenly Jane seemed stone-cold sober. She started to talk about me – about how fond she had become of me when we had worked together, how she had almost given up her job when she had heard that I was taking a long rest, about her selfish hope when my wife had phoned and she had realised that I had walked out on her.

She was silent for a minute or two, which, after what she had been saying, seemed a long time. Then she blurted out, 'You know, Tony, I ran into her in the launderette. I go to the same one she goes to, in Formosa Street. I expected her to be upset. But she wasn't – she wasn't at all.'

I didn't say anything, expecting her to go on, but after another hundred yards all she said was, 'I'm sorry.'

There was no need to be sorry, I said. I put my arm around her shoulder and gave her a gentle hug that was meant to comfort her. At that she stopped suddenly in the busy, noisy road and faced me.

'It's bloody cruel,' she said. 'I've never felt like this about anyone else. I bottled it up because I wanted to be fair. No, not just that, either – I didn't even dare to hope that you'd be interested in me, anyway. But we've seemed so close tonight. You haven't just been nice to be kind, have you?'

I said, and more than half meant it, 'I think the world of you' – though I knew it was a crazy thing to say.

She stood staring at me.

'Now you're going away,' she said, 'and really I don't know what I'm going to do.'

I could only say again, feeling that I was getting in deeper and deeper, how sorry I was, and promise to write to her. That seemed to make her feel a little better.

As we turned into the High Street it started to rain, and we had to run to reach my place if we weren't to get wet. Just round the corner was a brightly lit antique shop, and I asked her to shelter in the doorway while I went up to my room. Then she said that she wanted to see where I lived. Couldn't she come up with me?

'Jane,' I said, 'my room's a seedy, slummy place that I'd be ashamed to be living in if it wasn't just a port of call. It's in a hell of a mess, too. I'd rather not let you see it.'

Really I was worried about what might happen if we got up there and old-fashioned enough to care, especially now that I wanted so much not to be involved.

Jane stared at me as we stood in the antique shop doorway and said, 'You're afraid to take me up there, aren't you? You know how much I want you.'

'Yes,' I said, 'I am afraid,' and I put my hands on her shoulders. 'Listen, Jane, dear, I like you enormously – far too much to be casual with you. I know you wouldn't want me to be casual with you, anyway. If I made love to you it'd be for real. Because I feel in a bit of a mess, you're an awful temptation. But listen, and don't misunderstand. I left Jill because I wanted to be alone, and I'm going abroad partly to make sure that I will be alone – alone, and ... and anonymous. If I went to bed with you tonight I'd feel involved. I mustn't be involved. If that sounds selfish ... look, I *will* write to you and phone you as soon as I get back. That's a promise. Now wait here. I'll be only a minute.'

Before she could say any more I had run around the corner, fumbling for my key.

When I came back in my mac and with an umbrella, I could see that she had been crying. I put my arm round her and held up the umbrella, as we zig-zagged back to the main road in the direction of Baker Street station. Neither of us spoke. As we got near the bright lights of Marylebone Road, Jane suddenly said, 'I feel so cheap. I *wanted* to make it difficult for you. I *wanted* to trap you. I'm sorry, Tony.'

She seemed to be saying that rather often. It troubled me. I told her not to worry and that I understood. She clung to me, found my mouth, gave me a long kiss, and, as she hugged me again, said, 'That makes up for everything. Tony, don't see me home. It's too wet, anyway. I'll get the tube.'

She was all practical, and seemed to know that I knew so well the potential hazards of her late-night journey home.

31

'No, don't worry. I'll be all right. I won't go through that underpass at Edgware Road – it always frightens me at night – or across Paddington Green. I'll go to Warwick Avenue and walk back.'

We walked on again. At the crossing to the station she said, 'Leave me here.'

She kissed me again and held me very close and very tight. Then she was running across the road, and she didn't look back.

III

I felt shaken as I started to hurry back towards The Old Rising Sun. It was very hard to say 'No' to Jane's warmth and affection, but looking forward to having a drink alone I was as sure as ever that what I most wanted was to be away, to be abroad, where no one would know me. It couldn't happen too soon, before I could see Jane again and perhaps change my mind. I would leave on that 10.20 train in the morning. I went in at the Paddington Street entrance to the pub and then to the front of the bar and ordered a pint. I took a gulp and looked around at the seven or eight other people who were there.

Mr Krasko was sitting in the quietest

corner, talking with a young woman. Straight away, I envied him. I'd seen and had fantasies about girls like this one: the Continental refugee whom I remembered from films, and the same kind of girls in real life, too. Maybe this girl wasn't strictly beautiful if beauty has to have top marks for every feature, but I'd never judged women on a points system. Perhaps her pale face was just a little too pale in the lamplight, but, just for a start, there were those big, sad eyes and that lovely mouth. Honey-coloured hair hung to her shoulders.

She was wearing a light-coloured gaberdine raincoat and under it a black, polo-neck sweater. At a guess she was from somewhere in northern Europe.

I noticed that while Mr Krasko was drinking spirits, she had beer, or perhaps lager. I had seen her many times – girls like her, I mean – and if she wasn't sitting beside one travel-worn suitcase at a frontier station, then she should have been. Mr Krasko was doing most of the talking, completely absorbed, looking earnestly into the girl's face whenever she had anything to say.

The first bell rang. Mr Krasko emptied his glass as the landlord called for last orders. The girl drank down the little that was left in her glass, and Mr Krasko came over to the bar where I was sitting on a stool. He seemed almost surprised to see me but gave his gentle smile and said good evening in his courteous, patient voice. We finished our drinks at the same time, and I was buttoning my coat when they came towards me. I noticed that the girl had long, slender legs, and that she wore very smart, very high-heeled shoes. As that didn't quite go with the refugee thing, I wasn't surprised that it was *Je Reviens* that I breathed in as they passed.

Mr Krasko said, 'Good night, my friend,' and the girl, walking ahead, turned and gave me a faint smile. As they went out into the High Street I heard Mr Krasko say quietly, 'One of my fellow inmates, Nina.'

So that was Nina. She was almost an exact copy of the picture that I had been carrying around in my mind. When I came out into a fine night, washed clean and made fresh by the thunderstorm, I saw the two of them walking off north up the High Street. I crossed over and began to think about Jane again as I walked home.

My decision to go in the morning meant that I wouldn't have time to get any laundry done, and I felt reluctant and almost un-decided as I started to pack my few clothes. It was a bother, too, that now I would have to take my typewriter. I wasn't planning to write anything while I was away, and had decided to leave it somewhere in town till I came back. Now there'd be no time for that.

There was the rent, too. I stood in the

middle of the room, tired and discouraged and troubled by the thought of Jane, wishing only that I could go to sleep and wake up – refreshed, I hoped – in Amsterdam. It seemed to have been a long day. In the end I left the rest of the packing and set the alarm for six-thirty. Then I wrote a cheque for the rent and a note of explanation, and propped the envelope up on the mantelpiece where the landlady would see it.

As I undressed, I heard someone on the stairs. It must have been Mr Krasko. From the noises he began to make in the room above he also might have been packing, but not even Mr Krasko could keep me awake when I got into bed and pulled the sheets over me.

I woke early, but it wasn't the alarm that woke me; it was the telephone, ringing on the landing. I thought, when my head cleared, that it might have been Jane, and was half out of bed before I remembered that I hadn't given Jane my phone number. As no one else had it, the call couldn't be for me. The ringing went on. I was about to answer it when a door opened on the floor above, someone came down the stairs, and I heard Mr Krasko's voice say, 'Hello.'

That was all it did say. There was a silence of about three seconds. Then the receiver was slammed down, and Mr Krasko went up the stairs and into his room faster than I would have thought anyone could. I sat up as I heard the hubbub above. About five minutes later I head him come down the stairs even faster than he had gone up, past my landing, down and out through the front door.

I leapt out of bed and went over to the window. A small red sports car with a woman in dark glasses at the wheel had stopped across the street. I was just in time to see Mr Krasko throw a suitcase and an overnight bag into the back and climb in beside the driver. Then, with a touch of wheelspin, they were off, just as I heard the 'hee-haw' of a police car or an ambulance from the direction of the High Street. I had got only my trousers and vest on when I heard another car stop outside. The door-bell downstairs rang – once, twice, three times. I put my feet into slippers and went down to open the door. Two policemen in flat top caps were standing there. One of them asked me, 'Have you a man named Krasko living in this house?' We had, I said, but he wasn't at home. Before I could say any more they'd flashed a pass at me, pushed past me, and run up the stairs. The old woman who had the room next to mine had come out in a dressing gown. She looked bewildered.

'Krasko,' they said to her.

'Krasko?' she said.

'Krasko,' they said.

'He lives upstairs.'

I followed them up the second flight of stairs. Mr Krasko's door stood open. They didn't need me to tell them that whoever had lived there had left in a hurry. The room was in disorder. The older man swung round on me and asked, aggressively, as if he suspected I'd been holding something back, 'D'you know when he left?'

'I heard him come downstairs about' – I paused and pursed my lips theatrically – 'about quarter-of-an-hour ago.'

'He didn't own a car,' one said to the other, 'but he could have had someone to collect him. Might even have grabbed a cab.' He turned to me. 'You didn't hear a car drive off?'

Why did I feel I was on Mr Krasko's side as I considered the question and decided that in the quiet of early morning his escape car could now be a long way off?

'I did hear a car, come to think of it,' I said, as though I'd had to dredge it up from my memory.

'Which way did it go, d'you know?'

I thought again. 'It seemed to go thataway.' And, telling the truth in my fashion, I pointed in the direction the red sports car had taken. I hoped they wouldn't ask any more questions because I didn't want to tell any lies. The way I'd been conducting my half of the interrogation, I might have to say something that wasn't strictly true if my answers were not going to sound a little odd.

'Thanks,' the older man said. 'Let's get going.'

He closed Mr Krasko's door, and they ran down the stairs.

I went back into my room and across to the windows. The blue lamp on the top of the police car was starting to flash as they turned with squealing tyres in the narrow street. I wondered, as I went over and closed my door, what they would start to look for, though I had to admit that I'd heard of success from even less promising beginnings. I looked around the room, and, remembering the alarm clock, switched it off.

I was certainly up good and early and already wide awake. I looked in despair at the mess I still had to clear up. Then I went over to the washbasin, wondering what the hell it was all about, ran the water hot, and started to lather my face. I was thinking of Mr Krasko – Mr Krasko and Nina. I hated not to know what happened next, but I guessed that the action had moved out of my territory. I wouldn't be missing anything by going away.

I'd shaved and dried my face and put on my shirt and was knotting my tie when the phone rang again. I went out, picked it up, and said, 'Hello.' There was no answer. I said

'Hello' again a couple of times, a bit louder. Then a gentle, patient voice that sounded a long way off asked, 'Is that you, my friend?'

'Who's that? I asked, though I didn't need to.

'Listen,' Mr Krasko said. 'It is rather important. Could you do a thing for me? Nina – that girl I was with last night. Nina will be at The Old Rising Sun at nine tonight. Tell her I've gone. That I had to go away.'

He hung up.

I went back into my room. Why had Krasko trusted me? Perhaps he had no choice. My guess was that he was sure he knew his man. I hoped the police wouldn't come back and ask more questions. I looked at the untidy room again, sat down on my bed, loosened my tie and undid the top button of my shirt. I wished I had something to drink. In a scene like this, I thought, you always had a drink and lit a cigarette.

I came back to my own world abruptly as I remembered that I'd be in Amsterdam that night, crossing the canal in front of Central Station, at just about the time Nina came into The Old Rising Sun. What would happen if she sat and waited and no one turned up? Remembering her, I couldn't bear to think about it. Did it matter all that much to me, I asked, with a feeling of relief as I looked at my half-packed bags, if I left for Amsterdam not today but tomorrow?

I thought again about the police and decided to go out straight away and stay out. I had this feeling that Jane would go to Liverpool Street to see the morning train off to Amsterdam. To set my mind at rest I went down to see it off myself, but Jane didn't join me.

Then, feeling like a man on the run, I started a long, wide circuit of the city that took in a slice of South London. In the early afternoon I picked up a *New Statesman*, fresh on a news-stand at Piccadilly Circus – a day early, for some reason and stopped off at a Soho pub to glance through it.

I was back in Marylebone for supper, but I didn't go home. I pulled the *New Statesman* out of my pocket when I got to The Old Rising Sun at about a quarter-to nine. I sat down with my drink not far from where Mr Krasko and Nina had been sitting the night before.

At five to nine Nina came in. She was dressed just as she had been the night before. There really was something about her. I knew why I hadn't gone to Amsterdam. She looked into the corner and round the other side of the bar, then bought a bottled lager and took it into the corner. She took a sip and, just as if she had picked up my habitual curiosity, looked to see what I was reading. Then she seemed to recognise me, gave me the same faint smile as she had the night before, and went back to her drink. She had her priorities right. I finished my drink and went over to the bar for another. She watched the door. As I went back to my seat I stopped in front of her table and said, 'You're Nina.' She sounded just a little surprised as she said, 'Yes.'

I hardly more than murmured, 'Mr Krasko asked me to tell you' – she looked startled – 'that he has had to go away.' I sat down and picked up my *New Statesman*.

I glanced at her before I started to read. She gave me a long, anxious look.

'Can you tell me more?' she asked.

I was surprised that she spoke English so well, in a soft, well-bred voice. I had expected a foreign accent. I moved along and sat next to her.

'I have a feeling that Mr Krasko may be in some kind of trouble,' I said.

'Yes?'

'I live in the same house.'

She nodded.

'Yes, I remember. Peter said so last night.'

'He left in a big hurry this morning after getting a phone call. I couldn't help noticing,' I said apologetically, 'because the telephone woke me up.'

'Go on.'

'Someone picked him up, in a red sports car' – she started – 'and soon after that policemen came looking for him. After they'd gone, he phoned me and asked me to give you this message. He said it was important.'

'Have you told anyone else?' Nina asked. 'Have you told – have you told the police?'

I said that I hadn't, that I had been out all day. I said, 'I thought it best to keep out of the way.'

She looked relieved and then amused and gave a real smile, showing her teeth. It was a lovely smile. Then straight away she was solemn again.

'You've been very kind.' She paused for a moment, sipped her drink. 'You see, I told Peter not to phone me, but I don't want *you* to feel involved. I would be glad, though, I would be grateful, if you didn't tell anyone else about this.'

'Of course not.'

'You're very kind,' she said again. 'You must let me buy you a drink' – she looked at the one I had – 'presently.'

She sat for a silent minute sipping her drink without seeming to feel she should say anything. Then she gave another real smile and said, 'You've got your *Statesman* early. I never get mine till Friday morning. I'm always so curious about what people read, and I noticed your paper, your magazine, before I noticed you.'

'You mustn't flatter me,' I said.

She laughed. 'Now, you're probably' – she looked me up and down – 'a *Guardian* man, though I can't be sure. You're reading the competition. I suppose you look a bit literary. That may be the *Statesman's* attraction, and you may read *The Times*. You may not be a socialist at all.'

She looked at me and waited.

'Actually I am,' I said. 'Well, a socialist of sorts. If it comes to that I do read the *Guardian*, too, though I sometimes wonder why – you know, Peter Jenkins and all. But I don't think I could be anything but a socialist, the way I was brought up. Unless I'd rebelled and was the opposite, if you know what I mean...'

'Oh, I do,' she said.

'I'm the Roman Catholic type of socialist,' I said.

She looked shocked till I said, 'Oh, no, the absolute agnostic.' I laughed. 'A Roman Catholic type of agnostic, too, if you like. I mean only that they had me for the first seven years – my dear old Dad did for twice that – and I've gone on believing ever since.' I laughed again. 'I couldn't become a Tory if I tried – I was going to say even if I was convinced that they were right, but that's damn silly. But, oh well, I'm a believer.'

I finished my drink, and she picked up my mug, and said, 'It's just bitter, isn't it?'

When she came back I told her that she didn't look like a beer-drinker. She took it almost solemnly.

'It was the years in Germany, I suppose,' she said, and suddenly she looked almost forlorn as she added quickly, 'But don't let's talk about that.'

She took a gulp of her lager.

'Strange that they should have had you for seven years,' she said. 'They had me, too. They all seem so intellectual now – the socialists, I mean. Intellectual in – what's that awful word? – the pejorative sense.'

She smiled but straight away was serious again.

'Most of them I've met are pretty materialistic, too, in many ways. It's strange to recall.' And she began to chant, 'Love, we give ourselves to thee. May we live in thy spirit all this day, in our work and in our play, in our joy and in our sorrow.'

She started to smile as she spoke. I must have looked startled at what she was reciting. When she had finished she gave a little laugh.

'That was a thing called the opening declaration,' she said. 'We used to say it all together at the start of meetings of the socialist Sunday school that I went to right through my childhood – till I was about fourteen.'

She started to chant again, 'May nothing of ours that is unworthy stain the purity or spoil the sweetness of this good day...' She broke off as I laughed.

'You're not pulling my leg?' I said.

'No,' she said. 'There was a puritan sweetness and light thing about it that I rebelled against in the end.' She shook her head impatiently and said, 'Forgive me for this ... for this lecture but the ethical thing about all that English socialism, Keir Hardie and William Morris and all, was absolutely right and something we've more than half forgotten. As you said about being a Roman Catholic type of socialist, socialism for those people and for my Sunday school was a belief. It wasn't just a political *policy*.'

She hesitated just a moment when the door from the High Street opened and a young woman came in. She was wearing dark glasses. The woman ordered a drink and glanced in our direction. Then she sat just inside the door.

'Socialists believed then...' Nina was saying, and her voice seemed to trail away in a sort of vagueness. 'Socialists believed in goodness and gentleness and real equality... They meant what they said when they preached, when they ... when they advocated "From each according to his ability, to each according to his need."'

She had started to stammer slightly, and she said suddenly, 'Have you got a cigarette?'

When I said that I didn't smoke she said, 'I don't either. But every now and then – have you ever smoked?'

I said I had. 'And of course I remember,' I said, 'reaching for a cigarette when I suddenly felt I *needed* one.' It was just what I'd thought of doing when the police had gone after Mr Krasko's departure that morning.

Nina smiled gratefully.

I started to get up. 'I'll get you some cigarettes,' I said.

'No, no,' Nina said. 'It never works, anyway.'

She looked across again to the girl by the door, who had written something on a page of a notebook, torn it out, and was putting her pen back in her pocket. The girl went over to the bar, looked in our direction as she spoke to the barman, and handed him the piece of paper. Then she went out through the side door into Paddington Street.

Nina was saying, 'I heard a Tory candidate at an election meeting once. He said, "You know what these socialists teach in their Sunday schools," and I had an idea he was thinking of free love, atheism, and bloody revolution.' She laughed. 'It was really rather different.' But her laugh was a bit half-hearted, as though her thoughts were somewhere else. She was watching the barman as he opened the hatch and came across to our table with the piece of paper.

'Miss,' he said awkwardly.

Nine unfolded the piece of paper. Reading it upside down I could see that there was

46

just one word on it and some figures: 'Barcaglia 1330'.

Nina folded the note and put it in her purse. She gave an embarrassed laugh.

'You know, I haven't asked your name,' she said. 'Though why I should–' This time her laugh was real.

I said that it was Tony, and she said, 'What's your work?'

I told her that I was a journalist and, before she could ask the next question, that I was between jobs.

'Yes?' she said.

'Oh, there's no mystery,' I said. 'I'm just naturally indolent ... I'm lazy.'

I was about to say that I was going to Holland in the morning, but I didn't. She asked me if my last job had been any kind of political journalism. I said that I'd been doing a motor sport job, and that surprised her – I didn't look that kind of person. When I said that it had just been a job, she seemed disappointed that I'd been satisfied doing something that apparently meant so little to me.

'I didn't say I was satisfied,' I said, trying not to sound testy. I didn't really want to talk about myself. I was thinking about the name 'Barcaglia' on the piece of paper in Nina's purse and wondering where I'd seen it before and what it meant. I was wondering, too, whether I would, when it came to the point, be on the train at Liverpool Street the next morning. The mysterious Barcaglia and Nina's obvious unease about the note again made me very unwilling to walk out on the Krasko story. Besides, I was now almost irresistibly fascinated by Nina, by the paradox, it seemed to me, of the near-puritan socialist morality she'd given me a taste of, and her sensuality, by an openness that reminded me of the Danish women I'd met, and by the casual yet elegant clothes she wore and the way she wore them.

With a backward glance at my recent near-obsession with freedom, I knew that I had only to get up and say 'Good night' and it could all be over, but watching Nina get to the bottom of her glass of lager I was afraid that that was what *she* was going to do.

I looked at my watch.

'I've hardly eaten today,' I said. 'I'm going to have a bit of supper somewhere. Why don't you come and have something, too?'

She thought about it, looking at me with a faint smile.

'I'd like to,' she said, 'but on one condition.'

'Yes?'

'That I pay my share.'

I suppose I must have looked displeased, for she put her hand briefly, gently, on my arm.

'No, Tony,' she said, 'it's not women's independence or anything. I just don't want to feel involved, if that's what letting you buy me a meal is. I haven't asked you anything about yourself – well, only about your work – and I'm not going to. You haven't asked me, either. That could be unflattering, but, no, I've liked it. You haven't even asked me about Peter Krasko. All right? Shall we go?'

IV

Outside, Nina said, 'Let's walk till we find a place.'

'Let's try Baker Street,' I said.

As we started off down Paddington Street she said, 'If Peter Krasko *is* in any kind of trouble you're not involved – by coming to me with his message, I mean – because I'm not involved, either. Not really.'

We crossed over, to pass the garden that was a popular spot with people who liked to sit in the sun to eat their lunches. Nina seemed to shiver, as from a sudden chill.

'You're not afraid of old bones?' I said.

She started and said, tensely, 'What do you mean?'

'It's just that the garden was once a cemetery.'

'No, no,' she said. 'I didn't know. I was

49

thinking of something else.'

She was silent. I glanced at her as we came into the brighter area near Baker Street and saw that all the animation of our half-hour of conversation had gone. She was still like that even after we had found a restaurant in Baker Street, sat down, and ordered.

She was almost impatient when I tried to persuade her to have a steak. She wanted only a very small cheese salad – 'and not because it's inexpensive.' She wasn't the kind of girl, either, that you could try any cheer-up nonsense with. It suited me fine that she didn't want to get involved, but her melancholy made me afraid to start any conversation in case it invaded her private world.

She kept glancing at what I was eating – a very rare, very red, steak – and at last, to break a long silence, I said, 'See what you're missing? It *is* good.'

'I'm sure it is,' Nina said in a flat voice.

I tried again: 'Have I done – have I said anything wrong?'

She stared at the steak and shook her head.

'Then what is wrong?' I asked, more gently, and I reached out and touched a hand.

'Please,' Nina said. 'Don't go on, Tony. I don't want to spoil your supper.'

But, stupidly, as I remembered it later, I didn't give up.

'Please do tell me, Nina,' I said.

She gave a resigned sigh.

'It's just that I once had a holiday on a farm.'

'Yes?'

'You shouldn't push me, Tony,' she said. 'I didn't want this conversation. I'm sorry ... it's just – it's just that I've seen animals killed and then had to eat them.'

'Oh, I *see*,' I said. 'Go on – I'm not squeamish.'

She looked at me with very wide open, unwavering eyes. She really was beautiful.

'There was the old rooster. Ted. I was only eleven. One day while we were having a kind of chicken broth my uncle said, "Ted tastes good." I was sick and ran out and hid in the hayloft. I stayed there for hours. I can still smell that hay. Now I can't see a slice of bacon or a ham sandwich without hearing the squeal of a pig. I can't see a turkey hanging by its neck at Christmas...'

She really was going on a bit, I thought, and as she broke off I had a flashback to that moment in the pub when she'd recalled her socialist Sunday school days. What was it she'd said? Then I remembered. I said, '"May nothing of ours that is unworthy spoil the purity of this good day." Dear Nina, you're almost too good to be true.'

'Oh, yes,' she said, and almost smiled. '*Puritan* Nina. Don't worry, Tony. I'm also quite lusty. I want everything else to be lusty, too, or to have the chance to be – even the

51

poor old cat that my Dad, that good, gentle man, had castrated. Sounds silly, I suppose, but I still remember the compassion I felt for it, for what it could never have, when I first went to bed with a man – when I was fourteen.'

I winced, and remembering that I had pushed Nina into this unfortunate conversation looked down at my plate and suddenly saw it all through Nina's eyes, as I was to see so much else in the days ahead. This time it was my steak browsing contentedly on her uncle's farm. I pushed my plate aside.

'Let's go,' I said.

She let me pay the bill after all, when I asked her if I might. Out in the street she said, 'I'm sorry, Tony.' She paused. 'I'll take the tube from Baker Street.'

She didn't say anything else as we walked north, and I, too, was silent, wondering again whether I'd ever see her again and how I could make sure that I did. We stopped at the station entrance. I stood there feeling awkward, but Nina smiled into my eyes and I thought again how much like a Dane she was.

She was about to speak when two good-looking men, talking in French, walked by. She watched them go as a man might look after a woman. Then she looked at me, laughed, and said, 'I wouldn't mind being with either of them.'

'Probably a couple of queers,' I said.

She laughed again and said, 'Oh, no. But it's flattering that you say so – that you're jealous. It was a try-on, really, but it's true enough in a way. It's nonsense that women must always have a long wooing. Sometimes it's just fun, so long as there's a bit of affection, a bit of tenderness. Well, here ends the tour of Nina's pleasure garden.'

She waited for me to speak, and when I didn't she held out her hand.

'I'm going for a walk up the river tomorrow,' I said. 'Chiswick and Hammersmith. I wish you'd come with me.'

She smiled. 'I'd really like to. When?'

I said I'd thought of early afternoon, but she quickly said that she had an appointment at one-thirty. Could we meet at, say, four? We settled for that and said good night.

I wondered, going home, what sort of a fool I was making of myself and how long this was likely to go on. There was a note under my door asking me to call at the Marylebone police station. After worrying about it for five minutes I phoned them, but the man who wanted to see me had gone home. I promised to call in the morning.

In bed I started worrying about that 'Barcaglia 1330' note in Nina's purse.

In spite of her assurance I felt sure that it was part of a mystery in which Krasko was involved. And just as I was on the edge of sleep I decided that 1330 was probably 1.30. Hadn't Nina said that she had an appointment at that time? Where the devil had I heard of Barcaglia before? Who or what or where was it? I worried away at it, then tried to forget about it, but it was a long time before I could get off to sleep.

I had used, dozens of times, the short cut through the cemetery garden that takes you from Paddington Street to Moxon Street and on to the High Street and watering points south and east. About half-way through there's a piece of sculpture on a white stone pillar under some trees: a boy, a little street orderly, carved in white stone. He has a besom under his arm, and one of his feet is bare, with the shoe that he has taken off lying beside him. He seems to be examining his fingernails, or perhaps looking for a thorn or a splinter in a finger. I suppose he's a bit sentimental for these times. But he has charm and the wistfulness of a child worker of the bad old days. I was doing the short cut in reverse, from Moxon Street to watering points north and west, the morning after my meeting with Nina and my sleepless night, when I glanced again at the little street orderly. I looked also, as I had more than once, at the inscription on the base of the sculpture: D. Barcaglia, Milano. Barcaglia! Barcaglia at half-past one. Was it possible?

I had already been to see the Marylebone police and told them that I knew nothing more about Krasko. They seemed to be fairly indifferent, anyway. They thought he had left the country. I asked them – casually, I hoped – what they wanted him for, but of course they wouldn't tell me that.

It was already a few minutes past one. At The Old Rising Sun I bought a takeaway sandwich and walked back towards the garden. By now I had more than half written off my hunch about Nina. I didn't really expect her to show up.

I stood and stared at the Barcaglia sculpture in the hot summer sun and then sat down to eat my sandwich on one of the benches on the path that ran in from the western Paddington Street gate. I had a near-back view of the sculpture and could see the western gate of Paddington Street on the left and, on the right, nearly as far as the eastern gate.

Almost on the half-hour, Nina came in through the eastern gate. I was startled. She had her coat over one arm and a small black satchel under the other. She seemed to come straight towards me as I bent my head to watch the pigeons and sparrows that had been feeding on the crumbs that I'd thrown at my feet.

She came towards the little street orderly, sat on a bench just beyond him, side on to me, and put her satchel beside her. Right on the half-hour, a tall man with grey, almost white, hair, wearing dark glasses, and carrying a black satchel, came along the path from the western gate. He stood staring at the little orderly and put his satchel on the ground between his feet. Then he patted the pockets of his jacket, produced cigarettes and a lighter, lit a cigarette and drew on it as though deep in thought.

Presently he picked up the satchel, walked around the grassy plot, and sat beside Nina. He put his satchel beside hers. When he had finished his cigarette, he looked at his watch, stood up, and with a satchel under his arm walked around past me towards the children's playground and the Moxon Street entrance to the garden. Had they swapped satchels or was I being a romantic idiot? Nina remained where she was. I got up and began to follow the white-haired man.

He moved along quickly, with an easy stride, on his long legs. At the High Street he turned north by The Queen's Head, and after that took the short cut by the parish church to Marylebone Road. Afraid of losing him if we didn't cross together, I caught up with him at the traffic lights. He had a fresh face and those very red lips that look as if they might bleed at any moment.

On the north side of Marylebone Road I stopped and looked at my watch and let him get a little ahead of me as he turned into the short road that runs up into Regent's Park. He'd almost reached the Outer Circle when a sports car appeared from the right and stopped in front of him. The door on the passenger's side opened, and as soon as the tall man had got in the car accelerated swiftly away to the west. It was, I was almost certain, the same car that had picked up Krasko the day before.

V

I walked on into the park and then came back to meet Nina where I'd left her the night before. I saw her as I came around the corner from Baker Street, before she saw me. She had no satchel, but her coat was still over her arm. If the clouds meant what they seemed to be saying, she might need it. She gave me only a small smile and was very quiet. I looked at the sky and suggested that we take the tube to Chiswick Park – to make the most of what was left of the afternoon. She just said indifferently, 'Anything you like.'

While we waited for the train, she asked me what I'd been doing and looked troubled when I told her of my visit to the police station. On the noisy train she said hardly a word, but as we came off the station into the street she smiled into my eyes and said, 'I'm not very good company. I'm sorry. It doesn't mean I'm not enjoying myself. *You'll* see.' And, sure enough, when we came out on the river, by that little island above Hammersmith, she brightened up and, as we walked along, talked about the boats – she loved boats, she said – and the fine old houses and the roses in the gardens.

Presently she took my hand. I squeezed hers gently. She smiled happily, and after a while said, 'We've got skinship.'

I misheard. 'Kinship?' I said.

'Skinship,' she said. 'You don't know that word. I feel in touch with you – no, no, not just literally.'

'You've said something really nice,' I said.

She said, with a little laugh, 'Don't sound so surprised.'

Just before we got to The Dove pub and Hammersmith pier, I stopped and pointed to the inscription above the doors at the western end of Kelmscott House – the quotation from William Morris's *News from Nowhere,* which at the same time tells you that the Hammersmith socialists of Morris's day met at this house.

'Guests and neighbours, on the site of this Guest-hall once stood the lecture-room of the Hammersmith Socialists. Drink a glass to the memory!'

Nina was overcome with emotion. 'Oh, and I didn't know it was here,' she said at last. She read the inscription aloud in a voice that almost broke, and gently, softly, she began to sing Morris's words:

> 'Hear a word, a word in season
> For the day is drawing nigh
> When the cause shall call upon us,
> Some to live, and some to die.'

She looked again at his house. '"Drink a glass to the memory." Let's do that,' she said.

I looked at my watch. 'It's still twenty minutes to opening time.'

We walked round past The Dove and sat in the little garden by Hammersmith pier, though it was overcast now and not very warm. Then we went back to The Dove and drank our glass to the memory. We stayed nearly an hour and had French bread and cheese and sweet pickled onions with our beer. When we came out it was raining. We ran almost all the way to the underground at Hammersmith Broadway.

We got on the District line rather than the Metropolitan and found ourselves riding east past Earls Court instead of north to Edgware Road. It turned out to be a fateful journey. Nina had thought that she'd go home, and we'd been meaning to head for Baker Street. But we decided to surface at Embankment to look at the weather and, if it had cleared, to walk for a bit along the river there.

We came out into a dry evening, walked downstream past Cleopatra's Needle and over Waterloo Bridge to the South Bank. Just as we came down the steps to the river front it started to rain again. If it hadn't, and presently Nina had gone home, I think I would have gone to Amsterdam next morning. Curious as I was about her and Krasko and all, I had more than half made up my mind on the almost wordless ride east from Hammersmith that, although Nina wasn't an uncomfortable person to be with, I was getting nowhere and probably wouldn't get anywhere.

'Let's see what's on at the NFT,' I said, as the rain came down. So we turned away from the river and, with a bit of shelter on the way, went up to the National Film Theatre. Hitchcock's *The Wrong Man* was showing, and we went in. I'd seen it before, but it was soon clear that Nina hadn't. At the point where Henry Fonda, as the wrongly accused bull-fiddle player, is arrested and locked up, Nina clutched my arm. She didn't let go even when the film ended.

As we came out on to the river yet again, a

police launch cruised by, its blue light flashing. In mid-stream a big passenger launch, adazzle with lights and noisy with a band, was heading towards Westminster Pier.

I turned to speak to Nina and saw that her face was dead white. I said something trite about Hitchcock being an old spellbinder. Nina didn't answer.

'He seemed to have a thing about being locked up,' I said. 'He wouldn't even drive a car because he was afraid of getting into trouble. I wonder if it did all really begin when he was locked up once by the police for fun when he was a small boy.'

We were in front of the Festival Hall, and Nina, standing in front of me and staring into my face, said almost hysterically, 'What do you mean? What do you mean?'

'You don't know the story?'

'What story?' Nina looked wildly into my eyes.

'Well, just that when he was about five his father sent him to the local police station with a note. The police locked him up for five minutes or so and told him when they let him out, "That's what we do to naughty boys."'

Nina looked at me in horror.

'You're making it up,' she said.

I laughed.

'Why should I?' I said. 'No, Nina, it's all quite true. I remember Hitchcock told a fellow who wrote a piece about him in the

Guardian that he didn't know whether that had given him his fear of the police and his preoccupation, in his films, with ordinary people in trouble. He said that if you know the source of a phobia you're supposed to be freed from it. But he admitted that this film, *The Wrong Man*, mattered to him.'

'It's nonsense that you're freed from a phobia just because you know the source of it,' Nina said. She was still very agitated. 'There's much more to it than that. But what a monster his father must have been to do a thing like that.'

She stared at me again without speaking. Then she said, 'Let's go home.'

She took my hand again as we went up the steps to Hungerford Bridge. When we turned into the Embankment tube station she stopped again and said, as though she had suddenly made up her mind about something, 'Tony, everything I said last night about not being involved, about not wanting to be involved – I meant it all.' She looked at me, her face still very pale, her eyes still wide. 'But I'd like it so much if you'd see me home. I live in St John's Wood, you know. Not far from the underground.'

'I didn't know,' I said, and she almost smiled.

'No? But it wouldn't take you long. It wouldn't keep you late.'

No doubt she meant it, too. Of course I

said I'd love to see her home. She was almost herself again when we got to Acacia Road. As a fellow so recently warned that he wasn't to become involved, I was playing it very cool; and by the time she had said, 'This is where I live,' and had reached into her handbag for her key, I was dragging my feet.

'You can't go home without a drink,' Nina said with her faint smile, 'and I make quite good coffee. Or you can have Pilsener – the real thing, from Pilsen I mean.'

As she put the key in her door at the top of the stairs she said, apologetically, as though to a prospective tenant, 'It's just a bedsitter with a kitchen behind a curtain. Oh, and a bathroom, of course – I couldn't bear not to have my own bathroom.' She opened the door and led me in.

It was comfortable and it was feminine, and for a bedsitter it was almost unbelievably tidy – no clothes lying about anywhere. There were quite a lot of books, there was a pile of magazines, and some newspapers.

Nina hung her coat behind the door and said, 'It will be Pilsener, won't it?'

When I nodded she went behind a curtain in a corner of the room and came back with bottles and glasses to where I'd sat down on the settee. She opened and poured expertly. Sitting at the other end of the settee, she raised her glass, took a generous mouthful, and said, 'That feels better.' She looked at her watch. 'You don't live very far away, do you? Well, I know you don't. But you're not in an awful hurry to get home?' Without waiting for an answer, she went on: 'I'm breaking the rules if I ask questions, but were you very unhappy at school?'

'I hated every day of it – every hour.'

She gave me a look of the warmest gratitude.

'We're two of a kind,' she said.

She took a gulp of lager – it was always a gulp – and held it for a moment in her mouth before she swallowed it. She tipped the rest of the bottle into her glass, put it on the floor beside her, clasped her hands over a knee, and seemed to be pondering something.

When I'd finished my drink, she noticed and, without speaking, got up to fetch two more bottles. As she poured my glass and handed it to me with the rest of the bottle she said, 'I'm sorry about tonight. I do have a thing about being locked up, especially about being locked up *myself*. I did identify with that man in the film.'

She took another gulp, and I did the first of a lot of identifying that I was to do with her.

'How I hated school!' she went on. 'Not the lessons – no, it was having to leave the sunlit world of our big garden and the fields around. Shut in, even at lunch-hours and playtime, behind the high gate that I always thought was a prison gate. Shut in, in that big brick building, for the hours of lessons. Do you mind if I talk?'

'Of course not. I want you to. I like to listen to you.'

'You can have your turn later if you want to,' she said. 'I was afraid of punishment every hour I was there. I can remember every lie I told to avoid it. Not owning up when other children did if I knew I'd be punished ... that kind of thing.'

She stood up suddenly and went over to her kitchen again. Her voice came from behind the curtain.

'Come and talk to me.'

I got up. There was the same tidiness in her kitchen. She was cutting some cheese into little pieces.

'You hadn't finished,' I said.

'I haven't talked to anyone quite like this before,' she said. She was buttering some water biscuits. 'It's strange. I suppose it's because you don't ask anything or seem to expect anything of me, but seem interested.'

'I don't just *seem* not to expect anything. I don't just *seem* interested,' I said.

'It's just me,' she said, and smiled. 'I have to qualify almost everything I say – sometimes till it almost disappears.'

She was taking pickled onions out of a jar

and putting them into a little bowl. She put everything on a tray, pulled up a straight-back chair by the settee, and put the tray on it.

'I'm not going to feed you,' she said. 'Just have what you want.' She went on talking as she sat down again. 'Then, when I was ten, my mother died. My father was a trade union organizer. He used to go away a lot. He sent me to this boarding school. I still can't understand why. It would probably have cost him no more to have a housekeeper or someone, but he was a man who liked his privacy, and I suppose he didn't want anyone else, a stranger, around the house. Anyway, he sent me off to this school, this prison – I always thought of it as a prison. I've already said that, haven't I? I was there for five years. I suppose the discipline generally wasn't all that harsh, but I was afraid. I hated it.'

She put her hands over her face and said into them, 'I'm sorry.'

'Don't be sorry,' I said.

She'd run away once, just for a day. She'd paid dearly for it, but still remembered it as one of the happiest days of her life.

'Because it was unexpected, I suppose, and because it was stolen.' She was suddenly amused. 'Stolen, I mean, like a stolen kiss. There was a little hill not far from the school, with fields round it and some woodland. It was late summer. I had Thoreau with me, *Walden* – it was my bible then and still is, in a way. I sat in the sun against a tree and read it. I heard the bell ringing for lessons and felt such joy that I wasn't there to answer it. I picked fat blackberries, and I lay in long grass and went to sleep in the sun. But I made a mistake.'

She went back to her Pilsener, and when she didn't go on I said, 'Yes?'

'I went back to the school when I should have run right away. That night they locked me in my room. For the next night, too, and for two whole days.' She put her hands over her face. 'I could *never* bear to be locked up again. I'd tell any lies to avoid that. That's what I was thinking about when you told me that story about Alfred Hitchcock. Oh, the joy when I went out those gates for the last time! It was like crossing a frontier, but … but … now why did I say that? I hadn't learnt about frontiers then.'

She put her glass down and stared at me desolately. The suddenly she said, 'Oh, Tony, oh, darling, I'm so afraid.' She put her arms around me and lay tense against my shoulder.

'There's nothing to be afraid of,' I said, and I started to stroke her hair.

'Nothing to be afraid of?' she said. 'Oh, yes there is.'

With my mouth almost on her ear I said in a voice that I hoped was as gentle and sympathetic as Mr Krasko's, 'Are you afraid of the man who sat beside you today in the Paddington Street garden?'

Nina jumped up and stood staring at me, her eyes wide with horror. Then, in a fierce whisper, she said, 'You know! You're phoney! You're a *spy*!'

I started to plead, 'Nina, wait a minute...' But she rushed on. 'You're the smoothest ever. You really fooled me. I really trusted you, and I want so much to trust someone. I even hoped you'd want to make love to me tonight. And all the time... I should have known. It was just too good to be true. The socialist talk, the *New Statesman* and all. You were so patient – *God*, how patient you were!' She said it in a tone of heavy sarcasm. 'You just waited and asked no questions. That's what fooled me most of all.'

'Nina...' I said, as I started to stand up.

She rushed to the door, locked it, and took out the key.

'You won't get away with it,' she said. Her voice was starting to break. 'You can't get away with it. But what am I to do? God, I even told you *what* I am afraid of.' She started to cry.

'Nina, you've got it all wrong,' I said. 'Believe me. It's just as you thought it was. I don't know what you're talking about.'

She looked up almost hopefully and said, 'No? No, I mustn't believe you.'

68

She went over to the bed, sat on the edge of it, and sobbed into her hands.

I stood away from her and said, 'Listen, Nina. If I hadn't met you last night, if I hadn't felt I should give you that message from Mr Krasko, I wouldn't even be here. I'd have gone to Amsterdam and – and Berlin by now.'

She was suddenly in control again.

'Berlin?' she said, very coldly. 'You were going to Berlin?' She jumped up and faced me. 'Look, what sort of fool *are* you? What do you take me for? You're telling me to trust you and you mention–'

Her voice trailed away as if she had suddenly remembered something else, and almost in her old soft voice she said, 'Listen. I want to ask you some questions.'

We went back and sat on the settee. Nina looked at me. I waited.

'I'm no good at this,' she said at last. 'I don't know where to begin. I don't know how to tell whether you're telling the truth or lying. I always thought I was right in my judgments of people. It's something I'm almost conceited about. I felt from the start that I could trust you...'

I pulled back my cuff and took a calculated look at my watch.

'Nina,' I said, 'I can't stay all night. I suppose it doesn't matter what you believe, though I'm sorry you're upset. I'm sorry I broke the rules by – by asking you that question. Now listen.' I looked at my watch again. 'I'm going home in ten minutes, and I'm leaving London in the morning for – for the Continent. I don't know what you think I'm going for. I don't know what you're talking about. But I'm going to get away from everything and everybody, because I've had a bellyful of everybody. I'm going to Amsterdam and Berlin and Copenhagen because these are places I like – places I've been happy in, if I ever *have* been happy.'

She opened her mouth to speak, but I held up my hand impatiently.

'All that you've been going on about makes me wonder whether there's something political in this. It's just a suspicion, and I'm not going to *ask* you anything about it. I suppose you'll think that's just part of my cunning! Anyway, I'm not involved in political things in any way, and I don't want to be. I'm a socialist, but I'm an onlooker. I'll never be anything else, I hope. Till a few weeks ago I was leading a rather dull life as a sub-editor on a motor sport journal and living with my wife across in Maida Vale.'

'You've got a wife?' Nina said.

I held up my hand again and said, 'Yes. I walked out on her, and I walked out on my job and found a room in Marylebone while I tried to make up my mind to go away. Mr Krasko just happened to be living in the room above me. We had a phone on my landing, and I must admit that his calls fascinated me. But I know nothing more about him than that he left in a hurry in a sports car after getting a phone call, that the police called, that he phoned me later with a message for you. I suppose it was the only thing he could think of. He must have been desperate. Of course I was curious. But it was for some stupid kind of human loyalty – to Mr Krasko, I mean, and to you – that I put off leaving for Amsterdam, so that I could give you that message.'

I stopped and sighed, looked at my watch yet again, and said, with a feeble smile, that I was running over time.

'What else? I saw the message that you were given in the bar and, oh well...' And I gave her a rather confused explanation of how I had worked it out. 'So,' I said, 'I went to the Paddington Street garden on a hunch. You could have seen me if you'd been more observant.'

I stood up.

'Oh, and just so that you'll know I'm not holding anything back' – I had to play my little spy thriller out to the end – 'I followed the man who sat with you and saw him picked up by the same car that picked up Mr Krasko.'

I couldn't have chosen a better punch line. Nina started, and her face went white. She opened her mouth, gulped, and closed it tight.

'I'm going,' I said. 'I've liked being with you, and I'm sorry I've upset you.' I smiled. 'I hope we'll meet again some time – at The Old Riser, perhaps.'

She went to the door, remembered it was locked, and unlocked it. All the time she was staring at me in a frightened way. As she started to turn the door handle she said in a strained voice, 'I'm sorry, too. May I phone you in the morning if I feel I must?'

'Oh, yes,' I said, 'but very early. I'll be on my way to Liverpool Street by ten. Of course you know my number – the same as Peter Krasko's.'

She didn't say anything more as I went out and said good night, but she stood in the doorway watching me go. I was half-way down the stairs when she called, *'Auf weidersehen.'*

VI

I decided to walk home. As I passed the end of Lord's cricket ground, at the bottom of Wellington Road, I suddenly suspected that I was being followed. I hurried around the corner into Park Road. When I was sure that

I was out of sight, I stepped into a doorway. A man came by and – I was almost sure – noticed me. I couldn't really tell what he looked like because he was wearing dark glasses.

I waited and watched. Soon he slowed down, waited by a pedestrian crossing, then crossed the road. I picked him up as I got near Baker Street and tried the trick again. This time he waited across the road.

I wondered how honest I had been, with Nina, with myself, in saying that I was going to Amsterdam in the morning. My indecision was becoming a bit of a joke. I was yet again going through the 'I want to be alone, I want to be uninvolved' routine. At the same time I knew that I was more than half in love with Nina, and I was almost certain that she was unwillingly caught up in something sinister. I wanted to help her if I could. Simple curiosity about whatever it was that I had stumbled on in the past forty-eight hours was, anyway, getting the better of me.

I glanced back from time to time. My shadow was still there when I reached my turning out of Marylebone High Street.

At home I felt depressed by the grubby wallpaper, the stained wash-basin, and my untidy preparations to go away. I wished that I had got myself a better room – not that it mattered now if I was going. The old woman stirred and muttered in the room next door. Somewhere up towards the park a police car or an ambulance was hee-hawing, farther and farther away. A plane whistled by overhead.

I went over to pull the curtains and was startled to find that the fellow who had followed me was on the corner across the street, looking up at my lighted window. For the first time I felt that I really might be in danger, but as the man moved out of sight I was reassured by the thought that he was pretty clumsy. I sat on the edge of my bed and had just unlaced my shoes when the phone rang.

It couldn't be for me, I thought. Then I remembered Nina. I said, 'Hello,' and Nina said, 'Tony?' and, without waiting for an answer, 'Are you sure the car you saw today was the one that picked up Peter Krasko yesterday?'

'I'm almost certain,' I said. 'And it did look like the same woman driving it.'

'A *woman?*' Nina said. Then, again without waiting for an answer, 'Can you come to see me? I've got to trust you, Tony.'

'It'll have to be terribly early in the morning,' I said.

'The *morning?*' Nina said. 'I can't wait until the morning. I've got to see you now.'

I waited.

'Tony,' she said, with great urgency.

Again I waited.

'Tony.' She sounded really anxious. 'Are you alone?'

'Oh, no,' I said and forced a laugh. 'I have my shadow with me, the fellow who followed me home.'

'Are you serious?' she asked, in a scared voice.

'I'm quite alone, Nina,' I said. 'But I *was* followed home – shadowed – by a fellow who's still waiting across the street.'

'You must come to see me now,' Nina said. 'Please. And take care. You're in danger.'

I'd often thought, while out walking, of useful ways of using an umbrella, and I took mine with me now. In Baker Street I got a taxi.

Nina was waiting in her doorway. She gave me a brief hug and led me upstairs. She looked very scared, and she went to the window, pulled a corner of the curtain back, and looked out before she told me to sit down. She stared at me, then came to sit beside me.

'I'm involved with a lunatic espionage group,' she suddenly said. 'It really *is* lunatic. The top man is just about certifiable, but like many loony people he's very cunning. Do you really know nothing about all this?'

'Nothing.'

'The top man,' she said, 'is called Mr Winston. He's convinced that you do know and that you're dangerous. *Because* he's crazy I

75

don't know how we're gong to persuade him that he's wrong. We were seen together last night, at the pub of course, and again this afternoon. They started following us after we left the – wherever it was we saw that Hitchcock film. Mr Winston phoned me as soon as you'd left here tonight. He was *very* unpleasant, and very upset when I told him that you were going away in the morning. He said you wouldn't get far. I was afraid that they'd kill you.'

She was silent for a few moments.

'Mr Winston wants you to go to see him – tonight,' she said at last.

It was all so incredible – what Nina was telling me and the way she was telling me – that I didn't find it easy to take it seriously. A little bit of me was almost ready to laugh. I did feel afraid, but as one is afraid of some menacing lunacy. Well, hadn't she used that word herself?

'This is play acting,' I said. 'I'm not getting involved with any nutty spies. I'll call the police.'

I stood up, but Nina said in great alarm as she, too, stood up, 'You just can't.'

'Look, Nina,' I said. 'I'm not doing a bloody thing until you tell me *all* about it. If you won't I'll go to the police. I may go to them anyway.'

She was alarmed again, but suddenly taking my hands said, 'I'm innocent in all this,

76

as I can explain. Do you believe me?'

I told her that I found it hard to think of her as a spy.

'Then,' she asked, 'will you promise not to go to the police if I tell you the whole story?'

I thought about it. It was a hard thing to promise, but in the end I told her that I wouldn't go to the police if I thought it would harm her. Was it, I wondered, a promise that I'd come to regret?

Nina took a wallet from under her pillow, and from it a British passport. She opened it to show me her photograph and looked at me like a frightened child.

'It's phoney,' she said.

'Yes?' I hoped I sounded unimpressed.

'They could put me in jail for it.'

'It's possible,' I said.

'I'd do *anything* not to be put in jail.'

I nodded slowly. 'So it's as simple as that.'

'Not quite,' said Nina. 'No, no, not really – not at all, in fact. It's *not* simple. But that's how it began.'

As she returned the passport I said, 'Don't you think you'd better begin where it began?'

She sat beside me again and started to cry.

'Oh, God, Tony,' she said, as I put an arm around her shoulder, 'if you're not the real thing I'm finished now. I'd do anything – take poison, walk in front of a car. But I couldn't let anyone lock me up.' She dried her eyes. 'Do you know a man named Walter Marshall, a journalist?'

I said I did – he worked for the BBC.

'That's right,' Nina said. 'One of Mr Winston's men saw you with him at the BBC Club. At Bush House, I think he said. He listened to your conversation. He also mentioned someone called Kolchak – Peter Kolchak? Mr Winston says he's a spy. He's seen him with Walter Marshall, too.'

'He's another journalist,' I said.

'Mr Winston is pathological about the BBC,' Nina said. 'He thinks most journalists are left wing but that BBC journalists are worst of all.'

'Some people who should know better think that,' I said. 'But what about my talk with Walter Marshall?'

'This man was sure you were up to no good. You were talking about Berlin, East Berlin!'

'For God's *sake*,' I said. 'I'd just come back from looking around there for a few days on my way home from Copenhagen.'

'Never mind,' said Nina. 'When they saw me with you – twice in a day – it was enough to make Mr Winston feel that you were conspiring against him.'

She was silent for quite a while, staring ahead.

'Yes, but–' I said.

Nina came to life again. 'You know I was

born in Germany.'

I wasn't surprised, but to try to help her relax I said with a small smile, 'You're *always* telling me I know things that I don't know. I didn't know that you were born in Germany.'

'I was born in Dresden – you know,' she said. She really was incorrigible. 'My mother was German and my father was English, but he'd lived in Germany for quite a long time. He went there out of sympathy for the Germans – for the way they were treated at Versailles. He was right, of course. It led to the Nazi dictatorship, which he hated. He came back to England just before the war, soon after I was born. Later he hated Churchill for what British bombers did to Dresden. I still do, even though I never really knew the place. It was so unnecessary then, even if you believe that other German cities had to be bombed – earlier, I mean. I don't believe that, either. If the British way of life could only be preserved by killing all those innocent people, all those women and children, was it *worth* preserving? Anyway, in the end, because I wanted to know the country I was born in, I went back to Germany. But not to Dresden – I went to East Berlin.'

She went over to her kitchen and came back with glasses and two bottles of Pilsener. I looked at my watch. It was two o'clock. Nina seemed quite self-possessed again.

'It's been a rather bibulous evening,' I said, taking my glass. 'Won't Mr Winston be getting impatient?'

'Oh, he'll expect me to have a bit of trouble talking you into seeing him,' Nina said. 'He'll expect it to take some time.'

She took a mouthful of the cold lager, held it in her cheeks, swallowed, and said, 'I wonder if this will ever seem just a bad dream.' She seemed to ponder. 'You told me you were married. Why did you leave your wife?'

'Nina,' I said. 'Don't you think you should finish your story?'

'Of course,' she said. 'But just tell me that.'

I sighed.

'It's quite a long story. She'd lost interest in me. I need a lot of affection, and she used to give it to me. Of course I gave it to her, too – I still feel it for her in a sort of way. Then our little boy, our only child, was killed in an accident. And without affection and without children there seemed to be no point to it. I found myself wanting more and more to be alone.'

Nina rested her hand on my arm.

'I'm sorry,' she said.

She opened her mouth as if to ask another question but gave a faint, sad smile instead.

'I'll be good,' she said. 'I so much want to confess, but I so much don't want to talk about it. I was married, too. I went to East Berlin partly because I believed in the revolution in the East. Part of me still hopes it will come right in the end – that the state really will wither away, as Lenin said it would. Perhaps I'm just being naive. But socialism as my dear old Dad taught me to believe in it means more freedom for everyone, not less.'

I glanced at my watch. Nina noticed and looked a little hurt.

'Oh, I'm sorry,' she said. 'I do go on.'

Her apologies were becoming as frequent as Jane's.

She went on with her story.

'I was only eighteen when I married Willi. He was as idealistic as I was. I was very alone – perhaps that's why I wanted to get married. I was lonely and quite easily won. But I *was* in love. We were both active in the Party. Of course many people were against the Party because they saw it as the tool of Soviet imperialism.'

She ran her hands through her long hair, shook it loose, and said, 'This girl in the sports car – what was she like?'

'I hardly know,' I said. 'The first time I saw only her back, but she had long, blonde hair, and she wore a black leather coat. Today – yesterday – she wore dark glasses.'

Nina shook her head. 'They *all* wear dark glasses.'

'Even my shadow tonight,' I said. 'Where does Mr Krasko come into all this, anyway?'

'He doesn't,' Nina said. 'At least I *thought* he didn't. That's what frightens me.' She almost laughed at herself. 'As if I wasn't frightened before. No, Peter just helped – oh, well, I'll tell you about that when I get to it.'

I looked at my watch again. Nina put a hand on mine and looked at me tenderly. Then she emptied her glass, put it on the floor, and was back in Berlin.

'I probably influenced Willi. I talked to him – we'd talk all night – about the liberal socialist ideas I'd picked up in all those early years in England. Willi started to talk about these ideas, in the Party, among the people. That's why he was arrested.

'We had this shabby room in an old apartment block. The secret police came one night just as we were gong to bed. They were quite polite. But – but–' she covered her face with her hands again – 'they put handcuffs on him.'

When she looked up she rubbed her wrists.

'At first I wasn't afraid for myself – of being locked up, too – because I was so afraid for Willi. But they seemed to treat him quite well, though they questioned him a lot.

'Then he died. No, it wasn't their fault – at least not obviously. He caught a virus infection. I suppose he mightn't have caught it if he hadn't been in prison. Then suddenly, while I was still upset about Willi, I was terribly afraid for myself. I'd wake terrified in the night after dreaming that I'd been handcuffed.' She rubbed her wrists again. 'I wanted to get away, but I knew that if I tried to leave they'd stop me.'

Again she stared at me.

'You *do* know how terribly afraid I am of being locked up?'

As if she hadn't made it clear! It really was an obsession.

'Of course, Nina,' I said. 'Of course.' And I reached out and held her hand.

'Then one night, in a café I used to go to near the Friedrichstrasse station – I'd stare at the station and think of it as the gateway to freedom – this good-looking boy, Rudi, bought me a drink. We talked for a long time, but not about anything – well, not about anything sensitive. I went back to his room. He made love to me. In the very early morning, as we lay together, he woke me to say that he knew who I was and all about Willi and why Willi had been arrested. If I wanted to get away, he said, he could get me a forged passport.

'I suppose I should have been more suspicious than I was. *More* suspicious? I wasn't suspicious at all. I thought he was doing it for love.'

She stretched out her hands as if warming them at a fire and gave me a long, wistful, yearning look.

'I'm astonished now that I wasn't more afraid of being caught with a false passport,' she said. 'I suppose one fear cancelled out the other.'

It had all been quite cleverly done, she said. It seemed clever to her, anyway. The passport's pretence was that she had come from a visit to Denmark, across the Baltic and through East Germany, where she'd joined the train on its way to East Berlin. Apart from the nervous wait there, at the Ost station, that I, too, remembered so well, when guards with rifles watched the train, it had all seemed so easy. There were no awkward questions, no delays. Her dream about Friedrichstrasse station came true when she was through it at last to the West. It was even more wonderful when the ferry from Calais brought her into Folkestone harbour.

'I saw the green fields of England beyond the town, and I felt happy.'

VII

Nina gave her tiniest smile and put a hand on mine.

'I didn't even think about my false passport,' she said. 'Were the British going to question what the East Germans had accepted? Of course they didn't. I was so happy to be back that I walked all the way from Victoria with my suitcase, across the park, and to Sussex Gardens, where I knew I'd find a room.

'How good it was to put my bag down in my room and to listen to the music of London's traffic. I was going to rest for a while, then go for a walk, but there was this phone call that I'd promised Rudi I'd make – just to say that I'd arrived.'

She clasped her hands tightly, compressed her lips, closed her eyes, and when at last she opened them said in a toneless voice, 'I went down to the phone in the hallway. Oh, they were *very* pleased to hear from me. Rudi had told them so much about me. Would I come round for a drink? I was very tired, I said. Could I come tomorrow? Oh, no, they wanted to welcome me now. I'm not sure why, but that was when I felt the first chill touch of fear. They wanted to talk to me. They'd send a car to fetch me. It was Mr Winston's car...

'If they were people *playing* at spies they'd be too good to be true. It's one of the ways their lunacy shows. But they're not just a joke. They're quite efficient in their way. Take that passport of mine. They see themselves as the world's saviours fighting against Communism – an intelligence élite.

'But their B-movie gimmicks! I was so

scared when I got into the car. It was a big black Bentley with a uniformed thug at the wheel. Another sat with me in the back. The windows behind me and at both sides and between me and the driver were dark, one-way glass – but one-way so that I couldn't see *out* of the car. The gorilla just sat there beside me with a hand inside his coat, like Napoleon.'

Nina gave a wry smile as she held her right arm across her breast. Then she looked at her watch.

'You'd better go soon,' she said. 'You'll find Mr Winston – that's what he's always called, just *Mr* Winston – you'll find him behind a desk, in the shadows at the end of a long room. Of course he's wearing dark glasses, but everything tells me he's the young top executive type. That seems right. I suppose that's because I do so despise people who dedicate their lives to profit and loss accounts – to making money and to what passes for good living in the Sunday paper colour magazines. They see their corrupt, decadent lives threatened by socialism, and they're right. But Mr Winston! Intelligence élite! They've let it turn their heads.'

They'd given Nina a drink, and Mr Winston had come straight to the point. They were in the intelligence business in the fight against Communism. Nina had been in trouble with the Communists in East

Berlin. Mr Winston's people had helped her. Perhaps she'd like to show her gratitude by helping them.

'I was simple-minded enough to think I had a choice. So I looked into my glass and said that I *was* grateful, but I was sorry – I thought this would be something I would be no good at. Mr Winston said there were all sorts of ways in which people could help. He thought I *should* help. It would be bad for me if they – if the police – found out that I had come to England on a false passport after being active in the Communist Party in East Berlin. I thought hopefully about political asylum and mentioned Willi. Mr Winston was sounding all the time more menacing. He said I should not reckon that the sad story of Willi would help me. Rudi would take care of that.'

Nina suddenly stood up, went across the room, and looked out of the window before she went on.

'I stared at Mr Winston, and he smiled. I could hear the jailer turning the key in the lock, and I knew I'd do *anything* to stay free.' She laughed bitterly. 'Free!'

'But Nina,' I said, 'you weren't hooked as easily as that? You could do something about political asylum even now.'

Nina held a finger to my lips and went on to tell a bizarre story. Mr Winston, she thought, might have felt that she would pretend to agree to work for him, then disappear. So he'd suggested that she might pay off her debt with a small job they had to do that very night. When she had protested that she was too tired, he'd said there was nothing to it – they'd take her in the car. She'd been driven into the country – it must have been into the Chilterns – and told to knock on the door of a certain house and ask her way to Chalfont and Latimer underground station.

One of Mr Winston's men had gone with her to the door but had suddenly disappeared into shrubbery when her knock was answered – by a man in dark glasses. While this man had stood on the roadside with her, the better to give her directions, she'd heard a shot from the house. The man who was helping her had rushed back inside.

Had someone been shot? Had someone been killed? She didn't know, couldn't know, and no one would answer her hysterical questions when, back in the car, the man who had gone to the door with her and come back carrying a pistol sat wiping it with a handkerchief.

I told Nina that I'd seen a trick like that done in a 1940's gangster movie to lead someone to believe that they'd been an accessory to a murder, though there had been no murder.

But how could she be sure? Nina asked. I

had no answer. From conversations over-heard – because she had been meant to overhear them? – she believed that Winston's men did use guns.

Back in London, before taking her back to her hotel, they'd stopped outside the Paddington Street garden and pointed out the little Barcaglia street orderly sculpture, just visible in the pale moonlight. That was to be her rendezvous when, within a few days, she started her life as a courier.

Nina could make no more sense of it than I could. The black glasses that they all wore, the coded messages to the pub or wherever, her whole involvement – why her? – made her wonder, as I wondered, whether it was romantic nonsense. She couldn't, she thought, be value for money, either. But she kept coming back to the guns and the shooting in the Chilterns, if it was a shooting, which I kept having to admit I couldn't be any more sure about than she was. And if Winston and all of them were out of their minds, didn't that perhaps make them all the more dangerous? I hoped that, eventually, I'd find out.

There was also what looked like a personal thing between Winston and Nina, which worried me, as it worried her.

'Once a week,' she said, 'I get a sermon from him – a lecture. Then he says he's quite fond of me, and the look he gives me scares me. I ask him, "Haven't I paid off my debt?" Then he reminds me of Chalfont and Latimer, says they've got to take care of me, asks how I would get along if they *didn't* take care of me.'

She stopped with a helpless wave of her arms, and there was a long silence.

'Where does Krasko come into all this?' I asked.

'That's what frightens me almost more than anything,' Nina said, and not, I thought, for the first time. 'Are you quite sure that the car you saw yesterday was the one he was driven off in the day before?'

'I'm almost certain,' I said. 'And the girl at the wheel was dressed the same as the one who drove him away.'

'Peter was a friend of Willi,' Nina said. 'He'd been looking for me in London. A little while ago he found me. He just asked me, in quite a tentative way, whether I'd go back to Berlin. He said he could make it all right for me. He's always been a mysterious man who seemed free to come and go across frontiers, but he was worried about something that last night. So I wasn't all that surprised when you told me he'd had to go away. I liked him, though, and trusted him. If he should somehow be connected with Mr Winston – it's too awful to think about, too frightening.'

Nina looked at her watch.

'Oh, Tony darling – will you go to see Mr

Winston now?' she asked. She stood up.

'What does he want to see me *for?*' I asked. 'What will he expect of me?'

'Mainly reassurance, I think,' Nina said. 'I'm afraid for you, too. But knowing him I'd be more afraid for you if you didn't go. I'd be really afraid for you then.'

I thought it over for about half-a-minute. In the end it was the thought that knowing Winston might help me to help Nina that really made up my mind. Not that it needed much making up. I think I'd known for some time, and everything she said made me more sure, that for me it was all the way with Nina from now on.

'All right,' I said.

She opened a little cupboard above her bed, took out a telephone, and standing it on her dressing table started to dial. As I stood beside her she replaced the receiver and said, 'Of course you'll try to remember the number, but it won't do any good. It's changing all the time – very often, I mean. One day I tried dialing four or five of the old ones, but they were all dead.'

She turned and faced me.

'The strange thing is' – she shrugged helplessly – 'it isn't altogether a secret organization. It's interested in propaganda – I suppose *they'd* call it public relations – and somehow, sometimes, something gets into the news.'

She turned back to the phone and dialled. I stood close behind her and put my arms around her. She shivered and caught her breath, and her voice was very soft as she said, 'It's Nina. Tony Fredericks is at my flat. Yes, he's ready to see Mr Winston.'

'The car's coming,' she said as she replaced the receiver.

When she faced me her eyes were very liquid, her lips were parted, she was breathing very quickly. She stared at me. 'Yes, I want *you*, too, but it can't be now.'

I put my arms around her. She caressed my cheek.

'Now, Nina,' I whispered.

She just found my mouth and pressed herself against me. We were still standing like that when we heard a car stop outside, its engine running quietly.

Nina pushed me away gently and said, 'Oh, darling, come again as soon as you can.'

She went quickly to the door.

'I can't help you,' she said. 'You're on your own.'

I stopped by the door, but she compressed her lips and shook her head helplessly.

VIII

I closed the front door quietly and walked across to the big waiting Daimler. I wanted to look up at Nina's windows, but a front door of the car was open and I thought it might be better if I didn't. A man in a uniform and a cap, and wearing dark glasses, got out of the driver's seat. As he opened a rear door for me I saw a husky fellow in dark glasses in the back seat. Just as Nina had said, I found when the door closed that I couldn't see anything outside through the dark glass all around me. I felt very unhappy, and if my heart was beating faster than usual it wasn't, now, because I had felt so close to making love to Nina.

All the same, as the gorilla sat beside me, doing his Napoleon-at-St-Helena thing, I did think about Nina. I knew that I had a small problem, if 'small' was the right word, in wanting to be with her and wanting to be alone. It was the Jane problem, but rather more acute. I thought about it. I didn't want to come home to Nina every night if that meant always doing the things that *we* decided to do. I didn't want to make the effort to adapt to someone else's ways and, worse, the people in someone else's life, that two people have to make when they live together. But just then I wanted more than anything else to be with Nina, and quite as much for simple affection and tenderness as for what might come after.

When the car stopped I looked at my watch. It was four o'clock. We were in a big garage. I was hurried out of the car and into a lift. In a very big room, just across the corridor from where we came out of the lift, Winston was sitting in his dark glasses, in the shadows behind a table. He waved me forward and dismissed the gorilla. It was so theatrical! There was a seat in front of the table, but before Winston asked me to sit down he held out his hand to shake mine. It was – it had to be – a hot, damp, limp handshake. His face was flushed. Even if there hadn't been a bottle on the table I'd have known he'd been drinking.

He didn't take his eyes off me as he took a glass from behind the desk, asked if I'd have a Scotch, poured two without waiting for an answer, and pushed mine across the table. Then he offered a box of long, thin cheroots. When I said I didn't smoke, he lit one for himself. He was the kind of man you see in advertisements for spirits saying things like, 'I always think a brandy and a soda enhances a woman.' If vodka hadn't been a Russian drink, I might have thought he was another example of the shattering effect of Smirnoff. I already hated his guts.

He was probably in his mid-thirties, fleshy, with shiny black hair brushed close against his head. He had a cultivated voice with a fashionable lisp, and an unpleasantly insolent edge to it. Still, he began politely enough.

'We've seen you about with our Nina. We do not like to bother you, but we are somewhat possessive about our Nina. We want to make sure that you have good intentions.'

Then came a laugh that Nina had mentioned. I could see what she meant when she said he *began* to laugh. It was always only a beginning. It died away, as a laugh does when a man suddenly realizes that the joke is on him. It was alarming.

Suddenly Winston glared at me.

'How much has Nina told you about us?' he asked.

Before I could begin he snapped, 'Well, how much?'

'Look Mr Winston,' I said. 'I gather you've got some notion that I'm a dangerous left-winger or something. Maybe even a spy. I'm not interested in politics.'

'You read left-wing papers,' he said. 'You are a friend of Walter Marshall.'

I laughed in a way that almost convinced me that I was amused. It *was* funny, in a lunatic way.

'The *Guardian?*' I said.

'The *New Statesman,*' he said aggressively.

'It's a way of keeping in touch,' I said. 'Walter Marshall? *He's* no leftie, and even if he were' – I laughed again – 'he's a handy fellow to know when you're hard up, as I am. They do a good salad really cheap at Bush – at the BBC Club.'

He leaned towards me across his desk but didn't speak for quite a long time. All I saw was his pair of dark glasses, and I felt my return stare was very ineffectual.

'When were you last on the Continent?' he said at last.

I told him that it was about two years since I'd been there.

Had I been to Berlin? Yes, quite incidentally – though I imagine that nothing was incidental to him. I'd come from Copenhagen and spent a few days there. Of course – I thought it best to volunteer it – of course I'd gone to East Berlin to have a look.

With the voice of a man who was sure he'd caught me out, he asked, 'Is that where you met Peter Krasko?'

I gave a deep sigh and said, very slowly and patiently, 'I don't even *know* Peter Krasko. I've spoken to him a few times because he happened to be living in the building that I live in. I found my bedsitter' – I thought how absurdly irrelevant it was – 'by looking at cards in a shop window.'

Winston was silent for a while.

'That is not so unusual,' he said at last. 'The left underground uses many ways to communicate with its agents or even with fellow travellers.' He paused. 'Then how did you know that Krasko was in touch with our Nina?'

'That's easy,' I said, and I was thinking as I said it that this conversation would have been a whole lot easier for me if I'd had some idea how much he knew about the Nina–Krasko connection. 'I'd seen them in the pub, and they'd seen me.'

I waited for him to ask the next question, but he knocked the ash off his cheroot and waited for me to go on. I wished I'd asked Nina more and hoped I had my lines right. 'That's how I got to know Nina – if you can call it getting to know her. Mr Krasko went away.'

I paused and looked at him. He was nodding, quickly, impatiently.

'So was it strange–?' I wondered whether it was wise to make him seem unreasonable and changed my line in mid-sentence. 'Well, it didn't seem strange to me to speak to Nina when she was there alone in the pub. Of course we got around to Mr Krasko and his going away. He went, you know, in such a hurry. She seemed as puzzled about it as I was.'

He didn't pursue the Krasko line, which

surprised me, and when he asked me about my work I just told him the truth. In the end he stared at me for a long time, more than a minute, before he said, 'That is all. Go now. I might want to see you again. Do not try to be clever, Mr Fredericks. Does Nina know how to reach you?'

I knew that he knew she did, but I just said that, yes, she had my phone number. As he nodded, I heard someone come into the room behind me. I look round. The gorilla was holding the door open.

Winston said no word of farewell, but I'd just reached the door, without looking back, when he called: 'Fredericks!'

I turned round. Again he waved me forward theatrically and dismissed the gorilla. When I'd sat down he looked at me glumly in that stupid, sightless way.

'Many people know that we are working to free Eastern Europe from the Communist tyrants,' he said at last. There was a hint of megalomania in his voice. 'But we cannot have our enemies, or friends of our enemies, knowing how we go about it. It would put at risk our trusted friends and workers here and abroad.'

I moved impatiently and said, 'I don't…'

But he interrupted: 'Be quiet and listen,' paused, then leaned forward and snapped, 'You know Peter Kolchak, too.'

I remembered this small, serene, friendly

man, in his mid-fifties, who wrote on the Communist world for a Sunday paper. I said that, no, I didn't really know him, though I'd had a drink with him two or three times with colleagues who'd introduced us when I worked in Fleet Street.

'Would you help him if he was in trouble?' Winston asked.

'Listen—' I said.

'Would you?'

'For God's sake!' I said. 'For a start, what *kind* of trouble? It depends, can't you see?' I wasn't playing it very cool. 'And I wouldn't be likely to know if he was in trouble. I don't really know him, any more than I know Krasko. I haven't even *seen* him for, probably, a year.'

'He is a spy,' Winston said, dramatically.

I shrugged sceptically.

'He is gong to be arrested tonight,' he said. 'He has been far too clever to be caught with the evidence, but this time they will find it on him.' He gave a manic, frightening laugh, which this time went well beyond a beginning. 'It is your chance to help him, if you are one of his kind. I think we understand one another, Mr Fredericks.'

He waved dismissively.

I wondered, as I went down to the car, and sat in it on the journey back to town, what sort of impression I had made on Winston. Everything, I thought, depended on that. I hoped that I'd reassured him at least a little, and decided that perhaps I had. I didn't feel happy about the encounter, though, and what he had said about Kolchak left me very uneasy.

It was starting to get light when the car dropped me at my door. Back in my room I undressed, splashed some water on my face, and got into bed. I felt washed out. Even so, I lay awake for a long time going over all that had happened in what had seemed to be the longest day of my life.

IX

In a way, the meeting with Mr Winston had done me good. At least I had faced him now and no longer feared what had been unknown. During our second conversation, after he'd called me back, I'd felt cool and contemptuous, but I was still scared about what I had become involved in.

The Kolchak situation sounded especially sinister. Though part of me couldn't take it quite seriously, I felt that I must. Was Kolchak being framed? I half-suspected that. Should I warn him? If I did, that crazy man Winston would draw his own crazy conclusions about it. If I didn't, he might be reassured about me, though it seemed to me that it might tell him only that I was scared and wanted to stay out of trouble. Even if I had been a spy, would it seem all that strange if I didn't warn Kolchak, since I had my own survival to think about? Spies, I supposed, were quite amoral, but I knew so little about them that it wasn't easy even to try to think myself into their likely attitudes.

My inclination was to do nothing and see what happened. I could always come forward with my story if Kolchak was arrested, though anything I said then might not carry much weight. There was a risk, too, I thought, that Winston would try to frame me in some way.

I began to think again about making a run for it in the morning on the early train from Liverpool Street. I could even fly off somewhere else, to Dublin, perhaps, but didn't feel confident that I'd be safe. When I really faced it, I knew I wouldn't go if I felt that Nina was in any danger. I couldn't see myself, anyway, walking out on an unsolved mystery that probably would still be there, perhaps even more menacing, when eventually I had to come back.

I began to think about Krasko. I got out of bed, dressed, and crept up the stairs to his room with a torch. I was very surprised to find that the door was not locked. I went in and looked about. There was the usual litter left by anyone who has vacated a room. There were old newspapers, some of them from East Germany – all of these around the same few days about two months before, when Krasko must have been there. There were old bus tickets, a few crumpled envelopes, things like that. None of them told me anything that I didn't know.

It was quite light now. I went over to the window and looked down into the street. Across on the corner a man – in dark glasses, of course – was standing. I stood to the side behind the grubby curtains and peeped out, hoping that he hadn't seen me. Every now and then he glanced up at the building. Winston, I thought, must have a lot of people playing spies if he could afford to have one watching the place while I slept. It was going to be difficult to go anywhere without being followed.

I went down to my room and got back into bed, and eventually fell asleep. I had more than half expected to be woken by an early phone call from Nina, but when I did wake it was nearly eleven. I lay there hugging my pillow and thinking how completely unheroic I was. I hated the thought of ever having to get up to a day of such incredible difficulty. It was just as Nina had said. I thought of such mornings during my unhappy schooldays when I would lie wishing I could become so ill that it would be impossible for me ever to go to school again. I remembered the formula 'Everything will be all right, Mum, won't it?' as I went off to school, and the help her reassurance gave me in my despair.

I smiled now at the memory, thought, 'Well, I'm a big boy now,' threw back the covers, and got out of bed. Ah, the glorious freedom I'd found by leaving my wife and my job! I sliced open a couple of stale rolls, buttered them, lay some slices of cheese between, and made myself coffee at the little gas stove in the corner. As I ate and surveyed my untidy room, I was alert for a phone call. Then, unwilling to go out even for a paper in case Nina phoned, I packed with sudden resolution, tidied all the rubbish away, and left the few things I had to use neatly laid out on the table.

I felt better. My shadow was still across the road. I'd thought I could possibly get out undetected through a rear window, but there was no point now in trying to avoid him. At midday I decided to go out for a paper and a drink. In Blandford Street I found a newsagent who still had a *Guardian*, and, sure that I was being followed, I walked up the High Street to The Old Rising Sun. There, on the dull red upholstered seat in the corner where I'd first met her, was Nina. I was so surprised! It was a possibility I hadn't even thought about.

She looked tired and very anxious, but she

smiled with what I supposed was relief when she saw me. In my own relief I wanted to go straight to her, but with a great show of coolness I bought a pint of beer before I went to sit beside her.

She almost gasped, 'Oh, God, Tony, I thought you'd never come. I've been here an hour, since opening time.'

No one had followed me into the bar. I looked round at all the other lunchtime drinkers before I said, with forced calm, 'Why didn't you phone me?'

'I don't know how,' Nina said, 'but I think my phone's being tapped. It's just that Mr Winston spoke to me this morning and seemed to know what I'd said to you when I phoned you last night.'

'I doubt it, I really doubt it,' I said, almost impatiently. 'Anyway, there are call boxes. Or you could have come to see me – you do know where I live?'

Nina looked bewildered and gestured helplessly. She said that in fact she didn't know where I lived, and that she had thought it best for me not to be able to phone her. She looked at her watch.

'I haven't much time,' she said. 'I've – I've an appointment at – at twelve-thirty.' She gave me a frightened look. 'I was so sure you'd come here very early. It was something Peter Krasko said about you – that the pubs could never open too early for you. How did you get on last night?'

'I might have done worse,' I began, and before I could say any more she said, 'I'm so frightened – I'm terrified. Mr Winston said' – she looked around the bar in terror before she went on – 'Mr Winston said I'm to pick up some papers and instructions, some orders, at twelve-thirty for a job I'm to do this evening. He said I wasn't on any account to see you or get in touch with you until the job's done. Don't follow me, Tony. I'm afraid for me, and I'm afraid for you too.'

'I can't follow you, anyway,' I said. 'I'm being shadowed. There's a man outside.'

'Are you sure?' she said. 'Oh, God, what *are* we going to do?'

We were both silent for a few moments.

'I have a feeling he's going to start giving me dangerous jobs,' Nina said at last. 'Did he threaten you last night?'

'He says he doesn't trust me,' I said. I was just about to tell her about Kolchak when the door from the High Street opened, and the man who'd been following me came in. Nina saw him, too, and must have recognized him. She froze, looked at her watch again, said urgently, 'Darling, can you see me at eight-thirty this evening? It should be safe by then. I'll just have to phone you before then if you still mustn't come.'

Then she drained the half-full glass of lager in front of her, and walked out into the

High Street.

The man in dark glasses didn't seem to be taking any notice. I went to the bar and ordered a cheese salad. It was nearly one o'clock by the time I finished it.

I left quickly and went back to my room. I was worried about Nina and about Kolchak. I still hadn't made up my mind whether I should interfere. I decided to phone Walter Marshall at Bush House and ask him some questions about Kolchak, but the duty editor there told me that Walter was away in Vienna and wouldn't be back till the next day.

I thought about Kolchak, imagining him in prison that night, and then phoned his paper to ask if he was in town. The features department said that, yes, Kolchak was still in London, but he was leaving that night for Warsaw. That startled me. I asked if they could give me his home address. Of course I didn't expect it straight off, but after a few more questions they did give it to me. Kolchak's home number was unlisted though, and no, sorry, I couldn't have that.

Now I felt that in one way or another I might be involved if Kolchak was arrested, but at least that would make my story more credible if I came forward to try to help him.

I left my room and went up the stairs to where a window looked out over roofs and backyards. I opened it and leaned out. There was a fence below, a few feet from the building, and beyond that a four-storey building with a concrete driveway that led away towards the opposite side of the block. I could see that if I wanted to get away from the place undetected it wouldn't be too difficult to get over the fence, but I could see no way down the sheer wall to the inside of the fence.

I went up the stairway to the third and top floor and found a trapdoor, bolted on the inside, that opened out on to the roof. I climbed out and looked down into the back area. In one place blank backs of buildings would shield me so that I would probably not be seen if I got down the wall on a rope. Water pipes that ran across the roof looked a safe enough anchorage for a rope. It was years since I'd abseiled in the mountains, but I remembered the technique.

As I came back to the trapdoor I heard the phone ring two floors below. It kept on ringing. I got back inside, heard a door open and the voice of the old lady from the room next to mine. Then there was a tapping, and her cracked voice called my name. I started to run and almost fell. By the time I reached the landing the old lady had hung up and was standing in her doorway, looking frightened.

'Oh, Mr Fredericks,' she said. 'I'm sorry. I didn't know you were upstairs. A lady was ringing for you.'

'Did she leave a message?'

She shook her head.

I went in, sat on my bed, and tried to read the newspaper. It must have been Nina who had called. With what fresh alarm? I tipped on to the bed the contents of the air travel bag that I used for my few overnight things.

I looked at my watch. There was still plenty of time for the bit of shopping that I had to do. I wandered around the room, sat down a couple of times, and tried again to read the *Guardian*. I opened the door and stared at the phone as if that would make it ring. Sure at last that Nina had taken her one and only chance to ring me, I slung my bag on my shoulder, locked the door, and started down the stairs.

I'd just opened the street door when the phone upstairs rang again. I shot up the stairs like a rocket and lifted the receiver before the old woman could even open her door. Of course it was Nina. She was in a public call box and very distressed.

At her rendezvous in the Paddington Street garden she had been given a small sealed packet and an envelope addressed to herself. When she opened the envelope at The Baker and Oven pub across the street she had found a letter telling her to call on Peter Kolchak at half-past six that evening. The visit had been arranged by one of Winston's men who had begged Kolchak to see Nina because, he said, she had a cousin in Warsaw and wanted Kolchak to take a personal message to him.

Nina had got as far as that and was in mid-sentence when the phone went dead. Her voice had become more and more agitated, and I felt sure that much worse was to come. I waited beside the phone for about a minute, and back in my room for another two or three. Then I raced round to The Baker and Oven, but she wasn't there. Getting more and more anxious, I looked frantically for her in the nearby streets. I didn't find her. Had she been interrupted by one of Winston's men while making the call? It seemed more than likely.

When I got back I asked the old lady next door if there had been any calls. There hadn't, and after waiting impatiently in my room for only a few minutes I went out again.

The man spending all his time shadowing me flattered and rather amused me now. When I saw him standing across the street, I decided that, just for fun, I'd give him a bit of a run on my way to Gray's Inn Road, where I wanted to do my shopping.

So, starting in Devonshire Street, I set out at a good pace, weaving in and out of the various mews. Once or twice, with a short sprint as soon as I was out of sight, I almost lost the man. If I did want to shake him off, I thought, it wouldn't be impossible, or even very difficult, especially at night. This thought, and the childish pleasure I was getting from leading him a dance, cheered me up. I began to enjoy myself, plotting my moves ahead as I hurried along.

At Great Portland Street I looked at my watch, realised that The Albany, across the street from the tube station, would still be open, and dawdled till he almost caught up with me outside the pub. Then I darted through the corner door, shot across the door opening into Euston Road, and out into the street. Hurrying back to the corner door I managed to get through just in time to see him disappear into Euston Road.

I sat on a bar stool and ordered a drink. It was all of five minutes before the Euston Road door opened and he looked in but didn't come in. I left as the last bell rang, feeling subdued after ten minutes' thought. There he was, standing on the corner watching the entrances. I didn't feel like playing any more and walked across to the tube station, where I took a train to King's Cross.

It was a roundabout way to go, because it meant that I had to walk south the whole length of Gray's Inn Road before I got to the shop I wanted, Blacks of Greenock. The place fascinated me. I wandered around looking at the new light haversacks that had come on the market since I had last used one, at the gaily-coloured new tents, and the incredibly light ice axes. Then I bought what

I'd come for: a perlon climbing rope and a pair of Jumar clamps for climbing a rope. I was sorry to have to pay out so much money for something I expected to use for only a very short time and bought the cheapest anorak I could find. Then I walked west along High Holborn.

In Tottenham Court Road I bought a pair of dark glasses, took the tube to Bond Street, and walked the rest of the way home. My shadow was never far behind.

Back in my room I set the alarm for about an hour later, lay on my bed, and went to sleep.

X

It was, as I should have remembered, a silly thing to do. The alarm woke me to a state of nervous fatigue, negative and irresolute. I rolled over and hugged my pillow, then snapped my eyes open, stared for a moment at the unwelcome sunlit world outside my window, and got off the bed.

I still hadn't decided what I was going to do about Kolchak. I went to the wash-basin, held my face flannel under the tap until the water ran very hot, and sponged my face: it was a quick way to freshen up that I remembered from my first long flight. I washed my mouth and swallowed a glass of water. I did drink it sometimes. Then I closed the curtains, turned on the light, picked up my bag, and went up the stairs and out on to the roof.

When I looked into the area behind the building I couldn't see anyone. Before my luck changed I uncoiled the rope and quickly tied one end to a couple of water pipes. In minutes, paying the rope out around one thigh and over my shoulder, I'd walked backwards down the side of the building to the ground. I left the rope where it was, scrambled over the fence, and five minutes later I was flagging down a taxi in Baker Street.

I wished now that I had got rid of my shadow during the afternoon and had a look at the place, somewhere off Kensington High Street, where Kolchak lived. The taxi dropped me a hundred yards short of the corner of the street. Although it was still very warm, I put on the anorak as well as the sunglasses and hung the blue air travel bag over my shoulder. I hoped I looked like a tourist.

Kolchak lived in a pleasant terrace house in a narrow street. There was a pub on the opposite side, only about a dozen yards beyond Kolchak's house. I went in and ordered a pint. A tall blonde in dark glasses was sitting at the only table, by the window, from which Kolchak's house could be seen, so I stood in the open doorway, looking out on the street and sipping my beer.

I looked at my watch: it was six twenty-five. I glanced at the blonde and saw her look at her watch, and then, her gin or whatever it was poised half-way to her lips, stare tensely into the street. She must have realized suddenly that I was looking at her. She turned her head and gave me a brief but open smile. I smiled back and again looked up the street. I glanced back at the blonde. She had taken off her sunglasses and was looking at me with somewhat startled curiosity.

I heard footsteps from the direction of the High Street. Both of us looked up the street to where Nina had appeared. As she came up towards Kolchak's house I could almost hear my heart beating. Should I rush across and stop her? Then, only a few yards behind her, I saw her shadow. I gripped the doorway and took a gulp of beer as Nina rang Kolchak's bell. It was one of those things with a talk back beside it. I could see Nina put her mouth to it, then press the door and disappear inside. Her shadow had paused a few yards short of the door to light a cigarette. Now he walked on, looking over at the pub as he passed. I glanced back at the blonde. She was looking at me coolly, and when I tried a smile she didn't react. I was sure she knew that my interest was the same as hers.

I glanced back into the street. After three or four minutes Nina came out and looked up the street to where her shadow had stopped and was watching her. She glanced across at the pub. I thought for a moment that she was going to cross over to it, but she turned and walked back towards the High Street.

For a suicidal moment I thought I'd wait till she was out of sight and then go to see Kolchak, though I had only the wildest idea of what I might say to him. But just as Nina turned out of sight to the right a black Jaguar turned out of the High Street from the left and came towards us, stopping outside Kolchak's door. Three men got out. One rang the bell and spoke into the talk back, two of them went inside. The other waited, leaning against the car and every now and then staring up at the windows above Kolchak's door.

The blonde and I again looked at each other and back at the door. Ten minutes passed. At last Kolchak's door opened, and one of the men came out. He spoke to the man still waiting, who opened a rear door of the car and lifted out a photographer's gadget bag and a tripod. Then both went inside.

In another five minutes two of the men reappeared leading Kolchak between them. He was wearing a trench coat, was bareheaded, and looked frightened. I could see as he got into the car that he was handcuffed to one of the men. The driver got back into the car and reversed quickly back along the narrow street, into the High Street.

I felt shaken and sick and frightened. I took my empty mug back to the bar and ordered a double Genever, which I hardly ever drank, except in Amsterdam. The blonde had got up and was speaking to the second barman, who reached behind him and put a telephone on the bar. She made a call, cupping a hand round the mouthpiece as she spoke. I swallowed the gin in a couple of gulps while she was still talking and eyeing me at the same time. Then I went quickly out and, as soon as I was out of sight, ran to the busy High Street.

A hundred yards east, near Kensington Gardens, I called a taxi. I hadn't any idea what I should do next. Just short of the Albert Hall, I left the taxi and went into Kensington Gardens. Whatever else I did, I decided that I might as well be free of the men shadowing me until they picked up my trail again when I went to see Nina.

I walked as far as the Round Pond, sat on the grass, and envied three small boys playing with a yacht and a motorboat, two lovers kissing as though they were the only people in the world, and, most of all, three ducks diving for food in the shallow water near the edge of the pond. A girl, probably about eighteen, in a very short skirt above very long legs, was walking barefoot through the grass, carrying her shoes in one hand. As she went sauntering by, she gave me a smile of invitation. I smiled back and badly wanted to follow her, but what was the point? A week ago, I thought, I might have done so. Was this the free life that I had left my wife and my job to enjoy?

I looked at my watch: it was still only a quarter-past seven. From the direction of Mayfair the whistle of a big jet sounded above the muted roar of the city. I watched the plane climb above the trees, pass overhead, and disappear in the direction of Heathrow.

The two lovers had stopped kissing and with amused smiles were watching the small boys wading out to rescue their overturned yacht. I looked longingly after the girl with the short skirt and the long legs and the bare feet and the smile. Now a couple of hundred yards away, she had stopped to talk with a young man. I'd taken off my anorak and put it in the air travel bag. Using it for a pillow, I lay on my back, staring up at the traces of cloud that seemed to lie still high in the sky, and tried to make up my mind what to do. I couldn't think of anything. Playing, as I'd thought, for safety, I had let Nina become even more deeply involved. But, then, what could I do but play it safe, unless I betrayed Nina's trust and told the whole story to the police, or to someone else? Or was this just an excuse for doing nothing, which, for all my anxiety, was still the easiest thing to do?

I'd been lying with my eyes closed, feeling already an aching tiredness as the effects of the beer wore off, and half wishing that I would go off to sleep and not wake again. When I thought of the night ahead, the meeting with Nina, and the efforts to find a way out of all this, I wanted only to stay where I was.

I opened my eyes. The lovers were walking towards Notting Hill Gate. The small boys had rescued their boat and were playing some sort of tag game on the edge of the pond. The girl who had smiled at me was no longer in sight. I got up and started to walk towards Marble Arch.

I got to Nina's flat at about a quarter-past eight. I heard her running down the stairs as soon as I'd rung her bell. She was wild-eyed when she opened the door and almost ran up the stairs ahead of me to her door. Inside, she started to weep hysterically and wouldn't let me near her to comfort her. When at last she could speak, it all came out.

Just as I'd supposed, her call to me during the afternoon had been cut off, by a hand that suddenly appeared from behind her. She'd been taken to a car, driven home, warned in an angry phone call from Winston not to go out again till her assignment in the evening. When the evening came, she'd been dropped in Kensington, just around the corner from Kolchak's house. The man who had followed her to the house had let her see that he had a gun.

The car had waited for her in the High Street and taken her back to Acacia Road. The whole assignment had terrified her from the moment she had first been told about it. But it wasn't till she got home and Winston had phoned to thank her that she was told that the packet she'd left for Kolchak to deliver was in fact evidence that would lead to a charge against him of spying when he was arrested after she had left the house.

In her distress, Nina took a long time to tell me everything. What seemed to upset her more than anything was something that Winston had said right at the end. He told her that I had known all about Kolchak, knew that he was to be arrested as a spy, and had shown good sense by not interfering.

'Did you know?' Nina asked.

I looked away from her.

'Yes, I knew.'

She came close, took me by the shoulders, and looked at me with anguish.

'Why didn't you tell me?' she asked.

'I didn't know you were involved,' I said.

'Not till you phoned. What difference would it have made, anyway? We're caught like rats – like mice – in Winston's trap. It's incredible, really, that you'll do things like this, anything, rather than risk being exposed to the police – though, God knows, I do know how you feel about being locked up. I've promised you that I won't do anything that'll expose you, and I'll keep my promise. But now *I'm* being drawn in. I feel already that I'm an accomplice in Kolchak's arrest. I did nothing when I knew he was to be arrested. I stood by while they took him away.'

'Perhaps they haven't taken him,' Nina said. 'Perhaps they only pretended, just to test our loyalty and make us feel involved. You always thought they might have done that on that first night I was back in England, when they took me to the Chilterns, and I thought there was a shooting. Perhaps even Kolchak is one of them.'

She looked at me with sudden hope. I looked away again.

'No, Nina,' I said. 'I *actually* stood by while they arrested him. I was there. I was in a pub across the street. I saw you come. I saw you go. I had to know. And they know that I know. One of them, a woman, was there watching. I'm sure she knew who I was.'

Nina stared at me in fresh horror. Then she sat on the bed and again started to cry. I did my best to comfort her, and when she was calmer I said, 'I tried to think of a way out, but there was so little time, and I really knew so little – not much more than nothing – about what was going to happen tonight. I was going to talk to Walter Marshall – he's the BBC man Winston is so paranoid about. No, no, *no,* not about you. About Kolchak and the spy group here and all the rest, just to see what came out of it. Unluckily, he's away and won't be back till tomorrow. It just might help to talk with him if I could see him without Winston's men knowing. In the meantime, what can we do about Kolchak?'

Nina said suddenly, 'Mr Winston would like you to work for the organisation. I hadn't told you. He says that after another test you might be ready to start. A test. That means giving you something to do that'll really involve you, so that you daren't betray them.' She turned and looked at me, and said, as she'd so often said before, that she was sorry.

She kept looking at me. She was quite calm now, and she started to caress my hand. I looked down at her long, slender fingers. Suddenly she gave a deep sigh, then one of her helpless shrugs, let go my hand, and stood up.

'Don't go, Nina,' I said tenderly. I held her tightly around the shoulders. She started, and her eyes were very bright and mobile as they seemed to be taking in every detail of my face. I began, gently, to ease her down on to the bed so that I could lie beside her.

'Let's do it properly, darling,' she said suddenly. 'Let's get into bed.'

So we made love and then lay together. I was almost asleep when I gave a start. Nina asked what was the matter. I had thought of Kolchak in a police lock-up, just like Henry Fonda in *The Wrong Man,* but I didn't tell her. I said that nothing was the matter.

When I woke it was getting light. I looked at my watch: it was half-past three. My mouth was dry and stale from the day's drinking. Nina, still facing me, breathed deeply as she slept, her lips just parted. I looked down at her for a long time, and felt tender, unworthy, and sick with longing. I put my arms around her and presently slept again.

When we woke it was after seven o'clock. Nina kissed me, then sat up and looked down at me, at first smiling and tender, then grave, wistful, forlorn, and frightened. She sighed, got out of bed, put on a dressing gown, and went into her little kitchen.

I lay and faced the new day. It looked just as hopeless as the old one. Nina came back with coffee and a plate of buttered rolls on a tray, put it on the bed, sat beside me, and sugared my coffee. I sat up and put a blanket around my shoulders. We ate and drank without speaking. Then, without looking at me, Nina said:

'What a pity it was for you that you went to live in the same house as Peter Krasko. Everything seems so much worse for you than it was a day or two ago. For me too, in a way, but especially for you. I've got used to it all, anyway. When I come to think about it, I'm almost resigned. Wasn't it Thoreau who said that resignation was confirmed desperation? He wasn't exactly talking about my situation. Still–'

She sighed.

'But then if you hadn't met Peter I wouldn't have known you. Yes, I know, you'll say I wouldn't have missed what I didn't know, or whatever it is they say. Well, all right. But *I* say I wouldn't like not to know you – I would hate it. Anyway, you do in a sense miss something that you've never known if you have that empty feeling, an unsatisfied craving for something. For tenderness and affection, in my case. Now I've found them.'

She turned to look at me and said in a toneless voice, 'Darling, what's to become of us?'

Soon I got up and dressed. I told Nina I'd go out for a paper to see if there was anything in it about Kolchak's arrest. Just across the road a small saloon was parked. I knew straight away that the man in dark glasses at the wheel was one of Winston's men. He seemed to take no notice of me, but when I looked back as I got down towards the tube station the car was turning in the road.

Outside the station I bought a *Telegraph* and a *Guardian*. As I started to walk back towards Nina's room the car passed me and stopped outside the station, from where I could be kept in sight.

I didn't open the papers till I was back inside. I spread them out on the bed. Kolchak's arrest was there all right. In a small column six lead on page one the *Telegraph* said only that Kolchak had been arrested at his Kensington flat on suspicion of spying, that papers found at the flat were being examined by the Special Branch, and that he would make a brief court appearance in the morning. The *Guardian* had more detail and a picture of Kolchak. It mentioned that he had been due to fly out of London for Warsaw a few hours after the time that he was arrested.

Though there was nothing in the stories that we didn't know or hadn't guessed, I was shaken, and Nina was distressed. For both of us, I suppose, it was like the cold print announcement of the death of an old friend or the first telegram that you get when you have lost a member of the family: it made it so final. We didn't talk again about what we should have done or even about what we should do next. After promising Nina that I'd meet her in The Old Rising Sun at noon, I left soon after eight o'clock.

There was the same drill as before with the car. I knew it would follow me. I wondered what would happen if I made a quick exit by way of the tube station, but there was really no point. I was going home, and I wanted to walk.

It was a sunny morning and already quite warm. There were a lot of pretty girls about on their way to work, and my night with Nina and my tender feeling for her didn't get in the way of my appreciation. Kolchak's arrest, and the whole intolerable situation I had got myself into, did, all the same, preoccupy me. I chased my ideas around and got almost nowhere – almost, because I did at least decide to talk with Walter Marshall during the day and see if anything came out of that. Though I could probably reveal a bit about my entanglement, because I felt sure he would be discreet, I knew that I would have to be careful about linking my trouble with Winston's organization if I was not to break my word to Nina.

I had been keeping an eye on the car that was following me, and noticed it pulling into the kerb just off Marylebone High Street. A hundred yards ahead was the corner that I turned just before I got to where I lived, and on it a man was standing. As I got a little closer I could see that he was wearing dark glasses. It was so silly that I couldn't help smiling.

XI

I turned the corner by the antique shop and started to cross the street. A dark-haired woman was standing outside my door. She turned, probably because she heard my footsteps. I almost stopped dead as I saw that it was Jane. I gave a smile of sorts, but I didn't expect her to smile back, and of course she didn't.

As I took my key from my pocket I said, 'Hello, Jane. You'd better come in.'

At the bottom of the stairs she turned to face me.

'*Dear* Tony,' she said, 'you *are* a bastard.'

'Let's go up,' I said.

There were already tears in her eyes as I turned to her when I closed the door inside my room. Then she really started to cry.

Through her tears she said, 'Oh, God, Tony. There was no need to *pretend* that you were going away. I'd much rather you'd told me that I wasn't wanted. I hate dishonesty, and you make me feel even cheaper than I felt the other night, though God knows why. I felt really bad then, throwing myself at you. Now I despise you as well.'

She took out a handkerchief and tried to

dry her eyes, but she went on sobbing. I took her arm.

'Look, Jane,' I said, 'I *was* going away. I wanted to go away. I still want to go away. But everything's gone wrong, and, honestly, I don't know what to do next.'

She stopped crying and stared at me.

'What do you mean?' she said.

I told her to sit down and went over to the window and looked out.

'Did you notice that fellow out there wearing dark glasses?'

'So what?' she said, with fresh irritation.

'He's been following me around.'

'He wasn't following you when you arrived here this morning,' Jane said. 'He was there when I arrived half-an-hour ago. He was there when I came here last night.'

I'd walked back to the bed.

'You've not even shaved. Whose bed have you just got out of?'

I shrugged and sat down close to her, but she edged away.

'You were here last night?' I said. 'How did you know I was still in London?'

I put my hand over hers as it rested on the edge of the bed. She didn't take it away, and she looked at me with almost innocent curiosity.

'There was this phone call yesterday to the office,' she said. 'From a woman. I happened to answer it. She asked if we knew

126

how to get hold of you. I told her you'd gone to Amsterdam or Berlin or somewhere. She said that couldn't be so because someone she knew had been talking to you in London the night before.'

I must have looked suddenly alert or startled, because Jane then said, 'You know the woman I'm talking about?'

'No, no. It's just that I've spoken to hardly anyone.' I stopped and thought for a moment. 'The night before last I spoke to only about two people that I can think of. Did she say who she was or what she wanted?'

'Oh yes,' said Jane. 'Well, what she *wanted*, anyway.'

She opened her handbag, took out an envelope and handed it to me. I began to open it.

'They're tickets to dinner and the show tonight at a night club called The Blue Dahlia. It's off the King's Road. This woman said she wanted you to go. She remembered your pieces on racing drivers, she said, and some of the drivers were going to be at The Blue Dahlia tonight. It's the British Grand Prix tomorrow, you know. At Brands. I know because *I've* got to work.'

I stared at her. She looked back with her big, dark eyes, waiting for me to react. I was thinking hard. It was possible, I supposed, that someone had seen me, but I was sure that in the last day or two I'd spoken to no one who had anything to do with motor sport. I'd told Winston about my connection with a motor sport journal, just to show how neutral – how far from politics – I was.

'Are you sure this woman said someone had spoken to me?'

It was a silly thing to say, because I knew how reliable Jane was.

'Quite sure,' she said. 'I remember feeling so jealous that she might be another of your girlfriends.'

'And where did the tickets come from?'

'Someone brought them to the office about an hour later.'

'You didn't see who brought them?'

'No. I didn't. Does it matter? You should be pleased you still have admirers.'

'I'm not interested, anyway,' I said.

I shrugged and tossed the envelope on to the bed. Jane picked it up.

'I am,' she said. 'I'd love to go.'

She looked at me hard. I started to smile, and Jane almost smiled herself.

'That's different,' I said. 'If I have someone to go with.'

Jane turned, put her arms around my neck, and whispered in my ear, 'Oh, Tony, will you really take me?'

I gave a small nod.

'Oh, Tony,' Jane said. 'I love you so much that it hurts.'

It was a bit of a cliché, but it sounded nice

when someone said it about me.

I had put my arms around her, and Jane rubbed her silky cheek against my unshaven one and began to nuzzle me till she reached my mouth. I knew that I couldn't deny her this time. I didn't want to. But even while I savoured her affection I was thinking the thoughts of a man in despair, a man who so much wanted more than anything else to be alone but was now hopelessly involved not just with one woman, but with two.

It wasn't till afterwards, as we lay together for a long time, that Jane asked the question that I knew she had to ask before long.

'What's gone wrong, Tony? Why didn't you go away?'

I didn't answer but snuggled close to her. I could feel her stiffen suspiciously.

'Was it a girl?'

'It wasn't a girl,' I said, 'though there was a woman involved.'

I was going to say that it was almost a horror story but Jane cut me short as she rolled away from me.

'I'm so jealous. I don't want to be. I shouldn't be. But I'm so jealous.'

I rolled on to my back, clasped my hands behind my neck, and stared at the stains on the ceiling. They reminded me of the areas of chipped paint on the door of an old shed at my home when I was a child. I had always thought of them as lakes joined by rivers. I'd never felt very nostalgic about my child-hood, but lying there, wondering what to say to satisfy Jane, I thought how secure it had been and, in spite of the horrors of school life, how uncomplicated when com-pared with my life now.

The phone on the landing rang and went on ringing. I hoped it wasn't Nina. The old woman answered it, talked for a bit, and went back into her room. She started talking to herself, but I couldn't make out what she was saying.

'I can't explain it, really,' I said lamely. 'It's very hard to explain.'

'I'll bet it is,' Jane said.

She sat up suddenly, ran her fingers through her hair, and said, 'Anyway, I've got to go. I have things to do.'

I got off the bed and looked down at her.

'Look, Jane,' I said. 'I hope I can tell you all about it soon. I *am* in a mess. I *am* in trouble. I'm not sure that I'm even on the right side of the law. All because I delivered a message – I thought it was a harmless message – from a fellow who was living upstairs.' I nodded to-wards the ceiling. 'He seemed to be in some sort of trouble.' I raised my arms in a helpless shrug, and Jane softened.

'Don't worry, Tony,' she said. 'I keep getting possessive when I know I've no right to be.'

She got off the bed, came up to me, and

hugged me.

'I don't suppose anything lasts,' she said, 'but you've – you've made me so happy.'

She went over to the mirror above my wash-basin and started to comb her hair.

'It is a bit squalid,' she said.

'Squalid?'

'The room and all.'

She turned and smiled.

'Perhaps you weren't just trying to put me off the other night.'

I couldn't leave well alone.

'You do trust me?' I said.

'Oh, I trust you,' Jane said, with no conviction at all. She put her shoes on.

'What are you doing at Brands tomorrow?' I said.

'Oh, lap scoring, or some damn thing. Dogsbody for the great white chief who'll be covering the race. Why don't you come out?'

I shook my head. Jane repaired her make-up and picked up her handbag. We settled to meet at Victoria at eight o'clock, by the Calais platform. We went down the stairs and kissed goodbye, and I saw her out.

I'd thought from time to time of the rope still hanging from the roof, where I'd left it for my re-entry the night before. Now I went up the stairs, got out through the still unbolted skylight, and crossed the roof. I had a good look around but could see no one. I pulled in the rope and took it down to my room.

I thought again about Walter Marshall and wondered what I could possibly say that would not be some kind of betrayal, however well meant. I was getting to the point, anyway, where I had to talk to someone I wasn't emotionally involved with, even if it didn't lead me anywhere. Walter would do me as much good as any psychiatrist. I'd always thought of him as the best kind of BBC man – as solid as a rock, but sympathetic and sensitive. He was one of the old school, less interested in promotion and big money than in dedication to all the things that broadcasting as a public service stood for. How wonderful, I thought, that there was still such a good person around.

I phoned Walter's office at Bush House. Yes, they said, he was back from the Continent, but he'd probably be out of his office for most of the day. Still, if it was urgent... It was rather, I said. Well, he was going to see some documentary people at Kensington House, and after that he'd be with various people at Television Centre. If I rang in about half-an-hour, I'd probably get him there.

I went back to my room and started to shave. Looking at my face, when I'd washed and dried it, I saw that the strain was showing. I had a ragged look, and my skin was dry and chafed. My hands were a bit shaky, too.

I rubbed some lanolin into my face, put on

a clean shirt and tie, brushed my shoes, and went out. I walked over to Baker Street, to the restaurant where I'd first taken Nina what seemed like months ago. I was just going to order a steak when I thought of Nina and asked for a mushroom omelette instead. It was the first really good meal I'd had for a while. I realized that I needed it. It made me feel much better, and I took my time over the pot of strong black coffee.

Outside it was a wonderful sunny day. I strolled back to the High Street through the Paddington Street garden, pausing to look at the little street orderly. Suddenly I remembered that I was being followed. In the High Street I bought a loaf of French bread, cheese and butter and tomatoes and some small bottles of Continental lager. I felt as if I was laying in stores for a siege.

Back in my room, I phoned the number I'd been given for Walter. He was somewhere around, they told me, if I'd just hang on. Half-a-minute later he came on the line.

He seemed quite pleased to hear from me. When I got round to telling him that I was on the loose and suggested a drink, he said it was a great idea. Why not come up to the Centre and have a drink at the club? So we settled for one-thirty. I only hoped as, still a bit hungry, I cut a slice of cheese and halved a tomato and poured myself a lager, that Nina hadn't heard anything that would make it difficult for me to keep the appointment. I went over to the window where the sun was shining in. My shadow and I looked at each other across the street till he couldn't stand it any more and turned away.

At noon I went out to see Nina. My shadow came into the bar and sat round the corner, only just in sight. Nina had heard nothing since I'd left her in the morning and seemed more relaxed – except when, briefly and inevitably, we got on to Kolchak. She sipped a lager and looked at me tenderly and affectionately. Once or twice I thought of Jane and wished I hadn't.

Nina suggested a walk in the sun. She was disappointed, but quickly herself again, when I said that I had at last talked to Walter Marshall and was going to Television Centre to meet him. She was upset when we got around to talking of the evening ahead. She couldn't see why I should want to get involved in a motor sport occasion. Well, I'd promised now, I said, and couldn't get out of it, but I kept telling her that I'd go to her as soon as it was over, however late it might be. In the end, she was calmer.

So that's how it was when I left her at Baker Street station, went back to my room, and put the rope in my air travel bag ready for my second abseil exit.

I knew that I'd be in big trouble if Winston ever got to know that I'd gone to see Walter

Marshall. Did his crowd suspect that I'd slipped out by some other exit the day before? Or did they just kick themselves because they thought that somehow I'd got out of the front door undetected? It puzzled me, and troubled me more and more, that they should think me important enough to watch as closely as they did. It was flattery that I'd have been very glad to do without.

XII

I made a blind-side exit, and in half-an-hour, by way of Bond Street and an underground train to White City, I was at Television Centre. I had forgotten how crowded the club at the Centre usually was at that time of day and thought there might be a problem in having someone find Walter for me. As it happened, the commissionaire remembered me from earlier visits. He let me go in to find Walter, sitting over towards the terrace, and Walter went out and signed me in.

Walter was a quiet, rather romantic-looking man who, at around forty-five, was still youthful. He had a ready smile. I was sure women loved him. Though we didn't meet often I thought of him as more than an acquaintance. I hoped he thought the same about me. In my Fleet Street days we'd had long talks in The Punch Tavern or at Bush House Club after we'd finished work.

I felt that he must have been puzzled, perhaps amused, at my switch to a motor sport journal, and even more so at my interest in motor racing, though he would never have remarked on it.

We took our drinks back to his corner, and when he asked me what I was doing was interested in my plans to go abroad. He talked about his own visit to Eastern Europe and the political currents there, then broke off as if he'd suddenly remembered something, stared bleakly out in the direction of Wormwood Scrubs prison, looked at me and said, 'You know Peter Kolchak, don't you?'

I said that I did, though not well.

I watched a couple of young actresses come down the steps, pass us, and go out on to the sunlit terrace as Walter said, 'You saw the news about him, of course?'

I nodded.

'You know, I can't understand his arrest. It doesn't sound right at all. I can understand spies in a way, the dedicated men – or women – who are loyal to an idealogy, to their country, even to another country. But I'd have bet anything that Peter couldn't lead that kind of life.'

I must have shown my feelings, because Walter said, 'It has upset me. I can see you feel strongly about it, too.'

I was given time to think about how I'd answer by a welcome distraction – loud laughter from the next table, where two trendy young men were trying hard to impress a very young woman. They were so wrapped up in themselves that I was sure they wouldn't notice anything I might say, even if I announced the second coming of Reith.

I turned with a half-smile to Walter, who seemed not to have noticed the diversion. He was looking at me with the same troubled face, still waiting for my answer. I was sure that I had the very bright-eyed, guilty look that I'd seen in people expecting to be caught out doing wrong. I wanted to clasp my hands over the top of my head as I had as a child when I'd tried to pretend that I was innocent. Then, looking at Walter's strong, compassionate face, I felt that I wanted to confess. Perhaps he would even give me a kind of absolution.

'Walter,' I said, 'Peter Kolchak is one of the reasons I wanted to talk to you.'

I thought: Dare I betray Nina?

'I'm in the most god-awful mess,' I said, 'and other people are involved in a way that really binds me to silence. Could I talk to you about something that will shock you, and ask your opinion as though it were a hypothetical case?'

'I'm not sure that I understand what you

137

expect of me,' Walter said.

'I'm going to tell you something that you may feel you should do something about. Supposing I confessed to you that I'd, well, badly injured a child in a hit-and-run accident?'

'Oh, I see,' he said. 'You want me to promise to do nothing.'

I nodded uncertainly.

'You're asking a lot – but I'm touched by your trust.'

I waited. Walter sighed.

'I suppose so,' he said at last. 'Yes, I suppose so.' He sighed again and looked very unhappy. 'Who am I to play God, anyway?'

'It'll take a bit of telling,' I said. 'Are you in a hurry?'

He looked at his watch and said that he could spare half-an-hour.

'Peter Kolchak was arrested on planted evidence.'

I felt like a man unable to swim who has jumped into very deep water. I hadn't expected Walter to look quite so shocked.

'You know that, and you're not going to do anything about it?' he said. 'I mustn't do anything about it, either?'

'It's not as simple as that. I know something must be done eventually, somehow. Tomorrow, in a few days, next week,' I said, desperately inventing a timetable that I was almost sure I couldn't keep. 'If I speak out now about what I know I may endanger someone who has trusted me. Someone who is terribly afraid of the police and may have good reason to be afraid.'

I rubbed my hands over my face.

'Go on, Tony,' Walter said, more kindly.

'Don't misunderstand me,' I said, 'but I'm still not sure what I should tell you. I feel so bound by a promise.'

I stared out of the window at a Metropolitan line train that was racing up towards Wood Lane as if it wanted to plunge into it and commit suicide.

'Do you know a man called Winston?' I said.

Walter looked surprised. 'Winston?' he said. 'Winston?'

'*Mr* Winston,' I said. 'It's a surname.'

'Oh,' he said, 'oh. You don't mean the man who runs some kind of anti-Communist group that seems to have East German connections?'

That was the man, I said. Walter nodded.

'You don't know how seriously he's regarded?'

'Not really,' Walter said. 'Are you trying to tell me he has something to do with Kolchak's arrest?'

'That's exactly what I'm trying to say.'

'Any moneyed megalomaniac is potentially dangerous, I suppose,' Walter said. 'But – Kolchak. No, I didn't think of this Winston fellow in that kind of way.' He pondered. 'We've almost certainly got a note on him. I could have a look.'

Suddenly, to my great relief, Walter had dropped his good citizen's indignation and become the reporter ready to consider every point dispassionately and follow it as far as it was necessary to go to get his story.

'Look, Walter,' I said. 'I've *got* to talk to someone. I met a girl quite by chance. A comparative stranger asked me to give her a message because he couldn't keep an appointment with her. There was something odd about her – and, well, she confided in me, she confided in me so much. I hung around. This brought me under suspicion.'

'Whose suspicion?' Walter asked.

'Winston's,' I said. 'I'm telling this very badly. The girl works for Winston, though she has no sympathy with what he's doing or with his politics. *She's* a socialist. But she has been compromised. I'm still not sure how badly, but probably very badly.'

I was saying more than I really believed, because I wanted to play it safe in making out a case for protecting Nina.

'She's scared to death. Now Winston is testing *me* out – I've actually been to see him. The girl thinks I'd be in real danger if he felt I was working against him. I'm followed, shadowed, most of the time. God knows why Winston takes me so seriously. I think I gave them the slip today – I hope so, because I've been seen with you before, and you're reckoned to be a Red agent or something of the sort.'

Walter laughed and said to me, kindly, 'How seriously do you take all this? It sounds a bit like fantasy. You don't think the girl–?'

I shook my head vigorously. I looked again at the young people at the next table. It seemed so odd that they hadn't stopped to listen to the story that I was telling, as I was sure I would have done.

'This is the one thing I don't want to tell you,' I said. 'The girl planted the evidence that led to Kolchak's arrest – though she didn't know she was planting it. I saw her go to his flat. I was watching from a pub across the street when he was arrested.'

As I paused, Walter looked angry again. It didn't suit him at all. He seemed to be having trouble finding words, but at last he said, 'It's intolerable. It's *quite* intolerable. Your worries are one thing – yours and the girl's. Don't think I'm unsympathetic. I may be unjust, but–' He shrugged impatiently and made as though to get up, but he sat back again and said, 'I may be unjust, but it seems that you've *bought* trouble.'

'It's true in a way,' I said. 'Even of the girl, it's true in a way.'

'But Kolchak – well, of course we don't

know, we *can't* know,' Walter said. 'As I see it he's probably just been picked on by Winston because he's a liberal who sees that the East German Communists must have a point of view. But to have evidence of spying planted on him! To be in prison! He's probably suffering terribly.'

I nodded miserably. Walter put down his empty beer mug and looked at his watch. Desperately I asked him if he'd have another drink. I was a minute or two at the crowded bar, and as soon as I sat down again Walter said, 'Couldn't we get the girl away, out of harm's way?'

'While we do something about Kolchak, you mean?'

'I was thinking of him more than of anyone else. But for her own good, too. If she's afraid of the British police – it *is* the British police?'

I nodded. I didn't want to say that she was just as frightened of the East Berlin police.

'Then couldn't she get out of the country?'

'They watch her very closely,' I said pessimistically.

'You got away. *How* did you get away?'

I told him, and he gave a smile of wry amusement and said, but only, I felt, half seriously, 'Perhaps you could get her away the same way.'

I entertained the idea before I dismissed it

142

as he sat silent, staring over the roof-tops towards the city.

'It's intolerable,' he said, yet again. 'I've never been a conspirator, and I don't want to become one now. But I keep thinking of Kolchak. This girl, now. You're not in love with her?'

I said that I was afraid I might be.

'I don't want to be unkind,' he said, 'but you're probably a bit of an innocent when it comes to dealing with people in this kind of work... Anyway, I've got to go.'

He stood up. My anxiety must have been very obvious, because he said, with a very faint smile, 'Oh, all right. All right. I promised. Foolishly, I promised. I won't talk to anyone.' He paused. 'Not yet, anyway.' It was a very out-of-character threat. 'How can I get in touch with you, tonight or tomorrow? Without any of this steeplejack stuff, I mean.'

He took a note of my phone number.

'I'll stay here a bit,' I said. I hadn't finished my drink.

Walter went up the steps towards the door. I thought suddenly of Krasko and wondered whether I should have mentioned him. Perhaps it was just as well that I hadn't. I'd got a load off my mind but had said already more than I'd intended. To mention Krasko when he was so close to Nina would seem near to betrayal – if I hadn't already betrayed her.

I looked around and was startled that so many men, and women, too, wearing dark glasses were sitting eating and drinking and smoking and talking. I felt surrounded by people faintly disguised. Any of them might have been one of Winston's odious creatures.

I swallowed my drink and went out, looking behind me as I hurried towards the lift. I didn't slow down until I was outside in Wood Lane, telling myself that I was a bloody fool. I turned south towards Shepherd's Bush Green and then east to Holland Park tube station and took a train to Oxford Circus.

Back in Marylebone, I went up the back wall on the rope. The Jumar clamps were easier than the slip knots of my mountaineering youth, but even so it was an awful effort, spinning in space, banging repeatedly against the brick wall. But I didn't do myself any real harm. Back in my room, I took off my tie and my shoes, set the alarm, sponged my face with a very hot face flannel, and when I lay down went straight off to sleep.

I was woken by someone banging on my door. The old woman was calling my name. When I opened the door I saw that the phone receiver was off the hook. It was Walter.

'Is that you, Tony?' he asked.

I said it was.

'Then who is this?'

I said that it sounded like Walter Marshall. He laughed and said he was sorry but that he had to be sure.

'Tony,' he said, 'I can trust you, can't I, to be absolutely discreet with anything I tell you about Kolchak? Don't misunderstand me. I'm not telling you anything that I shouldn't, in a professional sense, anyway. But you seem to be – forgive me – in such a confused state.'

'I suppose I am,' I said.

'I keep wondering,' Walter said, 'about this girl. You're quite sure she's on the level – I mean, putting your personal feelings aside?'

I said I felt absolutely certain.

'It's just that I suggested that you should get the girl out of the country,' he said. 'It could come to a point, without our intervention – yours or mine – that she could be a vital witness here.'

I waited for him to go on.

'We've nothing on Winston that's not pretty generally known,' he said. 'You know – the wealthy fanatic who backs anti-Communist propaganda here and in East Germany. But I found out that Peter Kolchak had got interested in what Winston is up to.'

'Yes?'

'I wish to God,' Walter went on, 'that I hadn't promised you I'd do nothing about it.'

'You did promise,' I said.

'Yes.'

'And if you hadn't,' I said patiently, 'I

wouldn't have told you anything.'

'No.'

After a rather long silence, Walter began again, slowly, as if feeling his way.

'I called in to see Peter Kolchak's editor – I wanted to say how sorry I was. He's still very upset. He no more doubts Peter's innocence than you or I. We talked for a bit, got away from Peter on to more general things. I made a passing reference to Winston. Peter's boss was startled and asked me if I knew anything about Winston's organisation. I told him I just wondered whether it was perhaps more dangerous than people supposed.'

'Should you have done that?' I said sharply.

Walter went on as if he hadn't heard me.

'Peter Kolchak's boss – his name's Rowson, as you probably know – then said that this was Peter's view. Peter talked to him about it only a week ago and told him he'd been getting together a small file on Winston's activities. Last night, when he heard that Peter had been arrested, he went through his things. He noticed the file on Winston and even opened it, but like all the rest of Peter's stuff most of it was in shorthand. He went home, and at about one o'clock this morning a couple of Special Branch men called just as he was going to bed. They said they wanted to look at Peter's office. They drove him into town and went through everything very thoroughly with him. They read out the titles of all Peter's files as they went through them, gave him a receipt, and took them away. The Winston file wasn't among them. It was missing.'

'Good God!' I said. 'Did he mention it to them?'

'He didn't. He hasn't mentioned it since, either, but I think he will. Especially as the cleaner reported to him this morning that he'd found a window in the office forced open.'

'Yes?'

I waited for him to go on.

'I shouldn't be telling you these things,' Tony,' Walter said. 'But you trusted me. Now I'm trusting *you*. It might help you to make up your mind, though in what way I don't know.'

'It's a bit of a shocker,' I said. 'I'll have to think about it.'

'You do that,' Walter said drily. Then he asked, 'Are you staying in tonight – in case I should want you again?'

'I suppose it must sound crazy with all this going on,' I said, 'But I'm going to a night club. I promised to take a girl from the office – my secretary, in fact.'

'Crazy?' Walter said. 'Not at all. Relax, Tony. It'll do you good. I'm not likely to hear anything, anyway, but when do you expect to be home?'

I told him I'd promised to see Nina afterwards, so I hoped it wouldn't be too late. In the end, he gave me his home phone number and asked me to ring him when I got in, however late – just in case.

XIII

I went back into my room and looked out of the window. The men in their dark glasses were beginning to get on my nerves. I wondered what I'd do if I had the power to destroy the fellow standing on the corner across the street. Nothing, I thought – he was probably just a hireling or some misguided idiot. I wondered what he would do if I tipped off the police and they came to pick him up and question him and ask him to take them to his master. I hadn't thought of that before. Now it occurred to me that if it came to the point where I had to get away unobserved that was one way to do it. Still, there was no special point in going unobserved on my date with Jane. So when I'd shaved and washed I left by the street door.

I took the underground through to Victoria, where I found Jane waiting. She looked startlingly beautiful in low-cut, very short, black velvet. There were big silver rings in her ears, and she had a bright red cloak over her arm. I gave her a big smile and a tight, affectionate hug. She breathed, 'Oh, Tony, darling' into my ear. Then I stood back, admired her, gave her another big smile, and offered my arm as we went into the underground.

On the short run to Sloane Square I said, 'I've been thinking about this evening. It doesn't make sense. Racing drivers don't go night clubbing the evening before a world championship race.'

'What does it matter?' Jane said. 'Perhaps *you're* the celebrity.'

'You know I'm not a celebrity,' I said. 'It doesn't make any sense to me. Perhaps I'm just being too suspicious.'

'Of what?'

I shrugged and looked at our reflection in the window.

'I wish you'd trust me, Tony,' Jane said.

'It's not that I don't trust you,' I said. 'Perhaps I'll be able to tell you about things soon. You'd worry if I talked to you now. You might even be in danger.'

'Now?'

'No. But you might be if you knew about things.'

'What difference could that make?'

I shrugged again.

'What difference could it make?' Jane said

again, and, when I still didn't answer, 'I'm worried, anyway, and I don't mind worrying more. I don't even mind being in danger if I'm helping you.'

I looked at her and felt very tender. I smiled and said, 'You're nice. You're sweet.' I squeezed her arm, looked away, and said, 'But don't get too fond of me. I'm a lone wolf.' I was going to add, 'And I want to be,' but I didn't want to hurt her at the start of a night out – I didn't want to hurt her, anyway. I was relieved that the train was stopping.

There was no conversation as we started down the King's Road till Jane said in a small, slightly hurt voice, 'You don't act like a wolf. Still … I don't want to be a bother.'

I put my arm around her, squeezed, left my arm there, and said, 'You're no bother. You're sweet. I like being with you.'

It was true, too. The words meant a lot. I squeezed her again and said, 'Now, let's have a ball.'

We walked on through the crowded, bustling, noisy street. The night club was one of those intimate places that seem no larger than a very big lounge in a rather grand house. There were fewer than a dozen tables around the walls, and when we went in only about half were occupied. Between the tables was an oval dance floor, partly of glass tiles with coloured lights shining through from below. On a platform at the end of the room away from the entrance a dance band was playing – mainly Dixieland, I was pleased to hear. It made me feel more relaxed when I wasn't really feeling a bit like having a night out.

I had suddenly started to think of Nina. It already seemed such a long time since I had seen her, and I worried quietly as I wondered whether she was safe. And whenever I thought of Peter Kolchak it was like a physical shock, a missed heartbeat.

A waiter who showed us to our table addressed me by name and straight away offered a list of drinks. Jane ordered a gin and French, and I had just a Genever and water. With the drinks came *hors d'oeuvre*.

I looked around. They had a few motor racing motifs among the decorations. As for racing drivers, all I could see so far were a couple of very minor Formula 3 drivers who seemed already to be having what we used to call a gay time with two very pretty girls. Jane saw me looking at them and gave me a sulky glance. I laughed and said, 'Big deal,' and mentioned the drivers' names. She looked relieved and laughed, too.

The menu came. We saw that we could keep going all night if we wanted to, but neither of us was very hungry. Jane ordered chicken. I thought of Nina and again asked for a mushroom omelette. It was extraordinary the way Nina had troubled my conscience. When Jane's chicken came, recognisably a bird that could have been alive that morning, I looked at it with distaste. I hoped that Jane didn't notice.

We had a bottle of white wine, brandy with our coffee, then some port. I was relieved that at first Jane chatted away about office politics. By the time she got round to me and what I intended to do, tonight, tomorrow, and in the future, I was mellow and didn't mind.

Tonight, I said, as soon or as late as she liked, not too soon, but – I looked at my watch – sooner rather than later, I'd take her home and, whether she liked it or not, go to bed with her. I gave what must have been a rather alcoholic smile and wondered about my likely performance. She gave me a pleased, wicked smile and a very wicked wink and squeezed my arm.

As for tomorrow, I said, that was too far away to think about, the day after that was infinitely remote, and the day after that even more so, if anything could be more remote than infinitely.

Jane squeezed my arm again – it occurred to me that there'd been rather a lot of arm squeezing – then was suddenly, alarmingly serious.

'Will you go on seeing me?' she asked.

I would, I said, if I was still in London.

'Then you still think you'll go away?'

'I may have to,' I said.

The 'have to' upset her. She looked away but didn't say anything. When she turned back to me her eyes were moist, and she looked very unhappy.

'*Why* don't you come to Brands tomorrow?' she asked. 'We could have a drink between races.'

I felt myself weaken but shook my head.

'Why not?'

I said that I wasn't interested enough to bother.

I watched another couple of very minor Formula 3 drivers coming through the door with another couple of very pretty ash blondes. Racing drivers' girlfriends, I thought, were almost unbelievably alike.

'You're not interested enough to bother even for me?' Jane was saying. 'What if it was the other girl?'

'That's not the right question,' I said. 'It doesn't come into it. You're greedy. With all the goodies I've promised you in the hours ahead you're worrying about tomorrow. Let's see if the old fellow can still dance.'

Instantly ashamed of the tasteless self-denigration, I decided that I must be drunk, or even more drunk than usual. I doubted whether Jane was going to enjoy going to bed with me. I stood up and we went out on to the dance floor when the band was half-way through 'Begin the Beguine'. As I held Jane close I felt tender and sentimental.

The number ended, and with hardly a pause they started to play 'Louise'. The lights went even lower. As the band stopped playing, a yellow spotlight picked out the empty space just in front of it, and a girl came out on to it. She was tall and blonde and leggy, and she wore a short, skintight silver frock and black stockings. She had an authentic Bardot pout. She started to sing in French. At first it was something I'd never heard before, then it was 'The poor people of Paris'. There was another, whose name I'd forgotten, that Eartha Kitt had made famous. Altogether there were five numbers. She came down off the platform, and the spot followed her around the tables before she returned to the platform and the band started to play 'Louise' again. She did a little dance. Then she was gone, and the lights came up.

There was a lot of applause, but she came out only once to acknowledge it. I poured a glass of port for Jane and one for myself.

'She's very beautiful,' Jane said. I looked up and shrugged.

'Not beautiful,' I said. 'But she has got *something*. She's a good performer.'

Jane was looking at me hard, too hard. I laughed. As the band stopped playing, a waiter came across to our table.

'Mademoiselle Louise presents her compliments,' he said. 'She asks if she might join you and mademoiselle for a drink.'

I was surprised, but I said of course and that we'd be honoured. The waiter went away and came back with glasses on a tray and a bottle of champagne in a bucket of ice. As he again disappeared, I said to Jane, 'The woman who phoned, the woman who invited us here...'

Watching the stage entrance, Jane said, 'She didn't have a French accent, if that's what you mean.'

'I'm not sure that Mademoiselle Louise would have one, if we caught her unaware,' I said.

The band was playing, and people were dancing. Mademoiselle Louise came out wearing a long black cloak. The waiter followed her. I stood up and introduced Jane. Mademoiselle Louise asked if we would drink some champagne with her, and the waiter filled the glasses. She said how pleased she was that we had been able to come. I said how much we had enjoyed her act.

She was a little older than I'd thought, probably nearly thirty, if thirty is older than anything. She spoke with a charming French accent, but I couldn't make up my mind whether it was real or she was just a good actress. She said how much she had liked the pieces I used to write on motor racing people.

Which ones in particular? I asked. She pouted while she thought about it. Perhaps the one on René Arnoux, I suggested, laying a trap, because I'd never written about him. But, no, she hadn't seen that one. Before I could try again Jane said, 'The one you wrote about going around Silverstone in a sports car was easily your best.'

And, yes, yes, mademoiselle remembered that and was enthusiastic about it. I reckoned that it was about two years since I'd written it, and I asked Mademoiselle Louise had she, then, lived in England for some time? But, no, no. Only for a short time, on an entertainment contract. In fact, soon she would be going back to Paris. She lived in a quiet little street near the Porte d'Orléans. Did I know that part of Paris? As it happened, yes, I did, quite well.

In Paris, she said, she bought all the motor sport papers she could get. She'd been specially interested ever since France had really begun to make an impression again in single-seaters. She'd like to see what I'd written about René Arnoux. And, apropos of that, what did I think of his chances in the British Grand Prix tomorrow?

I told her I didn't really know. If she had asked me a month ago, while I was still in touch, I would have said the works Lotuses had the best chance – 'if they didn't have suspension failure'. It was a very old joke, but she laughed at it appreciatively. After the Lotuses, the McLarens seemed the likeliest, and the most reliable of all. As I'd been out of touch for a month, though, and had read almost nothing – I raised my arms and gave what I hoped was an expressive, perhaps even slightly Gallic, shrug.

I was going to the race, of course? Mademoiselle said. No, I wasn't. Mademoiselle pouted and looked disappointed. In any case, I said, I had no Press tickets and would have no chance of getting them now, the RAC being what it was. And I wouldn't care to go without them – one got used to the privileges.

I glanced at Jane and saw her mouth open, so I gently pressed her foot with the toe of my shoe, which closed her mouth and made her smile with pleasure at being part of a small conspiracy against another woman.

Ah, but Mademoiselle said, *she* had some Press tickets. She seemed to ponder.

'Now I wonder,' she said. 'It is my first Grand Prix here. You would not be my guest and help to show me what it is – how do you say it? – what it is all about?'

Jane looked very hard at me. I shook my head. In any case, I said, Jane would be working at Brands Hatch, and I had other things to do. When I added that, it was Jane's turn to pout and look downcast, so I pressed her foot again, and again she smiled.

Mademoiselle Louise dropped her persuasion and asked was I going back to motor sport journalism? I didn't know, I said, but if I did it wouldn't be for a while, anyway. I was thinking of going abroad. Where to? To Amsterdam, I thought, and possibly to Berlin. Not to East Berlin, though? I asked why not, and she looked surprised and said that she thought only Communists went there.

I laughed, and I had just asked her about the lack of celebrities among the patrons when the waiter came out and handed her a note. She put it on the table to read. I saw that it was in French. I considered myself expert at reading things upside down, but she didn't leave it there long enough for me to try my skill. She folded it slowly and thoughtfully, looked up, and smiled.

'I'm sorry,' she said. 'Please excuse me. I am so glad that you could come.'

She stood up and took our hands in turn. I held on longer than I needed to and gave her hand two warm squeezes while I said something nice about her act, and looked into her eyes. She gave me a grateful look and said, 'But nothing will persuade you to go to the motor race tomorrow? Nothing?'

I shook my head and smiled. I felt sure that Jane hadn't missed the handplay. As soon as Mademoiselle Louise had gone she asked if we might go home. I looked at my watch. It was still only half-past eleven, but with so much to do in the next few hours I was glad to go early.

I got Jane's cloak while she went to the women's room. As we went out the door-man offered to get us a cab, but I told him we'd walk to the King's Road and find one there. I put my arm around Jane. She held herself very close to me as she said, 'I wish I wasn't jealous, darling.'

'There's no need to be,' I said.

She said, 'No?,' and I said, 'No', and I stopped in the dark street, held her close, and gave her a long kiss. She was gasping when I let her go and started to laugh breathlessly.

In the taxi I held her close again. We didn't talk till she said, 'She's beautiful.'

'She's very sexy,' I said, thinking as I said it that we seemed to have been over all that before.

'Is that why you made such a fuss of her?' Jane said.

I laughed. 'Did I make a fuss?' I said. '*I* wouldn't have put it like that. No, there's something odd, strange. I don't know what. Perhaps I'm too suspicious.'

'I won't ask you what you mean,' Jane said. I thought: This is another conversation we've had before.

XIV

We went up the Edgware Road and, at the canal, turned west along it and into Park Place Villas. Jane had a studio flat in St Mary's Mansions, on the first floor. I kissed her as soon as we were inside, and she clung to me while I caressed her through her frock. She asked if I wanted a drink. I said I wouldn't have one unless she was thirsty. She wasn't thirsty. She showed me the bathroom and gave me a towel. When I came back she was already in flimsy pyjamas, brushing her hair. I stood behind her and watched without touching her. She smiled at me in the mirror and, without stopping her brushing, said, 'I'm sorry I've no nightwear for you.'

I laughed and said that I wouldn't really need any.

Jane laughed, too, then was solemn. She put her brush down, gave me a tender smile, and went out to the bathroom.

I took off my jacket and tie and sat on the edge of her bed to unlace my shoes. I looked round the room. It was wonderfully un-cluttered and tidy, apart from the creams and the hairbrush and other toilet gear on the dressing table.

I was a bit surprised to see on the wall opposite me a big, crowded bookcase. The books looked too numerous for a light-weight reader. I went over and started to look at them. Most were novels and poetry and drama in well-kept paperback editions, from Defoe to Graham Greene, Keats to Eliot, Shakespeare to Christopher Fry.

I was looking at the Alfred Hayes novella *In Love* when Jane came back into the room. She stooped to look at the cover and laughed.

'I was going to say "Jane the egghead",' she said, 'but perhaps I won't if that's as far as you've got.'

She took the top off a jar and began to rub cream into her face.

'It's good, isn't it?' she said. 'Or haven't you read it?'

I said I had and that, yes, it was good.

'Not that I'd have done what *that* girl did,' she said. 'If you remember.'

I looked up, found her looking at me, and nodded.

'I'd have stuck with the fellow who's telling the story,' Jane said. 'On balance, anyway. Though I must say' – she turned back to the mirror – 'she'd thought up a very keen way of having her bottle of bubbly and drinking it at the same time.'

'Keen?' I said.

'Yes,' Jane said. 'Don't you remember?

Wasn't that the word Marilyn Monroe used all the time in *The Seven Year Itch?* Wasn't it keen? Or was it delicate? Yes, it was delicate.'

I said I remembered that there was a word but wasn't sure what it was.

'That was a good movie,' she said.

She looked back at me and started to put the top on the jar.

When I said that I'd liked it, too, Jane gave a pleased smile.

'So we both liked *In Love* and *The Seven Year Itch*,' she said. 'That just about makes us soul mates.'

'You're getting rather smug,' I said, in a bantering way. As Jane's face fell I wished that I hadn't.

She looked away and said, 'Let me be pleased, darling. I'm not really smug – truly.'

'I didn't mean to be, um, censorious,' I said. 'To use a dirty word. I was only half serious anyway – thinking that the evidence was a bit, um, tenuous. But I'm sure you're not smug.' I started to walk towards her.

Jane looked up with a wry smile and said, 'No, no, Tony. You mustn't spoil me. Pick another book.'

I went back, paused in front of a half-shelf of poetry, and with my left hand took out Gerard Manley Hopkins and with my right an Eliot collection.

She came over and said, 'Jane, egghead.'

'Oh, no,' I said.

'Well, you are surprised, aren't you?' she said.

'I didn't expect it.'

In a low, soft voice she said:

'Margaret, are you grieving
Over goldengrove unleaving?
Leaves like the things of man, you
With your fresh thoughts care for, can
 you?'

I said:

'Should I, after tea and cakes and ices,
Have the strength to force the moment to
 its crisis?'

Jane smiled. '*I* didn't see you eating any ices *or* cakes,' she said. 'Or drinking tea, for that matter.' She giggled. 'Not bloody likely.'

Then she came up to me, took the books from me and put them in the bookcase, put her arms around me, and with her mouth breathing warmly into my ear said, 'Darling, let's go to bed.'

She kissed me once, walked over to the bed, and as she kicked off her slippers picked up a red rose from the bedside table, cupped it in her hands and held it to her nostrils.

'If it embarrasses you,' she said, 'I won't look,' and she turned away.

As she got into bed she said, 'Do you

really know "Prufrock"?'

'Oh, yes,' I said. 'I was Eliot's model. "I am not Prince Hamlet, nor was meant to be."'

Jane laughed and then said quietly, as if thinking aloud, 'And you don't think I'm a girl with glasses?'

'A girl with glasses?'

'It's the egghead bit,' she said. 'Girls with glasses don't get passes.'

'It doesn't seem likely,' I said.

'Seriously,' Jane said. 'I mean – well, I've read poetry and, I suppose you'd call it, good fiction since I was about thirteen. At the office I worked in before this one – you know, my *last* job – I had that Hopkins book. I'd been reading it in my tea break. The boss, who was only about twenty-five, picked it up and started to read – well, he started to *try* to read – one of the "terrible" sonnets. "I wake and feel the fell of dark…" Do you know it?'

'Not that one,' I said.

'The boss laughed and said he didn't think I was a culture vulture. Do you?'

'Of course I don't.'

'I was afraid,' Jane said, 'of what you'd think when you came here tonight.'

She snuggled against me and sighed contentedly.

'Somehow, though,' she said, 'I don't dig politics. My brother was a Communist – not a real one, but almost. Still, I don't want to be rich, I really don't. And I don't want a lot of *things*. I don't even much want to go to swanky places to eat, unless it's with someone nice like you. So perhaps my heart's in the right place.'

'I'm sure it is,' I said and put my hand over it. 'Just as I expected,' I said.

Jane shivered. I held her closer and was just about to find her mouth when she said, 'Tony, are *you* interested in politics?'

'Not specially,' I said. 'Why?'

'It just seemed odd. That woman who rang yesterday, you know, from the night club. She said were you the Tony Fredericks who'd taken a special interest in politics when he was in Fleet Street?'

I felt suddenly tense as I said, 'She must have been thinking of someone else.' I tried to sound indifferent. I ran my fingers down her spine. 'What did you have to say to that?'

'I said that I didn't know anything about it. So she just said–'

I waited.

'Yes?'

'Oh, she just said something about it not being important – oh, yes she said that it wasn't important enough to mention to you.'

Jane wanted me to stay the night, but I said that I'd go sooner or later, and at about one o'clock, when she'd gone to sleep, I got out of bed without waking her, dressed in the dark, and let myself out.

In the half-hour since we had made love, while I'd snuggled against Jane and waited for her to go to sleep, I had started worrying about Nina and tried to think of a way in which Winston might be connected with the invitation to the night club. I'd got nowhere.

Out in Park Place Villas I wanted to run, to get quickly to Nina, but I knew that at that hour it would mean that I'd be questioned by any policeman who might see me. I remembered my shadow and realized that I hadn't seen him all evening, and there was no one in sight now, which was odd. It wasn't all that far to Acacia Road and Nina. Even so, I hoped I'd see a cab.

I'd got well up towards the canal when I heard a car coming from behind me. It was accelerating when it passed, and as it went under a street light just ahead I almost jumped at the reminder of the so-similar red sports car that had picked up Peter Krasko the day he disappeared and then the courier whom Nina had met the day after.

It had hardly gone out of sight round the corner – towards Edgware Road – when the sound of its engine died. As I turned the corner myself I saw it at the kerb only about twenty yards away. I came abreast of it and looked into its dark interior. It could have been a woman at the wheel, I thought. The next moment she spoke.

'May I give you a ride?'

It was Mademoiselle Louise. I stopped and tried to make out her face in the dark.

'This *is* a coincidence, and actually I *am* in an awful hurry,' I said.

But I just stood there.

'You'd better get in ... Tony,' she said, and she opened the passenger's door.

I got in, and as she started the car she said with a laugh, 'You do take a long time to get home. Now, where are you going?'

I looked at her as we moved under a street light. She was wearing a black leather coat. She smiled at me.

'Which way are you going?' I said.

'I will run you home anyway,' she said.

'I want to go to St John's Wood,' I said. 'Do you know the tube station?'

'Perhaps you will show me the way,' she said and, getting it right for a start, turned north into Edgware Road.

'Second on the right,' I said.

She looked at me again, smiled again, and said, 'I thought you lived in Marylebone.'

'I'm not going home,' I said.

She nodded in a knowing way and said, 'Jane is a nice girl.'

I said she was. Mademoiselle Louise drove past St John's Wood Road, just quietly cruising. Presently she said, 'I called you Tony. You do not mind if I call you Tony?'

'All my friends do,' I said.

She turned and gave me a big, grateful smile.

'I hope you will call me Louise,' she said.

I said I'd like to.

When she turned into Hall Road I gave her the next direction.

'Tony,' she said at last, 'I wish you would come to the Grand Prix tomorrow.'

'I'm sorry, Louise,' I said. 'I don't want to. Anyway, I'm likely to be busy.'

'Only likely,' she said. 'And what if you are not?'

I didn't answer, and suddenly she pulled in to the kerb and stopped the engine.

'I am not going to be here – in London, I mean – for long,' she said. 'Is there nothing that I can do to persuade you?'

We looked at one another very hard.

'Louise,' I said at last. 'I'm grateful for the ride and flattered by your attention. But I really am in a hurry.'

She laughed, touched my cheek with the back of her gloved hand, and said, 'Do not be so nervous.'

Then she sighed, started the car, and drove slowly on. Now that I thought I knew who she was, I had made up my mind to go to Brands. I would say so as soon as she asked me again. Perversely, I wanted to hear just one more plea from her for Winston.

We were in sight of the tube station when she said, without looking at me. 'You do not want to come home with me?'

'I'd love to,' I said. 'But I've promised to see someone else. I'm sorry. There's the tube station. Could you drop me there?'

She stopped the car outside but left the engine running and said, 'It is closed.'

'I'm visiting a few doors away,' I said. 'Can you find your way from here?'

She looked ahead up the street and nodded. I started to open the door. She turned quickly, kissed me, gave me a hug, then looked at me and pleaded, 'Do come to the motor race with me, Tony.'

I smiled and pretended to think it over.

'All right,' I said at last, with a half-sigh. 'If I can I'll come. Ring me at eight in the morning and I'll let you know for sure.'

Louise kissed me again and told me I was a darling as she reached into the glove compartment for a notebook. I wrote down my number. Then I got out of the car, and she swung around and drove off south along Wellington Road.

Well, I thought, not for the first time, as I hurried along Acacia Road, I did seem to be finding a lot of obstacles to the solitude that I had been looking for when I left my wife – though I didn't think of Mademoiselle Louise as personal in the way that Nina and Jane were. I wondered how much I should tell Nina of all that had happened since I'd left The Old Rising Sun all those hours before.

Supposing, I thought for the first time, Nina was not to be trusted, but I put that thought out of my mind as quickly as it had come into it.

There was a light in Nina's window, and just as I was about to press her doorbell I heard a phone ringing somewhere above. I didn't see anyone watching the place, though I couldn't believe that they'd given up. I rang the bell and waited a long time, wondering whether I'd pressed the wrong one. I was just about to press it again, making sure this time, when I heard a door close and footsteps on the stairs. Then Nina opened the door and let me in.

She went straight up the stairs ahead of me, and I was in her room before I could really look at her. When she turned around to face me I could see that she was very tense.

'You're very late, Tony,' she said.

She sounded overwrought, but she didn't wait for me to answer before she said quickly:

'They've just phoned me. Just this minute. Just as you rang my bell. I've waited in all day. Somehow I felt that they were bound to ring. I was just about at screaming point.'

She brushed her hair away from her face, first with one hand, then with the other, and rubbed her eyes nervously.

'They want me to wait in all day tomorrow,' she said. 'They say they might have

170

something important for me to do. I can go to bed now, though. Big deal.'

I thought she was going to cry. I went towards her and was going to comfort her, but she turned away and sat on the bed and put her face in her hands.

'I'm so tired and distraught,' she said. Then she looked up and asked, 'What's been happening to you, Tony?'

I squatted in front of her and said, very quietly, 'Are you quite sure this room isn't bugged, Nina?'

'Bugged?'

'Are you quite sure there aren't any concealed microphones or anything like that?'

She shook her head and said, 'I'm as sure as I can be. I'm pretty sure. I chose it all on my own and all that, and I think it wouldn't be easy to interfere with it. You've probably noticed the double-locked door, and I always keep the windows locked.'

A double-locked door and a few locked windows weren't likely to deter a determined Winston hireling, I thought.

Nina seemed calmer now that she was talking about practical things. I'd decided to say nothing for now about my meeting with Walter, unless she asked questions that might lead to it, nor about all that he'd told me about Peter Kolchak. I started to talk about my evening at the Chelsea night club and the meeting with Mademoiselle Louise, though I said nothing about Jane and my visit to her flat.

About what happened later, I just told her that I'd been coming across town on my way to see her when Louise had come along in her sports car and noticed me. I was still squatting, like a cobbler, in front of Nina. She had lifted her head and rested her chin on her palms while she stared at the floor a few feet in front of her.

But when I came to the red sports car and my suspicions about it, Nina was startled, then horrified, as I went on to tell her of Mademoiselle Louise's persistence and my eventual promise to go Brands Hatch.

When I'd finished I just squatted there and looked at Nina, and Nina looked back. At last she said, 'Do you find this woman – this Mademoiselle Louise – very attractive? As a woman, I mean.'

'Listen, Nina…'

'*Do* you?'

'Of course she's attractive,' I said. 'Didn't I say she was like Bardot?'

'Is that why you're going with her to the motor racing?'

'Listen, Nina,' I said. 'I'm as susceptible as the next man. I love women. I really do.' She looked almost contemptuous. 'But I'm going to Brands Hatch with Louise, with Mademoiselle Louise, tomorrow – damn it, today – because I'm sure she's been asked to take me. I can't imagine why, but I'm sure it has something to do with Winston's plans.'

Nina nodded.

'I think so, too,' she said. 'Yes, of course. I only wish that I could guess what she has to do with Peter Krasko. That really frightens me. And the other thing that frightens me – oh, well' – she gave a helpless gesture and sighed – 'I feel that I can't trust anyone, and I wonder if I'm losing you. You've no special reason to be loyal to me. You're crazy about women – in the plural. Your woman might just as well be Mademoiselle Louise as me.'

I stood up, almost sprang to my feet. Nina, startled, drew her feet quickly up on to the bed, retreated to the wall, and sat there, looking defiant.

'No, Tony, no,' she said. 'Don't touch me, please. I don't want you to make love to me tonight. I'm at the end of my– I – I feel I can hardly keep going any longer.'

'It's all right, Nina,' I said. 'Just, please, try to believe that I want to help you. Your nightmare has become mine. But do believe that I want to help. That's the *only* reason that I'm going to Brands, to the motor race. Do you think I shouldn't go?'

She stared back for half-a-minute before she said, 'No. You *should* go. Of course you should go.' She looked at me silently again. 'Have you heard anything more about Peter Kolchak?'

'Not really,' I said.

'Not *really?*'

'No,' I lied quickly, 'I haven't.'

Nina got off the bed and walked over to the door.

'It's strange,' she said. 'I've wanted all day to see you. But you'd better go now. I'm sorry, darling. I do believe you.'

She opened the door but straight away closed it again as she asked, 'When will I see you tomorrow – today?'

I told her that I'd come as soon as I got back from Kent. It might be about eight o'clock. She nodded, opened the door, and offered her cheek. She didn't resist when I put an arm around her and held her close and tight. In the end she hugged me, too. I didn't try to go any further. Then I squeezed her hand and went out and down the stairs.

When I let myself out there was still no one in sight watching the place, and as I walked south towards Marylebone I was sure that no one was following me. What surprised me more, no one seemed to be watching my room.

XV

After I'd let myself in I wondered if I should ring Walter. Well, I had promised, and – what the hell! – two o'clock shouldn't be uncomfortably late for a news man. I dialled his number. The phone went on ringing at his end for what seemed ages, though it probably wasn't more than half-a-minute. Next door the old woman stirred and muttered.

I had dialled very carefully – something I had taught myself to do when making very late calls from Fleet Street – but, even so, this time I suspected uneasily that I'd dialled the wrong number. I was just about to hang up and try again when a woman's sleepy voice answered. It was Walter's wife. Before I could apologise, for ringing so late, she apologised, for not answering sooner. She was a terribly heavy sleeper, she said. Had I been waiting long?

It was such an unusual reaction at that time of night that I was amused. It seemed that she had been expecting me to phone since Walter had been called out on a shift an hour ago to relieve a sick man, and had told her to say when I did call that he had no news for me. She sounded so nice, so young, that I wanted to meet her. Oh, well. I told her to tell Walter that I'd be out all next day.

In bed I went straight into a deep sleep and didn't wake till the old woman pounded on my door at half-past seven. It was Louise on the phone. She sounded anxious when she asked if I could, after all, go to Brands, and relieved and grateful that I could.

Where would I meet her? It was my question, and I was surprised that for someone so mobile she should suggest – no, she *asked* me if I would meet her at Waterloo. That was fine, I said, and we settled for half-past nine. I went back into my room and looked out of the window. Yes, there he was, standing on the corner. If they hadn't bothered last night, why were they bothering this morning if they knew, as they must know, that I intended to go to Brands with Louise? I could only suppose that they knew also of the small doubt that I'd left in her mind.

When I'd shaved and washed and dressed I went out for a newspaper and some fresh rolls. As I expected, I was followed down to the High Street and back again.

It must have irritated me, because afterwards, when I thought about it, what I did next was silly and pointless. When it came time to go I let myself down the back wall. I felt childishly pleased that my shadow was still waiting, watching my door, as I swung the umbrella that I always took to Brands Hatch, and in the bright summer sunshine zig-zagged across Marylebone.

At Oxford Circus I caught an underground train. When I surfaced again, and came out of Waterloo station, there across the road was Louise in her sports car.

She had let the top down, and with her long blonde hair loose she looked like an ad for getaway people. She seemed delighted to see me – warm and eager – and, as we drove south towards the Elephant, she kept giving me big smiles in the mirror that she had angled so that we couldn't help looking at one another.

I was glad that she had worn a skirt rather than trousers. If I was going to be with a woman all day I might as well enjoy all the good things about her. I spent some of the time when I wasn't looking in the mirror looking at her legs, and she knew and was pleased.

She said hardly a word till we were well down the Old Kent Road, and the traffic was a little thinner. Then she said, 'Do you ever read any French newspapers or magazines?'

I said that I didn't because my French wasn't really good enough, but that I looked through the weekly *Le Monde* sometimes, and at *Paris Match*.

Le Monde seemed not quite the kind of

paper she expected a motor sport journalist to read. I shrugged.

She looked in the mirror, this time with a doubtful smile.

'I haven't said something I shouldn't have said?' she asked.

It was my turn to smile. 'Oh, no,' I said. 'It's what I expect, in a way. People don't expect motor sport writers to be interested in anything else, in anything serious, anyway – like art, or – or politics. Of course it doesn't have to follow. I was interested in other things long before I was interested in motor racing and before I became a motor sport writer.'

In fact, I said, in a really professional sense I wasn't a motor sport writer at all. I'd gone into motor sport journalism as a sub-editor looking for a quiet life.

But, said Louise, I had written those articles – the ones she had read.

I started to explain how I had got interested, but she interrupted.

'Just before you tell me about that – what sort of journalism did you do *before* motor sport?'

I told her that as a sub-editor on a daily I'd done just about everything except finance – *and,* I laughed, sport. As a reporter… I interrupted myself, pretending to be distracted by a passing truck.

'Yes?' said Louise. Her voice was unexpectedly urgent.

'Well, again,' I said, 'I ranged pretty widely in general news.'

'General news. Politics?'

'A little,' I said. 'Not much.'

'Then you are not interested in politics?'

I shrugged and pursed my lips. She looked in the mirror at me anxiously, obviously wanting an answer.

'You mentioned going to East Berlin,' she said.

I laughed and said, 'Oh, I have a thing about Berlin.'

'A thing?'

'It fascinates me. I'm a bit – hooked on it. But it's not a political thing.'

'It is not a political thing?'

'I don't go there because I'm interested in – Communism.'

'You are not interested in Communism?'

I laughed again and said, 'That isn't what I said. Though I'm not specially interested.'

Louise remained silent for a couple of miles.

'I would like to go to Berlin myself,' she said at last. 'Do you know good places there to stay?'

'In the Eastern zone?'

She seemed to think it over carefully before she said, 'Yes.'

I said I'd never stayed there.

'And in the West?'

Well, it had all been years ago. There was this little place in Dahlem that I'd picked out from a guide to cheap accommodation.

She was silent again, perhaps thinking that she wasn't being very subtle.

'Of course my interest is entertainment,' she said. 'You do not have any friends there?'

'In entertainment?' I said.

She said, 'Well...' and waited for me to speak.

'Come to think of it,' I said, as if I'd just made a discovery, 'I haven't any friends there at all.'

Louise again drove on for a while before she spoke again.

'I interrupted you,' she said, 'when you started to tell me how you got interested in motor racing. How was it, then?'

'They wanted a personality piece written,' I said. 'An article about a person, a driver. When the man who was to do it had an accident I offered to do it instead. He was a young fellow, the driver I went to see, named Peter. Or was it Patrick? Something like that. He gave it up later when he got married. He talked to me about the finer skills of the racing driver, and I could see that there was something in it quite different from just driving a car fast. He took me out to Brands and drove me around and tried to show me in practice what he'd been talking about. The

180

other thing about it: he was a quiet, gentle fellow. I hadn't expected that. Then I found out that other drivers were like that, too.'

I stopped talking. Presently Louise looked into the mirror again, almost expectantly. Now she was quite solemn. When she saw that I wasn't going on she said:

'I think I know what you mean, though I do not know any drivers. You probably thought I did.' She paused. 'I am not intelligent.'

'Come, now!' I said.

'I really mean that I am not – what is the word? – intellectual. Two or three of the men I know in Paris *are* intellectual, and they all thought it was very funny – a big joke – when I got mad on motor racing. But you know they used to go out to Colombes on Sundays to watch the football – the rugby – and that was quite all right, that was not strange or funny!'

I gave Louise what was meant to be a grateful smile. I felt grateful.

'That's *exactly* the point,' I said. 'I know lots of intellectuals who are interested in football. They watch it on television on Saturday nights with devotion – with as much devotion as they would go to church, if they were the kind of people who went to church. Perhaps it takes the place of church. Rugby, you know, which I played myself when I was a boy, is quite a coarse game, whatever they say about its skills, which of course it has.

Look, damn it, it's even in order, all right, OK, to be an intellectual and interested in *bullfighting*. I suppose there's a sort of raw athleticism about these sports that makes them different from motor racing.'

I nearly choked on the word 'athleticism' but I didn't stop. 'I don't know what it is. I know I dislike car club people' – I didn't stop to explain who car club people were – 'but these intellectuals who think an interest in motor racing is such a joke haven't seen or heard those people anyway. So they haven't *that* reason for being superior. And the professionals are quite different from car club people.'

Louise's close attention to what I was saying was flattering. She kept turning to me with a nod or a smile and had slowed down a little. I paused while she let a couple of impatient drivers past.

'Perhaps it's the noise,' I went on. 'People say to me, "You're a quiet fellow – how can you stand the noise?" But then they just see a race as a lot of cars chasing one another around.'

Again I paused. The man behind in an ageing Rover no doubt thought it a bit much that our sports car was taking its time on race day, when so many people fancied themselves as Grand Prix material. Louise waved him past.

'Now, look. Perhaps *that's* it. If you understand what's going on, even a procession – I mean a race that isn't very competitive – is interesting. If, for instance, you know what happens when a driver takes a single-seater through a fast corner: the dab on the brake pedal, the rear starting to break away – to go sideways – the foot down on the throttle and the drift across the apex of the corner till the car's pointed up the straight. And all the time he could lose the whole thing, spin or whatever, go out of control, if he didn't know, feel, exactly how far he could go. *That* kind of skilled handling of a piece of intricate machinery, with the driver really a part of it – you'd think it would appeal to people who like to be modern, sophisticated, in their interests and tastes.'

I stopped for breath. Louise laughed.

'You *do* go on,' she said.

I thought: Here I am talking about soccer fanatics treating *Match of the Day* like a church service, while I preach a sermon. But all I said with a grin was, 'Ah, well, we *are* going to Brands.'

'*Vive le Brands!*' said Louise.

By now we had got well down into Kent, and as we again drove on for a while without talking I started to wonder again why Louise had so much wanted me to go. I felt sure by now that she liked my company. Since I was a man, I suspected that that was not unusual for her. Of course I was certain that there was a reason connected with Winston's operations. It seemed that I would have to wait to find out what the reason was.

'Do you know a man named Peter Krasko?' I asked suddenly.

We were going down a gentle slope fairly fast, and there was quite a lot of traffic going both ways. I'd decided that Louise was a good driver, but as I spoke the car suddenly veered towards the oncoming traffic, and for a moment, till Louise quickly corrected, I thought we were going to hit something.

'I'm sorry,' she said tensely. She gave a faint, strained smile into the mirror.

I said it was all right.

She remained tense. I decided to say nothing more, but after a while Louise said, 'You were saying?'

'Yes?' I said.

'You asked did I know someone.'

'Oh, yes,' I said, as if I had forgotten all about it. 'Peter Krasko.'

'I do not think so,' she said, quite calmly. 'Should I know him?'

With a bit of a laugh I said, 'Oh, I don't know. Perhaps you should. He's a very charming man.'

Louise laughed, too, but she was not very convincing.

'There are many fascinating men, many charming men,' she said. 'One cannot know all of them.'

I knew from her silence, and her tense, set face, that I had her worried, and it wasn't long before she said, 'This man Kosko.'

'Krasko,' I corrected.

'Krasko,' she said. 'Is he one of your friends?'

I must suddenly have felt that I had her at my mercy, because I said in a bantering way, 'Not so much a friend,' and was about to add, 'more a fellow conspirator,' when I realized in time what an idiotic show-off I was making of myself. The words I'd spoken hung in the air for a few moments before I said lamely, in a quite different tone, 'He just happened to live in the same building as I do.'

I knew that I was telling her something that she must already know. Of course she didn't react, but after another silence she said, 'Then you did not *really* think I might know your Peter Krasko?'

'I just thought you might,' I said.

She shrugged and sighed at such incomprehensible reasoning as she looked ahead up the road.

'But *why?* Because he was a foreigner?' And she actually laughed, indulgently.

'No,' I said. 'Because he left his room one morning in a tearing hurry in a red sports car just like this one, driven by a beautiful girl with long blonde hair, and wearing a black leather coat.' I didn't look in the mirror this time but sideways at Louise.

Again the car veered, even more alarmingly this time, towards the oncoming traffic. When she had straightened up, Louise glanced at me in the mirror.

'I hope you have not told anyone about this, Tony,' she said.

She looked ahead up the road. I waited till I caught her eyes in the mirror before I said, with a shrug. 'Whom would I tell? Who would be interested?'

Louise looked back at the road again and then, briefly, back at me. She must have been wondering how far to go, but all that she said was, 'Oh, well. It is just that Peter did run away. I do not suppose you saw him again. I did not, either. But I knew that he had been breaking the law. I suppose I was breaking it, too, when I drove him down to – to Gatwick to catch a plane to – to France.'

I didn't say anything.

'So you did not tell anyone,' Louise persisted.

I looked in the mirror and caught her anxious look.

'About me, I mean,' Louise said.

I smiled reassurance and shook my head.

The route Louise had followed had taken us into Swanley. As we went along the main street past the road that led off to the railway station a crowded bus with a Brands Hatch destination sign up front trundled out of it. Louise said, 'It is a slow way to get to a motor race.'

'Oh, no,' I said with a laugh. 'I've gone that way more than once. We've been lucky with the traffic this morning. Tonight the race fans who go down there and catch a train back to Victoria – to London – will be back in town long before you and I.'

For all the notice she took, Louise might not have been listening. Even when we really got into the race-bound traffic and found ourselves stopping often, she remained subdued and said little more than a few words about how much she was liking the pleasant, green, rolling countryside all about us.

I began to feel sorry that I'd mentioned Krasko, especially as it didn't seem likely to get me anywhere. And Louise animated had been such good company that I felt I'd spoiled my day – and hers, too.

At Brands I talked her into the circuit, and we drove to the Press car park. When Louise had switched off the engine she put her hands over her eyes, just as Nina had done the night before, and then without saying anything she started to open the door on her side.

I reached across and took her hand. She faced me unhappily. I held her hand tightly and said, 'Don't be unhappy, Louise darling. I haven't told anyone.'

'I wish I could be sure,' she said.

'It's true,' I said, and we looked at one another for what seemed a long time.

Then I released her hand, and again she reached for the car door.

'I wish I knew what it was all about,' I said.

Half out of the car, Louise looked back and said, '*You* do? Well, I do, too.'

I got out and went around the car to join her. She looked at my umbrella and smiled. I smiled, too, and looked up at the cloudless sky. I took her hand, and we started to walk towards the road that ran around the back of the stands towards the paddock.

XVI

Out on the track the big saloon cars flashed by on their practice runs. Brands was easily my favourite circuit. Although I had no interest in saloon-car racing, the snarling cars, their engine notes rising and falling, the staccato gear changes as they ran up towards top in the finishing straight, put an edge on my appetite for the racing ahead. I squeezed Louise's hand. She gave me a smile.

'Let's go to the paddock,' I said. I had suddenly remembered Jane. She would probably already be in the Press box, and I didn't want to go near it if I could help it. Louise wanted to look in the shops on the way to the paddock, but I talked her out of it.

Going to motor races as a Press man had spoiled me for going as an ordinary spectator. I had learned not to trouble drivers, mechanics, team managers, and components people when they were busy, but I enjoyed the freedom a reporter has to ask questions and knew enough about what was going on not to ask silly ones. I took a juvenile pleasure in being remembered by star drivers and, as we wandered among the cars in the paddock in their usually partially dismantled state, it pleased me to make an impression on Louise.

She in turn was able to help when I showed some curiosity about a big job being done on one of the Ligiers. I tried my French on the mechanic who was supervising the job. He wanted to be helpful, but we got almost nowhere. He looked more and more bewildered until Louise intervened and found out what I wanted to know.

The place was already far too crowded. We had to peer over the heads of people surrounding some of the cars even to see what cars they were. At the end of the paddock closest to the track the Ferrari team had roped themselves off in splendid isolation that not even Press photographers were allowed to invade.

A few of the drivers were in anxious conference with their mechanics. Jacques Lafitte, surrounded and pursued by autograph hunters, was finding it difficult to make his way from his car to the Williams transporter, where Frank Williams was sorting it out with his mechanics.

Two or three of the cars were already running up and down through the revs while mechanics listened to the tune. It sounded like feeding time for the lions at Regent's Park. Over the years it had become music to me, but I knew what people meant when they said it was a noisy sport.

I stopped to talk with one of the privateer Formula 3 drivers I knew who was sitting alone and disconsolate on one of the rear wheels of his car. There'd been some misunderstanding about his tyre order, he said. The tyres with the new tread hadn't arrived, but he was still hoping to get some before his race, in an hour's time. Otherwise he couldn't see himself being competitive.

As we talked, he kept glancing at Louise. He smiled happily when I introduced her. Among the usual dozens of pretty girls who were part of the paddock scene she was still striking enough to be noticed. As we stopped nearby, I noticed that Stirling Moss was keeping an interested eye on her while he listened to what John Bolster was telling him about a shunt at Druids in unofficial practice, which had quite badly damaged one of the Grand Prix cars.

I kept worrying about Jane. I knew that Louise would want to go to the starting line when the racing got under way. If we were anywhere in the Press stand Jane might see us. My tactic was to persuade Louise to watch the preliminaries from the slope above Clearways, then go into the Press stand only when there were plenty of people about. Once the big race had started we'd be all right: Jane would be too busy lap scoring to notice anything else.

I looked at my watch and suggested a drink, and we went out to the nearest liquor tent. We had to stand there in the crowd with our drinks, which I didn't much like. Louise, settled with her gin and tonic, suddenly noticed someone looking at a map of the circuit in a programme. Couldn't we get a programme? I was just about to say that we'd get our complimentary copies in the Press stand, but remembering that Jane would be there I got one from a programme seller.

Louise straight away looked for the map and started to ask me questions about the circuit. Where were we now? Where was the starting line? Which were the good places to watch from? I pointed out two or three – Druids, Clark Curve. I laughed at her eagerness.

'You'll see them soon enough,' I said. 'Finish your drink, and let me get you another.' My mug was empty.

But, no, she didn't want another – not yet, anyway. She was still studying the circuit map, turning it this way and that, when I came back with my beer.

'Where is the start of the straight where it leaves the small circuit and goes out into the country?' she asked.

I was surprised. From a Frenchwoman on her first visit to Brands, it sounded very much a rehearsed sentence.

'You do sound clued up,' I said, then wondered whether she would know what I meant. I pointed it out to her.

'They say it is a good place to watch – to spectate,' she said.

'Spectate' jarred a bit, but I let it pass and shrugged.

'Do they?' I asked. 'And who are they?'

'People,' she said. 'People at the club.'

I said that of the places not too far from the start-finish line and the pits and Press stand, Clark Curve – I pointed it out on the map – was the best place to be. Without too much off-putting enthusiasm, I suggested that we might go there for the preliminary races. She brightened. She thought it a good idea.

So about twenty minutes later we found ourselves well up in the crowd near the exit from Clark Curve, with the whole wonderful panorama of the small circuit spread out in a kind of basin below us: the main straight running off to the left past the pits and the crowded stands, Hailwood Hill beyond Paddock Bend but Druids just out of sight, bits of Cooper Straight behind the pits visible below the colour-splashed, car-covered South Bank, the turn out of Cooper Straight that took the circuit out into the country, and the gap in the trees where it came back again at Clearways. Louise asked again where the start of the straight out into the country was. I pointed to it across the circuit.

The cars came out for the saloon-car race, strung out along the straight, snarled off in a crazy, crowded pack through Paddock and up Hailwood Hill, disappeared and reappeared behind the pits, and raced out into the country. Louise was animated and excited and immediately put her money on Tony Lanfranchi, who had grabbed the lead at the start and held it to the finish. When the Formula 3 cars came out, streamed past on their warm-up lap, and began a fantastic race-long dice for the lead, she could hardly contain herself. I hoped that she wasn't going to find the Grand Prix a let-down.

We went back to the paddock after that, had another drink, and bought some sandwiches. Louise said that she didn't want anything more, and I wasn't hungry. It was very hot. I felt an idiot with my umbrella, though I wasn't the only idiot.

We found somewhere to sit down and looked out over the paddock to the countryside outside the circuit. The flags on the component tents could hardly raise a flap, there was so little wind. Louise's two drinks had mellowed her. Now, almost indifferent to the scene around her, she talked nostalgically of her childhood just outside Paris and laughed affectionately about a very early love affair.

A quarter-of-an-hour before the Grand Prix cars went out to the track we went to the Press box. We had left it late – almost every seat was taken – but, in a way, that suited me, because we had to squeeze in high up at the very back. Sad, I thought, that the bar was at the opposite end. Still … I had felt anxious about Jane. Now I was less anxious. I knew that she nearly always worked at the opposite end from where we were and on the front row – she couldn't have been farther away from where I stood with Louise. We had a good view, though, of activity on the grid. I pointed out drivers, mechanics, team mangers, Press men whom I knew.

There had been for me, from almost my first motor race, something tremendously dramatic and blood-stirring about the start of a big Formula 1 race. So when the cars came back from their warm-up lap and lined up again on the grid, the helpers were waved away, the hooter sounded, and the five-minute board, raised high above the field, began the countdown to the start, I couldn't take my eyes off the track – not even to look at Louise.

The high-pitched, pulsating revving of the engines, rising and falling faster and faster as the last half-minute ticked away, moved me deeply. When the light turned green and with a great surge of sound they streamed away in a suicidal pack towards Paddock, I let out a gasp of pent-up feeling so loud that Louise turned and looked at me. I felt too overcome to say anything. Louise must have realized it. She smiled, squeezed my hand, and said affectionately, 'You are a funny man.' I smiled at her and squeezed her hand.

In the usual way, the field was already strung out by the time the cars came past for the first time, but the leading bunch – two Ferraris, a Ligier, a Williams, and a Brabham – were still in tight formation, with one of the McLarens not far behind. You always hoped that they would stay like that. They seldom did, and this time, after only five laps, the McLaren was in the pits.

Louise watched for about eight laps, saying hardly a word, turning her head to watch the leaders disappear at Paddock, stretching forward to watch them go up Hailwood and into Druids, following them in the little bit of Cooper that she could see and out into the country, and catching them again as they came into view at Clearways.

Then suddenly she looked at her watch and said, 'Could we go now?'

I was startled.

'Go?' I said. 'Go where?'

She looked at me with a slight, strained smile and said, 'To the straight out into the country.'

The leaders came into sight again. I watched them race towards us, pass, and disappear, but I knew that Louise was watching me. I looked at her as the cars streamed up to Druids. She was staring at me, her face tense and anxious. She tried to smile.

'Okay,' I said as I picked up my umbrella, and we went towards the exit. We squeezed our way past the back of the watching crowd and through the door. When we got out on the road behind the stand, far enough away from the noise of the cars to talk in comfort, I turned to Louise and said with a laugh, 'You've got a bee in your bonnet about the straight out into the country. There's nothing very special about it.'

I didn't think she would understand the colloquial phrase, but she didn't say anything. As we walked towards Clark and came back in sight of the track I took her arm. She smiled at me and seemed happier.

High on the bank near Clearways, at the end of the small circuit, a fellow I had known years before, watching with his lady, noticed me and turned to speak. I stopped for a couple of minutes and introduced Louise, and we stood talking while we watched the cars passing below. I had half an eye on Louise. I felt almost certain now that I was soon going to find out why she had so much wanted me to come to Brands. She had become tense again. She looked at her watch and stared over the circuit towards where we were going.

I said goodbye to the couple, and we walked on, over the bridge that crossed the circuit. We came at last close to the point where the cars left the sweeping bend out of Cooper Straight, rocketed into the section where the old pedestrian bridge had once been, and accelerated up the straight that went out into the country.

We turned up along the straight. I had been keeping an eye on the race, but my real interest was now in Louise and what she was doing. She seemed no longer to have any interest in the race.

The crowed that lined the fence just above the track was not specially heavy. It might have been possible to find a spot where we could watch. But Louise walked on. She seemed to be looking for someone in the crowd. After we'd gone about a hundred yards she said suddenly, 'Oh, there is André. He told me that he was coming.' She almost ran to where a tall, swarthy man was standing by the fence, looking towards us. He turned and spoke to the woman beside him, and she, too, striking, black-haired, and foreign-looking, turned towards us and smiled.

Just before we reached them, Louise said, 'André has come from Paris for the race. Yvette is his secretary.'

She introduced me to them as a journalist. They insisted on making way so that we could stand by the trackside. There was some conversation in French about mutual friends, which I didn't completely understand. Louise asked a question about dinner. André said that he would talk about that later.

We were all watching the race now. The three all seemed quite excited whenever a Ligier came by. When no cars were in sight for a few moments, André, I noticed, would look across to the other side of the track in a curiously intent way, while the woman, Yvette, kept up in French an animated conversation with Louise.

After watching for a while, I was almost certain that what interested André was a photographer directly across the track from us. He was a bit of a trendy, in black leather, almost like the gear of a racing motor-cyclist. Strangely for a photographer, he wore dark glasses.

On any other day at Brands, I wouldn't have given him a second glance. But it suddenly struck me, after he had panned a few times as cars passed, that the equipment he was using was very unusual for what he seemed to be trying to do. He had an expensive-looking 35mm camera of a make that I couldn't identify, on which he was using a quite exceptionally long, slender telephoto lens.

If I understood it aright, it could easily take a close-up of the nose of any of the drivers the photographer happened to be interested in, yet he never used it for its more obvious purpose – to pick up a car coming up the straight under the bridge, or going away into the distance towards Pilgrim's Drop. After each pan he'd sweep it into the air and bring it to a stop pointing towards our little group across the track. Was this what interested André?

The leaders came by. The two Ferraris were still out in front. I watched them, not all that far behind three back-markers, with the following Williams and Ligier, and the Brabham, now in the slipstream of the Ligier.

I looked sideways at André as the Ligier passed. He was watching not the car but the photographer. I looked at the photographer. I felt certain that, through his reflex finder, he was watching *us*. Again he swept low and panned as the McLaren that had had the brief pit stop went by. And, watching him closely, I was sure that when he again fixed the camera on us he didn't refocus, though we were much further from him than the car.

Suddenly I noticed that Louise and Yvette were no longer talking. I looked at Louise beside me. She was staring across the track with a look of terror. I could hear the Ferraris in Cooper Straight. This time I would only pretend to watch them. They came out of the corner and accelerated towards us, a good hundred yards apart.

The photographer again went through his act. This time I knew that we were all watching him. There was a bellow of sound from Cooper. I looked down towards where the old bridge had been and saw a Ligier, a Williams, and a Brabham in line astern, looking like one three-driver car as they passed the back-markers that the Ferrari had overtaken on the last lap. The six cars filled the roadway. The crowd along the fences on both sides of the straight craned forward to savour the splendid sight as the cars came racing towards us.

I looked across at the photographer. His lens was pointed steadily at us. Just as the cars came opposite to us, and the sound of their engines drowned every other sound, Louise swung towards me. With a scream almost in my ear, she pulled free from the closely packed crowd. She had been half in front of me. In breaking free, she sent me

200

reeling sideways into a young woman standing beside me.

As all this happened, I saw a bright flash in the lens of the camera across the track. Louise screamed again and stumbled on to her knees. I could see a spot of red spreading on her right arm just below her shoulder.

XVII

I looked back over my shoulder and saw the camera across the track still trained on us. I dropped quickly to my knees beside Louise. The bellow of the six dicing cars was dying away up the track. There was a muted scream from other cars approaching along Cooper. The area where we were was otherwise quiet.

I tried to help Louise to her feet, but as I lifted her shoulders I could see that she had fainted. Yvette was kneeling on the other side of her. The crowd nearby had turned away from the track and surged around us. I glanced up and saw André looking down at me with cold eyes.

'I'll get an ambulanceman,' I said to Yvette.

I started to get up and saw the exposed fence and the photographer across the track, his camera at the ready on his chest. At any moment I would be exposed to the bullet that would surely follow the one that had been meant for me but instead had wounded Louise. I half-stood behind the protective crowd. Then, without straightening up, I started to run back down the track.

I saw another man running in the same direction about fifty yards ahead of me. He must have raised the alarm because, just as I got to the corner, two ambulancemen rushed past me, with a policeman close behind. I looked back as they passed, a little sorry at what I was doing, but I didn't hesitate as I went on round the corner of the path towards Clearways.

At the bridge I slowed to a brisk walk. I hoped Louise would be all right. There was nothing, anyway, that I could do for her that wouldn't be better done by someone used to this kind of thing. The farther I got away from the target area that Louise had led me to, the safer I would be.

Even with a policeman on the spot, I couldn't feel sure that the bogus photographer across the track would not have another go now that he had failed to get me after all the trouble they had gone to to set me up: the invitation to the club the night before, Louise's meetings with me, the meeting with André and Yvette to which Louise had led me... Now that they had missed me, and almost certainly knew that I knew that they wanted to get me, they would be all the more eager to finish the job.

I felt sorry for Louise. Of course she was working for Winston. She had nearly led me to my death. Even so, I felt sure that there had been nothing more to her assignment than the meeting between me, André, and Yvette. What was her connection with Krasko? It puzzled and worried Nina. Now it puzzled and worried me.

I had got to the exit from Clark Curve – the point where it ended in the pit straight – and looked back across the club circuit. An ambulance was turning out of the long straight where Louise had been shot. Below me the two Ferraris, slipstreaming through Clark, screamed by.

I started to run towards the entrance to the circuit. I didn't know quite what I was going to do, but I wanted to get away from the circuit as quickly as possible. I could see, just inside the entrance, a couple of buses already waiting to ferry back to Swanley the spectators who had come out from London by train. I didn't think either would move off for quite a while yet – not until it was full.

I looked across to the traffic streaming up the Dover Road towards London. Still three or four hundred yards away was a Green Line bus. Already very tired, I put on all the pace I could. The southbound traffic also was heavy, but, feeling like Graham Greene living on the dangerous edge, I crossed it in a suicidal dash, raced in front of a Jaguar in the other lane that looked hell bent for London or wherever, and reached the bus stop when the bus was only yards away. I flung up my arms. The bus raced by.

I had remembered, as we'd arrived at the circuit, a walk that I'd once made across country from Brands to Swanley, with a stop for a drink somewhere on the way. Now, on a rather desperate impulse, I hurried the few yards from the bus stop to the little side road that led to the open country and turned down it.

It was a crazy thing to do. I wasn't even sure that I could remember the way, but at least I felt sure that no one would look for me there. For a while, I even enjoyed it, but when, hours later, I came at last to the outskirts of Swanley, I felt worn out. The race must have ended long ago. I looked up anxiously when a helicopter, coming from the direction of Brands, passed low overhead. It was, I thought, just the kind of transport that Winston might charter for a hit-man.

I looked for a bus on the way into Swanley. None came. When at last I got to the station I found that there was no train direct to Victoria for more than half-an-hour, but in ten minutes there would be one going through Bromley South, which was well on the way. With half-a-dozen or so people on the platform, I stood back to a big poster on a wall, looking from one face to another and watching the steps that led down from the road to the platform.

I felt singular and exposed. I was so sure that I must look different – the man someone had just tried to kill at Brands Hatch – that I expected everyone to be looking at me. But no one took any notice, and no one came down the stairs, and after what seemed a very long time the train came in.

I sat at the front end of a coach from where I could look out of the window and keep an eye on the stairway until the train moved out, which it did very soon.

When I thought about it calmly, it seemed unlikely that anyone would have followed me to the station and on to the train, although given Winston's lunatic thoroughness it was not impossible. Anyway, I was now neurotically fearful and jumpy after the physical effort that had kept me going for the last few hours. While trees, houses, and fields sailed away from me on either side, I kept looking nervously between the two double rows of seats, towards the back of the coach, to make sure that no one was hiding there, ready to emerge with a gun.

I hadn't bothered to notice the train's final destination, and at Bromley South got out and let it pull away before I discovered that it was going to Blackfriars. As I waited anxiously, I began to wish that I had stayed aboard. I didn't *have* to go to Victoria.

Again I found myself standing with my back to a wall and a good view of the platform. A tiny girl, in a bright red dress and a white bonnet, running away from her mother, came up to me and smiled. I smiled back, but nervously, half afraid that the child was a bait in a trap. I almost jumped when the mother turned to find the child. She was a smart, red-lipped blonde – wearing dark glasses. I said 'Hello' to the little girl as the mother came up to us, smiled at me in her eyeless way, bent down to take the child's hand, and led her away. She half turned to give me a puzzled glance as she went off down the platform. I wondered about her glance – did I look badly under the weather?

I heard a train coming. When a station attendant told me that it was leaving for Victoria from a platform that had to be reached over a bridge, I raced across and got aboard just as it was pulling out. Again I sat with my back to the engine and stared anxiously at my fellow passengers. I began to wonder, too, whether Victoria was not a rather obvious place for Winston's people to watch, if they were going to watch any place. It was the station most people came back to if they had been to Brands Hatch. So, as we got up into London, I decided to get out at the Elephant and take a tube through to Regent's Park. Then, suspecting from earlier journeys that the train didn't go through the Elephant, I got off on an impulse at Herne Hill just as I had made up my mind to phone Walter as soon as I left the train.

Closer to the station I found a pub and phoned Walter. His wife answered. He wasn't in, she said, but he was on his way home and expected soon. I told her who and where I was, and that I badly wanted to see him. I would walk on towards Camberwell Green and the Elephant and phone again soon.

Venturing out, and looking up and down the street like a child about to cross the road, I set off down Herne Hill. I had walked for about twenty minutes before I saw a call box, and realized that I was noticing hardly anything about me. I was still thinking about my narrow escape from a bullet. I had also begun to think about Nina and to wonder whether she was involved in any way in Winston's latest plot. What if he had decided that Nina also was better dead?

I dialled Walter's number, fumbled with my money, and finally got it into the slot. It was such a relief to hear Walter's voice. I told him what had happened. I got a bit incoherent as I looked out fearfully through the call box window at everyone who came along the street. I had the jitters badly. I didn't want to die.

Walter got it right in the end and was silent for so long that I had to ask him if he was still there.

'You're an idiot, Tony,' he said, after another silence. 'You'll have to do something about this. Someone's going to get killed, and it's as likely as not to be you.'

As if I thought he had not heard what I'd told him, I said that, for God's sake, it nearly *had* been me. Then, matter-of-factly, he said that he had a little bit more to tell me, and would like to talk again about what I had told him. Would it be all right if he came down and met me at some place where we could talk? Would I just keep on heading for Camberwell Green and the Elephant, even Waterloo, if necessary? Somewhere along the way he would pick me up. He would also, he said, phone his newsroom for anything they might have about the shooting and let me know when we met.

Only a hundred yards or so down the road I turned into a bar and ordered a double Genever. I asked a young fellow alongside me, listening with ear plugs to a transistor radio, if he knew who had won the Grand Prix. He didn't, he said, but did I know that there had been a sensational shooting while the race was on? A woman had been taken off to hospital with a bullet wound. No, it was not, apparently, very serious. No one had been arrested, but spectators said that the woman had been with a man who had disappeared by the time police and ambulancemen arrived. Now the police were looking for this man after questioning a French couple, friends of the wounded woman. They, it seemed, couldn't give them any help.

Louise, I thought, would be out of favour with Winston's crowd for spoiling their set-up at Brands, but my feeling was that they would probably not harm her. Unless, of course, they were afraid that she might talk, which I supposed she might, if she had only just realized how ruthless Winston was.

What could I do, anyway, to help her without having to explain more than I felt free to explain? I was no Prince Hamlet. Poor Louise! Poor Kolchak! Poor Nina! Poor me, if it came to that – on the run now from Winston's men and at the same time wanted by the police.

I wet my lips with my tongue and could feel the sweat running down the back of my neck. The young fellow had gone back to his radio and his beer, but he must have thought my vacant, preoccupied air odd, because he gave me a couple of curious glances.

Perhaps now I should get out of the country at last, forget about everyone else, even Nina, and save my own skin. I thought of Amsterdam. I always did when I drank

Genever, remembering the first time that I had drunk it there, in the Dutch way, in a bar on the edge of the red-light district, tossing down the brimful glasses like a cowboy drinking whisky in a saloon in a Western film.

I went to the door, looked left, looked right, and walked on towards the Green. I was a little way past it when a car pulled up beside me. Of course I jumped, and of course it was Walter, with his wife driving. Walter got out, but she stayed at the wheel while we were introduced. She was quite good-looking, very suntanned, with the sensitive, intelligent face that I had expected. She gave me a strange half-smile – was there a bit of rather unwelcome pity in it? – then kissed Walter and drove off.

As we walked on, I told Walter what had been given out on the radio. He said that that was just about all his newsroom had told him. I started to tell him, in detail, all that had happened, from the time that Louise had first come to my table at the night club. Before I could finish he said that he could do with a drink and supposed I could too. So we went into the first bar that we came to.

I was beginning to relax by the time I'd finished my story. Walter asked a few questions.

'I can't make it out,' he said at last. 'What they're doing seems so – so–' He shrugged helplessly. 'They just must have decided, and goddamn it I'm not saying anything original – they just must have decided that you know too much to be left alive. Surely that can only be because you know about the Peter Kolchak plot, and you might talk. Then, if that's so important to them – important enough to kill for – why did they tell you in the first place that Kolchak was going to be arrested? You *did* nothing, so why don't they trust you? Is it because you've been seen with me?' He laughed. 'I don't believe that. Do they think that the girl has told you too much? Perhaps the girl is more important than she seems, and knows more than she admits.'

He had been filling his pipe, finished tamping it, and lit it.

'Anyway,' he said, between puffs, 'you're going to have to be bloody careful all the way if you're going to stay around and still do nothing about all this – though I don't suppose you need me to tell you that.' He looked at me and shook his head sorrowfully. 'You really *are* a god-awful bloody fool,' he said. He took a sip of beer. 'Kolchak, now. He has talked to the police and told them that evidence was planted on him. Well, of course. He thought they were not impressed. And Kolchak's editor, Rowson, has spoken to the police about that file of Kolchak's on Winston's activities that was apparently stolen – that went missing, anyway – after Kolchak's arrest. Fortunately Rowson talked to the police about this before he saw Kolchak, so there's no question of collusion.'

'They *could* reckon,' I said gloomily, 'that Rowson was in it from the start.'

Walter thought it very unlikely that they would. Of course they would have to suppose that everyone had his price, but Rowson had an incredibly pure background.

He shrugged. Anyway, the police were very interested in the stolen files. They had gone round straight away to look for fingerprints or other clues. Perhaps the missing file would lead them to take Kolchak's statement about planted evidence more seriously. In the meantime, they had told Rowson not to mention the missing file to Kolchak.

'Of course they didn't say a thing when Rowson asked them about Winston,' Walter said, 'but they're bound to ask Kolchak about his inquiries.'

As Walter talked I had been watching the door, and presently a fellow in dark glasses came in. I knew at once that he was one of Winston's men: I had seen him before. He seemed to take no special notice of me, but of course I knew why he was there. Walter stopped in mid-sentence.

'Is something wrong?'

'Don't look,' I said. 'It's one of Winston's men.'

'Are you sure?'

'Quite sure – I've seen him before.'

'You'd better come with me,' Walter said. 'Jean's coming in the car to pick me up' – he looked at his watch – 'in half-an-hour. Reminds me: I must phone her to say just where we are. They'd hardly cause trouble if you were with both of us.'

I shook my head.

'I'm sorry, Walter,' I said. 'It's not on. I'm sorry he has seen you with me, today of all days.'

'Tony, for God's sake,' Walter said. 'Why *don't* you go to the police? Come with me. Or phone them from here. This *can't* go on.'

I thought of Nina and again shook my head.

'Listen,' I said. 'In a very short time I'm going to the toilet. I don't suppose that there's a back way out, but there just might be. I want you to get up and order two more drinks. Make sure that you let that fellow on the left just inside the door see that you have *two* drinks. As you come back to the table I'll excuse myself. If I don't come back–'

Walter nodded.

'Does this look like leaving you holding the baby?' I said.

'Don't be bloody silly,' Walter said. 'I'm not really worried for myself, though I see that this is a new complication. Jean'll be here with the car, as I said. Right?'

'Right.'

He stood up and got the drinks. When he got back to the table, I told him I was going to the toilet and walked towards it. I suddenly realized that my umbrella was still over my arm, but I didn't do anything about it.

The toilets were at the end of a passage about six yards long. I went into the urinal. It had only a high, barred window. I looked in the cubicles on either side. They were dead ends with only ventilation louvres.

I'd noticed a door on the left near the end of the short passage that led to the toilets. Behind it a radio, or perhaps a record player, was playing loudly.

I came out of the toilets, thought a moment, still hesitated, then tapped on the door. There was no answer. I turned the handle gently and opened the door a foot. In the room a young woman was sitting on a bed, her feet drawn up, reading a book and eating an apple.

She still took no notice. I stepped into the room but kept the door half open behind me. I was very glad that she had turned her record player so high. Then she saw me, her eyes opened wide, her mouth fell open, and I was sure that she was going to scream. I put a finger to my lips, and she just left her mouth open but made no sound.

I had already noticed that there was a

window in the back wall, beside the bed. I said as quietly as I could, 'I'm sorry I frightened you. I want you to help me.'

I had put my left hand into my jacket pocket, and I pulled out my Press card and threw it on to the bed. Without taking her eyes off me, she reached out and picked it up.

'I'm a newspaperman,' I said. 'I'm on a very important job. Understand?'

She had glanced at the card and now stared at me with big blue eyes. After a moment she nodded. I lifted my umbrella a couple of feet in the direction of the window and said, 'I've got to get away from here without being seen. Where does that window lead?'

She put my Press card down and eased her feet over the edge of the bed to the floor. Still without looking away from me, she said, 'You'd better close the door, or you'll have me in trouble.'

I closed it, and she faced me and said firmly, 'Now what do you want?'

'Just to get away from here without having to go out the front door,' I said.

'You're not in trouble with the police?'

I laughed. 'Lord, no.'

'All right,' she said, and started to unlatch the window. 'There's a yard out there, and there's a path leads to a side street on the left.'

She turned to face me, holding her hands out helplessly at her sides, and looking from one to the other.

'Left, right,' she said, with a nod in either direction with her head. 'No, the path leads towards a side street on the *right*.' She looked up. 'You've got me confused. I don't know my right hand from my left.'

'Hurry,' I said, 'for *God's* sake.'

'Oh, *His*,' she said, and grinned. 'You *are* in the big league.'

She passed a leisurely tongue over her bottom lip.

'The gate to the street is locked,' she said, very patiently. 'But you can climb over it. *I* can anyway.' She gave a big smile. I had time to think I was sorry that this was going to be such a brief encounter.

She opened the window and looked out. I grabbed my Press card and pulled a five-pound note from my breast pocket. As she turned back to me I said, 'You're a good girl. Take this, and don't tell *anyone*.'

She shook her head and waved the money away. I dropped it on the bed. Then she stood back as I climbed over the sill. I could see the path leading off to the right, just as she had said. I glanced back as I started along it. She leaned out of the window and gave me a wave.

It was a high wooden gate, but there was a bar half-way up. When I stood on it, as I imagined the girl had done more than once on illicit exits and entries, I could see no one in the street. I swung quickly on to the top of it, dropped to the footpath, and reached my umbrella down from where I'd hung it on the gate.

XVII

I knew that it was risky to dive in among the back streets. I didn't know the area, and I wouldn't have to be very talented to get lost in it. It was even more risky, though, to go back to the main street. I wondered, as I hurried along, how they had tracked me down to the pub. I guessed that they'd been following Walter, and as likely as not on his own account, though they might well have had it in mind that sooner or later we would meet again.

I hoped that I hadn't let him in for anything unpleasant, particularly when he was being so loyal to me. I took a navigator's look at the sun, still visible in the evening sky, and turned at the next corner in what I reckoned was the direction of the river.

I decided to avoid the Elephant. The subways there always confused me. I knew, too, that a subway could be dangerous. Instead I would head straight for Waterloo and take the tube either from there or from the Embankment station across the river.

I began to think of Louise and hoped that she was all right. I had a tender feeling for her. I hoped that I would see her again. It wasn't just that she had saved my life. I couldn't believe that she was deeply involved with Winston's gang – in the sense, anyway, that she would be a party to their deeper villainy. Perhaps she was just like Nina, a victim of some blackmail plot, such as the shooting that Nina was supposed to have been involved in, but which I was more and more sure was just a pretence of a shooting set up to scare her.

I was walking in a very quiet street. I turned to look back on a long stretch. Although in a way I felt more secure when people were around me, it was a relief to have no one in sight, no one following me.

My aim had been good, or perhaps lucky. I came out into busy main streets again just south of Waterloo station. I'd been turning over in my mind whether it was safest to go home quickly by underground or to stay on the surface. I did feel afraid of being trapped in an underground passageway, on a platform, even on an escalator.

Then, I thought, wasn't it possible that someone at Brands had taken a photo that included Louise and me at the trackside, and that by now the police would know what the man they sought looked like?

I had turned into Waterloo Road, south of the Old Vic, when I noticed a man wearing dark glasses on the opposite side of the road. He was standing near the edge of the pavement, looking in the direction of the Elephant, and he seemed to be watching carefully every car that passed. Was it possible that he, too, was one of Winston's men? I hesitated, not sure whether to hurry on past him or turn back. As I hesitated I thought he looked across and saw me. Straight away he started to cross the road. I hoped that he hadn't realized that I'd seen him, as I hurried on towards the station.

I decided to get a taxi at the front entrance to the station and wondered why I hadn't thought about a taxi sooner, but when I reached it there were no taxis waiting. I went quickly into the station. Just as I was about to turn out of sight of the entrance, I looked back. A taxi had pulled up, and the man I had thought was following me was getting into it.

Well, that was the end of one pursuer, I thought, even if only an imaginary one. Better be suspicious than not, I supposed, but there must occasionally be someone in dark glasses who wasn't a Winston hireling.

I had thought that if I could keep out of sight of the man I'd supposed was pursuing me I would throw him completely off my tracks, by taking the elevated route to the Festival Hall, crossing the river, and catching a train at Embankment rather than at Waterloo. Still preoccupied with the thought of a pursuer, I did just that. I even found myself looking anxiously back from time to time as I crossed the bridge high above York Road. I came down to earth again by the Festival Hall and ascended again for the Hungerford Bridge crossing of the Thames – *that*, I thought, was one place where I wouldn't like to have to make a fight for it, or a run for it. But no one did appear. By the time I got to Embankment station I was thinking calmly enough to abandon the idea of a further tactical detour on the Northern line and went straight down and caught a train to Baker Street. I didn't even feel specially anxious now, though I stayed alert.

At Baker Street I surfaced cautiously and hurried a little anxiously along Marylebone Road on a route home that avoided the Paddington Street garden and, particularly, The Old Rising Sun.

When returning home up the wall I'd got a certain pleasure and amusement from approaching my terrace house in sight of Winston's sentry, though far enough off not to be recognized. This time I made a safe, blind approach and turned with relief up the driveway that ended at the fence behind the house.

I was over it in half-a-minute and ran towards the house. Then I stopped suddenly. No rope hung down the wall. I felt like a man on a sinking ship. I stood for a few seconds, my skin pricking, looking up and along the wall for a point of entry that I might have missed. Of course there was none.

I wondered desperately whether I dare try to enter the house by the front door but knew it would be a crazy, perhaps even fatal, thing to do. I stood still and thought hard. Suddenly I remembered Jane. Hers was the one place I could think of that would be welcoming and safe – if only I could get there without being noticed. If she wasn't home? I thought of my wife's flat, another half-mile beyond, and wondered what she would think if I turned up with the story I had to tell.

I pulled myself on to the top of the fence, dropped to the ground and, hugging the wall on one side of the driveway, made my way back to the street.

I followed the old 'look right, look left' drill, crossed over, and turned in the direction of the High Street. I'd gone only a few yards when a big, sleek car that looked uncomfortably like the Winston pick-up passed the end of the street about a hundred yards away. It seemed to slow and pause half-way across the intersection, then pulled away. When I got to the corner it was almost out of sight in the opposite direction from the one I was taking.

It was, I decided, another false alarm. I was just getting too jumpy. Now that I was a wanted man, the policeman strolling on his beat a hundred yards ahead of me was probably more to be feared.

There was a mid-evening quiet about the area, and I had got well along Paddington Street before I sighted a taxi, which I now saw as my escape mechanism, but it turned away before reaching me.

Peering right and left down each side street as I came to it, I saw few people and even less traffic. Once, in the rather dim distance towards Marylebone Road, I saw a car stationary, then suddenly and swiftly mobile. I thought it could be the big car that I'd seen near my room. This time it was going, as I was, towards the Edgware Road. Even in my anxiety I soon dismissed it as just another imaginary menace, no more real than that man in dark glasses who had got into the taxi at Waterloo.

At Homer Street I turned north towards Marylebone Road. I had crossed Old Marylebone Road and started down Chapel Street towards the tube station when I saw another taxi. Though I had begun to feel almost safe now, I raised my umbrella hopefully. It bowled past.

I went on to the Edgware Road and turned north to the subway that would take me across to the west side and the short walk up through Paddington Green to Jane and safety. At the top of the steps that led down into the subway two young fellows in leather jackets and wearing dark glasses leaned on the rails, talking. They turned and glanced at me as I started down the steps.

The long subway corridor that ran under the flyover was deserted. The sound of my footsteps echoed off the walls. I was about a third of the way along it when two men appeared from the exit that led up to the Edgware Road tube station and came towards me. Almost at the same time I heard a clatter of footsteps behind me on the steps that I'd just descended. I glanced back. One of the young fellows who'd been leaning on the rails had turned into the subway corridor.

I felt straight away that it was a trap. Was it coincidence? Or had Winston's hand reached out again? Had the car I'd seen on my way over from Marylebone been shadowing me?

The two men approaching me stopped suddenly. One of them patted his pockets as he turned to the other. He had a cigarette in his mouth and could have been looking for matches. His companion felt in his own pockets, shook his head and pointed at me.

They walked on towards me.

In the few moments of what I saw as their little bit of play-acting I imagined them seeing me, within half-a-minute, being asked for a match, my umbrella over my arm, my hands feeling in my pockets, as nearly helpless as I could be, with my escape route back along the subway cut off.

I could see now that the two men approaching me also wore leather jackets and dark glasses. The Winston uniform was almost comic, though I didn't feel much like laughing. Now they were within a few feet of me. The one on my right tilted his unlighted cigarette up towards the roof with his lips, reached up and took it out of his mouth, and said, quite politely, 'Excuse me, sir. Have you a light?'

I gripped the umbrella tighter in my right hand, clenched my left tentatively, and shook my head. Behind me the footsteps seemed very close. The two men in front of me, both taller than me, stood their ground only about a foot apart.

'Okay,' the man with the cigarette said, and as he said it the man on the left swung his right fist in an arc that was aimed at the left side of my jaw. As I swung my umbrella up to fend off the blow, I lunged sideways to the right so that I almost fell on the man with the cigarette as he sprawled backwards on the concrete.

My umbrella had connected violently with the arm of the man attacking me from the left, and he yelled in pain as I stumbled past him and started to run along the subway towards the steps that led up into the Harrow Road. I heard the footsteps of the man who'd been following me pounding quite close behind. I hoped that no one was guarding the entrance that I was heading for.

I wondered what had happened to the other fellow I'd seen at the entrance to the subway. If he had travelled diagonally along the Edgware Road he could be at my exit as soon as I was. He would be lucky, I thought, to guess accurately which exit I was making for, though Winston's gang – if this *was* Winston's gang – probably knew enough about Jane to guess that I might be looking for refuge with her.

I wasn't feeling very fit and knew that the man behind must be gaining on me. Before I faced any danger above ground I'd probably have to deal with him, anyway. So at the foot of the steps I suddenly changed direction, grasped the umbrella near the bottom with both hands, and swung round. As my pursuer leapt at me with arms outstretched, I brought the crook of the umbrella handle down on his shoulder. He gasped with pain and stumbled against the wall, holding the spot where I'd hit him.

Behind him the other two were coming on. I turned again and ran up the steps.

I could see no one at the top, but as I came out I looked over my shoulder and saw the other fellow standing in the middle of the Edgware Road, as though waiting for a break in the traffic. He saw me immediately, dashed behind a passing car, and headed towards me.

It was ironic, I thought, as I sprinted up the Harrow Road towards Paddington Green, that I was passing the police station and praying that no one would come out of it and see me. Scared as I was of the men behind me, I was almost more scared, in a crazy way, of all that might happen if the police stopped me, questioned me, and discovered that I was the man they wanted to ask about the Brands Hatch shooting.

My pursuers, too, must have been apprehensive, because the clatter of running footsteps suddenly stopped. When I looked back I saw all four of them, about twenty yards behind, in a line across the wide pavement, now just walking briskly.

I slowed to a walk myself until I was just past the recruitment entrance at the other end of the police building. Then I started to run again, as fast as I could, to give myself a good start as I swung past the telephone call box and into the path, with fences on either side, that crossed the Green.

Half-way along the path, I saw a policeman turn in at the other end and stride slowly on towards me. I slowed to a trot, then to a brisk walk, and looked at my watch. The policeman gave me a hard look as I passed, but he didn't stop or speak to me. Once I'd passed him I felt glad that he had come along. It gave me a chance to get my breath back and keep my distance ahead of the men following me. I didn't think that they would try to overtake me until they were past him and out of his sight behind the church.

By then I was in the street that ran down past St Mary's Mansions to the canal. I started to run again and had turned into the short private roadway that led to Jane's flat before my pursuers came in sight. I hoped desperately that Jane would be home. I pressed her bell hard and kept my finger on it. In the still, quiet night I heard a door open somewhere above. Then Jane's voice came out of the little speaker by the bell push. She gave a little gasp when I spoke, and in a surprised, pleased voice told me to come in.

XIX

At the top of the stairs, Jane was waiting for me. She was wearing a workman's boiler-suit and a self-conscious smile to go with it. I said, 'Hello.' She put her arms around me, buried her face in my shoulder, and held me tight. Then she moved back a little, looked at me tenderly, kissed me quickly on the mouth, took my hand, and led me along the corridor to her room.

As soon as she'd closed the door she looked down at herself and said, 'I'm not crazy or anything, or going in for plumbing. I'm in a play. I have to wear this thing. I put it on this evening to try it for size and left it on to get used to the feel of it.'

'That's a good idea,' I said.

She looked at me and started to smile again. Then she was anxious and puzzled.

'What's wrong?' she asked.

I hoped my smile was reassuring as I said, 'Wrong? Nothing's wrong.'

She shrugged and looked hurt.

'Oh, well,' she said. 'The mysterious Tony. Still more of that.'

She walked silently into her little kitchen and ran water into a kettle, and I heard her

228

put it on the stove. She reappeared and said, 'You would like some coffee?'

I said I'd love some.

Again she looked at me very hard and noticed the umbrella.

'You *do* play safe,' she said.

'Oh, I've been out for the day and haven't been home yet,' I said.

'To Brands?' she said.

With what I knew must be a caught-out look, I nodded.

'With Mademoiselle Louise?' she said.

I didn't answer, but I knew that it was no good lying.

She went into the kitchen and turned off the gas. When she came back she looked very angry.

'Oh, I know I don't *own* you,' she said. 'I've got no rights at all. But your old, full-time runaround act really does give me the stitch. Now, would you like to go?'

She turned to the door and, with her hand on the knob, said over her shoulder, 'Why the hell did you come here, anyway?'

'Listen, Jane,' I said. 'I only went to Brands with – with Louise because I realized last night that she's mixed up with this bunch that I'm trying to get information about. I–'

'Pull the *other* bloody leg,' Jane said. She turned and faced me. 'Do you think I can swallow that?'

I started again, 'Listen Jane…'

'I'm *all* bloody ears.' She put her hands in her overall pockets and looked at me with a bitter, sarcastic half-smile.

'Louise picked me up after I'd left here last night,' I said.

Jane laughed, very bitterly.

'Louise picked you up, huh? It couldn't have been the other way about?'

'May I sit down?'

'I thought you were going,' Jane said. 'I'm not in the mood for bedtime stories.' She turned again and began to open the door.

I didn't move and was trying with desperate haste to decide how much I should tell her, and how little I could. She looked over her shoulder and said, quite loudly and very angrily, 'Well?'

The door was wide open. I blinked and, with one eye on the corridor, said, 'Jane, someone tried to shoot me today. They're waiting downstairs for me now. They tried to shoot me. They got Louise instead.'

Jane gaped and backed to the door, closed it with her bottom, and stared at me.

'At Brands? Was *she* the woman who was shot at Brands?'

I nodded.

'And I'm the man the police are looking for,' I said.

I told her what had happened.

'But – but why don't you go to the police if you're in danger?' Jane said. 'What have you got to fear? From *them*, I mean?'

She sat on the edge of the bed. She was pale, and she looked shocked.

'It's not as simple as that,' I said. 'There are other people involved. There–'

Jane had recovered quickly.

'You keep saying these things,' she said. The colour had come back into her face. She stood up impatiently. 'Can't you explain *anything* to me? I might even be able to help.' She stood frowning at me, waiting for an answer.

'I'm sorry, Jane,' I said. 'I'm sorry I came here. But I couldn't get into my place. Someone had taken the rope–'

I stopped.

'What are you *raving* about?' Jane asked.

'Have you got a phone here?'

She shook her head.

'I don't know what to say, what to tell you,' I said. 'I couldn't get into my room because they're watching it. Now they're watching this place, waiting for me to leave.'

Jane looked startled, but all she said was, 'Who the hell are *they*?'

I sat down and put my head in my hands. Jane breathed out long and heavily. Then I heard her walk away, the pop of lighted gas from the kitchen, and a rattle of cups. When I heard her footsteps coming back I looked up.

'Do you mean you want to stay here now,

tonight?' she asked.

'I don't know what to do,' I said. 'I'm afraid for myself, and I'm afraid for others, too. There's this woman I'm supposed to be seeing...'

'What woman?'

Then, in desperation, leaving out the names of the people and places, I told her about Krasko and Nina, a bit about Winston, nothing about Kolchak or Walter. It was quite a virtuoso performance.

Half-way through, the kettle began to sing, and I stopped talking while Jane turned off the gas. When I'd finished, with the story of my journey from Marylebone to her flat, she looked white and shocked again.

'Are you in love with this girl?' she said at last.

I shook my head. She stared at me. I didn't think she believed me. Then she turned and went into the kitchen and lit the gas again, and soon I could hear her making coffee. She came out and, without saying anything, took off her overall, put on a frock, and combed her hair. When she brought out the coffee, she sat beside me and put her cup on the floor.

'I think you should go to the police,' she said. 'At least, I think *I* should. They're just around the corner. I could bring someone here to talk to you. I know it sounds awfully square, but–'

I shook my head. Then, without telling her in so many words of Nina's phobia, her false passport, and other compromising facts, I tried, very inadequately, to explain why it was impossible.

As we talked, I was thinking all the time of Nina waiting for me, possibly in danger. I'd almost reached the point of suggesting that Jane should go to see her, but I knew that, whatever had happened, Nina wouldn't want that. There was, anyway, the risk to Jane in involving her. A little dishonestly, I used it to settle the argument in my own mind. For the same reason, I decided that I wouldn't get her to phone Walter.

In spite of my tense anxiety, I'd begun to feel helplessly tired. When Jane suddenly found, just before ten o'clock, that she was out of butter, and went out to buy some in one of the late-night shops in the Edgware Road, I took off my shoes and lay on her bed. I felt so relieved to be alone and free to sleep. If there was anything that I liked as much as – perhaps even more than – drinking or making love, this was it.

I was half asleep, thinking, inconsequentially, of Jane in her boiler-suit, when suddenly I remembered her remark about not being a plumber. I sat up, wide awake, and put my feet to the floor. I stared at the door. I was still staring at it when I heard footsteps on the stairs and the rattle of a key. As Jane came back into the room, I jumped up.

'What's wrong?' she said. 'What is it?'

'Do you think you could *really* pose as a plumber,' I asked. 'In your blue overall, I mean, if you didn't have to talk?'

Jane looked at me.

'Of course I could,' she said. 'Even if I did have to talk. That's the whole idea. What are you getting at? What–?'

'It's Nina,' I said and I almost bit my tongue as I mentioned her name. 'The girl I was talking about. Listen. I've been thinking. No, wait.'

I sat down again and stared into space. Then I started again.

'If you were to dress up really to look like a plumber – a plumber's boy – go out and hire a van and go to where – to where Nina lives, no one would take any notice of you.'

'I'm not with you,' she said. 'What good would that do? What's the point in me – in *my* going there unnoticed?'

'You do realise that they're watching the place – *her* place?' I said.

'I didn't,' Jane said. 'These spy people, do you mean. Even so–'

I rushed on impatiently, 'You get into the place – Nina lets you in – pretending that you're going to do some plumbing, and Nina changes into your clothes. She's about the same height and build as you are, the same size. You could make her up to look like a boy, couldn't you?'

'I suppose I could,' Jane said. 'What then? Nina comes here, I suppose, while I stay there, and you and Nina live happily ever after.'

'Nina drives to Heathrow,' I said, 'and catches a flight to the Continent – to Paris or Amsterdam or somewhere. *Then* I can talk to the police – when she's out of the way, I mean.'

'Tony and Nina finito,' Jane said.

I didn't say anything.

'Finito?'

'It's the only way,' I said, without much conviction.

Jane took her parcels into the kitchen and came out with a half-bottle of brandy and two glasses.

'Let's drink to it,' she said, pouring generously. 'When do I begin?'

I would have liked her to do it right away, to put my mind at rest about Nina, but I felt that it would be a bigger risk now than in the morning – much more likely to make Winston's watchdog suspicious. It seemed faintly possible also that Jane might be followed at night if anyone watching her flat had recognized her. So we settled for her going to work as usual in the morning and on to Acacia Road from there.

Jane became almost coldly practical and matter-of-fact about it. She produced her make-up box to show me how quickly she could turn herself into a teenage boy. I was very impressed, a bit startled, even. When, looking like a boy, she tried to kiss me, I turned away in horror. She thought that was very funny but suddenly was solemn. She went out to her bathroom, washed off the make-up, came back and kissed me tenderly.

'It's bedtime,' she said.

I woke very early in the morning. Jane had a slight flush as she slept, and her lips were parted, just showing her very white teeth. I wanted her very much, but I'd woken sick with anxiety. Now, as I looked at her, I felt sorry for her because of what I knew I would soon do. I rolled away and watched a sparrow that had settled on the window sill. I envied its freedom.

I began to think of the practical details of Nina's escape. Would she have enough money? Most of my available cash was hidden in my room. I couldn't risk sending Jane there for it, and of course there could be no question of my going there. I was sure that they'd made up their minds to get me, and they wouldn't care where they did it.

I couldn't bear to be inactive, so I got out of bed and was making coffee when Jane woke. I took a cup to her, and she sat up drinking it, a sheet around her shoulders, snuggling against me. I mentioned the money. She said that she had fifty pounds if that would help. So, with her fifty pounds and about forty that I had with me, she left for work soon after eight o'clock.

To carry her change of clothes, she had a very battered overnight bag that would look near enough to a tool bag when she left the hired van at Nina's flat. Her plan was to change into her overall in the back of the van in some quiet street on the way to St John's Wood. To make absolutely sure that she wasn't seen and suspected, she promised to stay in Nina's flat for at least four hours and not to use the telephone in case it was tapped. She made me promise not to leave the flat until she came back, in the afternoon.

I wasn't sure how much she feared for my safety and how much she wanted to make sure that I didn't somehow manage to run away. It was not a good idea to follow Nina, anyway. She should decide where she should go. She would know where she would feel safest. I put this in a short note to Nina that I let Jane read.

After Jane had gone I tried to read but found it difficult, even though I'd picked up a Simenon thriller. It occurred to me, presently, that Jane might, after all, go to the police, not so much from jealousy of Nina but because she thought that it was best and safest for everyone.

It was unlikely. Even so, I worried quietly

about it. I wondered what the news was of Louise and whether anything more had happened in the Kolchak case. I wished that Jane had got a morning paper, but there hadn't been time. I heard a phone ring on what seemed to be the floor below and a woman's voice answer it, and I wondered whether I might go down and ask if I could use it, to phone Walter.

I washed and made myself otherwise presentable and opened the door. I could hear the hum of a vacuum cleaner and the voice of a child. I walked slowly down to the next landing and along to where I guessed the phone might have rung. I tapped on the door. A little girl opened it, the hum of the cleaner stopped, and a woman of about thirty appeared. I hoped my smile was as diffident as I felt as I asked if she had a phone. Yes, she had, she said, as she looked at me rather uncertainly. Would it be asking too much–? I paused and said that I was visiting upstairs. She hesitated, then smiled, led me in, and left me in the lounge.

I found Walter's number in my diary and, as I waited for an answer, looked around. A copy of the *Express* lay on the settee a few yards away. There was a picture on the front page of Louise being put in an ambulance at Brands Hatch and, beside it, a mug shot of her. One of the headlines said that she had been wounded.

There was no answer from Walter's number. He wasn't at Bush House either when I tried there – they said he wasn't coming in till the afternoon. I went out into the hallway where the woman had started up the cleaner again, thanked her, went back to Jane's room, and had another go at Maigret. It was going to be a long morning.

Jane came back just after three o'clock. I had stood up anxiously as I heard the key in the door, but she came in with a big smile, put her arms around my neck, and said, 'Oh, darling, now you're really mine.'

I said tensely, 'What happened?'

She stood back, and still smiling, said that everything had gone just as we had planned, although she was sure that at first Nina didn't trust her. Until Nina was ready to go she had half-expected her to change her mind.

'There was a car parked opposite, with a man sitting at the wheel, just as you'd said there would be, and he didn't follow. I looked out from behind the curtains – oh, no, no, I *was* careful – as soon as I heard the van pull away, and the car was still there. It was still there when I came away. I took the number.'

She laughed and produced a piece of paper.

I was relieved, so relieved, but shaken. I sat down heavily on the bed. Jane was tender again.

'Poor darling,' she said. 'You look done in. Have you eaten?'

I shook my head.

'I haven't, either,' she said. 'All I could find at your friend's was a crate of Pilsener. I'll make sandwiches and coffee.'

She was busy in the kitchen for a few minutes before she reappeared, wiping her hands on a towel.

'She's very beautiful,' Jane said soberly, looking at me hard. She put her hand in a pocket. 'I forgot,' she said. 'She asked me to give you this.' She paused. 'I haven't opened it.' She handed me an envelope. I tore it open and read.

Darling,

I am so frightened. Mr Winston told me what happened yesterday. He says now they must kill you. Oh, darling, be so careful. I didn't know what to do when your friend came, but I must trust you now because I love you so much, and I must trust your friend with this note because you've trusted her with my life. I'm going to Paris, to one of the little hotels I know in the rue de Malte. If you can, look for me there. It's not a long street. But be careful.

Nina

I must have smiled as I bent to read the note. I knew the kind of smile it would be. I looked up and started to fold the note. Jane was looking at me very hard.

'She's gone to Paris,' I said.

She kept on looking at me hard, and I almost gave up and handed her the note. But just in time she shrugged and went back to the kitchen.

'Finito,' she called out. 'Remember? Nina and Tony finito.'

In all the circumstances I thought she was being incredibly big about everything.

She came to the kitchen door again.

'Oh,' she said. 'There *is* someone watching this place. There was a Mini at the corner of the building, in sight of my entrance, when I went out this morning. It was still there when I came back. The fellow was reading a book both times when I passed, but I'm sure he was watching. Anyway, who the hell wants to read a book through dark glasses?' She paused. 'It's pretty cheeky. They must be very sure that you won't go to the police. Or at least that you wouldn't go. Now you can, presently. How long are you going to wait?'

I didn't answer right away, and she went back into the kitchen and lit the gas. When she came out with the coffee and sandwiches I said, 'I'll wait – I'll have to wait – till I can talk to this – this fellow.' I felt awkward about not naming Walter. 'What's worrying me is how to go about doing that. I've got the wind up about this gang.' I was about to mention what Nina had said about Winston's threat but realized in time that it would be best, safest, not to have another embarrassing moment about the note. So I just finished, 'I don't know how I'm ever going to get away. I just don't know.'

Jane shivered and sipped her coffee. Presently she giggled.

'Your girl made a lovely boy,' she said. She giggled again. 'Perhaps you'd make a lovely lady.' She was solemn again. 'Are you still going away? Are you going to – to the Continent, to Amsterdam and all, when all this is over?'

I shrugged. 'I can't even think about that.'

Jane left at about four o'clock to go back to the office but returned before getting half-way down the stairs.

'How could I have forgotten?' she said. 'There's no one watching *your* room now. Of course they must know that you're holed up here. I came past in my cab on the way back.'

She went out again.

At six o'clock she came back excited.

'Do you think that they'd clear out if the police turned up?' she said.

'They?'

'The people who are watching this place, of course.'

There was no question of calling the police until I had spoken to Walter, I said. And now that I thought about it, I realized that I couldn't have talked with Walter as I needed to talk if I'd used the phone downstairs in the morning.

'No, no,' Jane said. 'I'd call them for my own reasons. Listen. Supposing a police car with hee-haw, blue light and all came round to my door. Don't you think our boy friend would withdraw?'

'So what?' I said.

'I follow them in a taxi – the police, I mean. You grab the taxi and skip. You could lie on the back seat if necessary. Then go to the office. Look, I got the keys on a pretext of going back to catch up with the work that I didn't get done today.' She held up the keys. 'You've got a phone there. You could call your friend. There'll be no one else there – I made sure of that. By the morning you should have it all sorted out. I think we should wait for dark, anyway. If there's any-thing that you need I could pick it up before then from your room.'

I thought about it and reckoned that she was well out in her optimism about what could be done in a night. Still, I had come up with no plan of my own and thought that there was a chance that hers would work. I said so. She was delighted and hugged me. She talked over the details. She wasn't at all worried about bringing the police on a wild goose chase. Then she went off to Marylebone to get my hidden wallet and my shaving gear, promising not to go into my room if anyone was watching. In half-an-hour she was back and made some supper. Then, at about nine-thirty, like a child going on a picnic, she went out to make her call.

I put on my coat and waited tensely. In about a quarter-of-an-hour I heard the hee-haw of a police car away towards the Edgware Road. As it came nearer I went down the stairs, opened the street door an inch or two, and peered out. I could see the watching car parked where Jane had said it was. Presently it was lit up by the headlights of an approaching car. With its blue light flashing, a long white police car swung in behind the mansions.

Jane's timing had been better than I'd believed possible. Her taxi had turned in behind the mansions before the police car had found her entrance. The taxi almost hit the watching Mini as it started up abruptly and shot into the exit drive towards the road. As the police car overshot and reversed, I stepped casually out of the doorway and walked to where Jane was getting out of the taxi about ten yards away. Minutes later I was bowling along Marylebone Road on my way to Fleet Street.

XX

My old office was just off one of the streets that run from Fleet Street down to the river. It was very strange to be opening the door again. It seemed a long time since I had been there, though it was really no longer than some holidays that I'd had. But, then, even the past few days seemed to stretch back a very long way.

I went into my old room and turned on the light. Whoever was using my desk – I hadn't asked Jane – was less tidy than I was. I felt almost a compulsion to tidy it up before I phoned Walter, but I didn't.

I got Walter first try. He was relieved to hear from me but was just finishing a bulletin and said he'd phone me back in about ten minutes' time. I wandered through into the main office and glanced at the familiar bits of paper in my colleagues' trays: raw copy, half-subbed copy, sliced up galleys, paste-ups, photographs, a programme for the British GP – that historic event! – an old, well-thumbed copy of *Mayfair*. I still felt glad that I didn't have to go back to all that – not yet anyway.

As I went over to the window, the phone

rang. I told Walter what had been happening. He said that he had been tailed after he had left the pub where I'd last seen him. He couldn't be sure, but he had a feeling that they were still watching him. No, there had been no developments in Kolchak's case, and he had heard nothing on the grapevine. Kolchak was still on remand in custody. Walter asked me what I intended to do – about myself and about the whole situation now that Nina had given Winston's men the slip.

I said that of course I would go to the police presently – sooner or later, I thought, but later rather than sooner – now that I was the only one involved. Walter didn't answer for a bit.

'I think you're right, of course,' he said at last, then was silent again. When we both started to speak at once, then stopped, Walter said: 'Yes?'

'Who do you think I should see – well, get in touch with?' I asked.

Again Walter was silent before he said, 'Tony, I shouldn't say this, but I'm not quite sure how far you're hoping to go with this alone. I know you've been concerned for the girl's safety – that's Nina, I mean. But you know – well, you *must* know – that you can't expect the police not still to be interested in her. Not after her part in the Kolchak affair. Do you know where she is? Is she still in

Western Europe?'

I said that of course she was. I wondered why I had said 'of course'. I was beginning to feel scared again.

'Tony, I'm sorry,' Walter said. 'I suppose I've been thinking all along of your concern for the girl's safety. God knows why, when I think of poor bloody Kolchak. Still … anyway, even if you don't know where she is, even if you do know and don't tell, they're almost sure to put Interpol on to it. If she *is* innocent – and really I take your word for that – she'll come to no harm if she comes forward. I'm sure they won't lock her up or anything, not for long, anyway.' I winced. 'But they can't just forget about her.'

'But Walter…' I said. I was about to tell him that we could easily have gone that far here in London, simply by asking the police to go and fetch her. I hadn't got her out of the country just to get her away from Winston, although that was the big thing. I had got her away to get her out of the whole damnable situation – though I couldn't for the life of me say how I was going to do the right thing by Peter Kolchak without Nina to back me up. But I didn't say any of this. I was aware as I said 'But Walter' that I was making a despairing gesture in the air with my right hand.

Neither of us spoke for a while. Then Walter said that he was going to the club for a drink before he went back to work, but that he didn't think we should meet there. Perhaps I would go up to his office at Bush House when he knocked off at eleven-thirty, if I thought I wasn't exposing myself, and we could talk about it again. We settled on that.

I sat at my old desk and stared into space for five minutes. I badly wanted a drink. Dare I go out for one? Then I looked in a drawer of my desk for a Paris hotel list. I was relieved to find it and started phoning the hotels in the rue de Malte. They didn't speak anything that you could call English, and I spoke little that you could call French. So I could hardly believe my luck when, at the seventh call, I found the one where Nina had booked in. She wasn't there, though. She had gone out to meet a friend. That was the message that she'd left.

I opened the bottom drawer of my desk and looked up flights to Paris. No, it was crazy. I half expected Jane to phone, but she didn't. Just before eleven o'clock I very deliberately put the office keys in the drawer of Jane's desk where she kept her make-up – I had a brief, heady breath of her *Je Reviens* – and let myself out of the office in time to have one drink, perhaps two if my swallow was all that it should be, at the nearest pub before closing time on my way to Bush. I sank two beers and walked up to Fleet Street, then west towards the Strand.

But I didn't go to Bush House. I had been wondering, anyway, whether it was a good idea to go there if Walter was being watched. Instead I turned down to the river, walked along to Embankment tube station, and caught a train to Piccadilly Circus. From there I took another train to Heathrow.

As we got out of town and rocketed westward through the dark countryside I had a fine feeling of freedom. I recalled other times that I'd made the journey to and from Heathrow by the underground – but the only time that I remembered really vividly was a journey, about a year before, back through the spring sunshine after I had seen my wife off to Spain on a fortnight's holiday.

I supposed I remembered it because then, too, I had had the feeling that I was escaping from something: the fields had never looked greener, the daffodils more yellow. This time, though, I had to remind myself, I was escaping for only a few hours. In Paris I would have all over again the worry about Nina.

At the airport I found that I'd made a mistake about the flights to Paris and would have to wait till the morning. It wasn't the kind of place I wanted to be. If the police had a description of me and still wanted to see me, it was one of the places that they might look, though I hoped that by now Louise would have put that right. It was also a place that Winston's men might watch if they had any idea that I might have got away from Jane's flat – especially if they suspected that Nina had fled the country and that I might follow. I felt pretty sure, though, that they suspected none of this.

I sat in one of the lounges and talked with a girl who was leaving for Kenya in the morning. She reckoned that she could live a long time on the sale of the hashish she would bring back in a couple of weeks' time. I dozed a little but was too uneasy really to sleep. Each time I came wide awake I felt in my pocket where my wallet and my passport were. I was glad that, from my days as a reporter, I had always carried my passport because I never knew when I might need it. I was relieved, although I felt like nothing on earth, when the morning came, and I bought my ticket and at last was on the plane taxiing out towards the runway.

Paris on that summer morning was as wonderful as Paris is on any sunny morning. I wondered, as I always did, why I didn't come more often, and hoped, as I always did, that this time I wouldn't become disenchanted in a day or two, or perhaps a little longer. That had nearly always happened in the past. Was the language problem that I had had with a bad-tempered ticket-salesman in the Gare du Lyon on my first visit anything to do with it? They always said that nothing told you more about a foreign country than the difficulties that you had there.

I reached République at about nine o'clock and walked toward Oberkampf and the rue de Malte. The hotel was open, and someone was sitting at the reception desk. In my halting French I asked if Nina was in. The man behind the desk gave me a long look, shook his head, and waited. I said that she was expecting me. He still looked at me. I told him my name. He started to reach towards some letters in some pigeonholes, but his hand stopped before it reached them. He seemed to be listening.

Someone was coming down the stairs. The man at the reception desk asked me to sit down and wait. He looked towards the stairs. I did, too, and the man we saw turn the corner was Mr Krasko. I stood up as he came towards me, with a diffident smile.

'Ah, my friend,' he said, offering his hand. Although I had begun to feel hot and angry, I took his hand as he stopped and looked at me intently, but still with a slight smile.

'You are looking for Nina,' he said. I nodded and swallowed hard. 'I will tell you about her,' he said. 'But I want to thank you first for all that you did for me in London – in – in Marylebone.' He didn't pronounce Marylebone quite right. He shook his head, and now his smile was wry. 'That was a rather difficult situation, rather difficult.' He waved me to sit down and sat beside me on the settee. He looked at his hands and rubbed the back of one with the palm of the other. He didn't speak.

'Mr Krasko,' I said, and I knew that my voice was angry.

He looked at his watch. 'I have an appointment. I have to go in a moment. You wanted to know about Nina.' He looked away from me, out into the sunlit street, and then at the man at the reception desk who had been sitting writing and had just picked up the telephone.

'Nina,' said Mr Krasko, very quietly, 'has gone back to Eastern Europe.'

I grabbed him roughly by the arm. He turned and looked at me.

'You do not understand,' he said, in that infinitely patient voice. 'You will not. I am sorry, but you will not understand. Not really. But if you wait here for me' – he looked at his watch again and gave a resigned look at the man at the reception desk – 'if you wait here for me, or go for your coffee and come back in an hour, I will tell you what I can. Not much, but what I can. I know that Nina told you a little – not much either, I imagine, and I am not sure what. But she told you a little. What *could* she tell you? It's much more difficult, much more complicated, than even she knows.'

He stood up, and I stood up and faced him angrily.

'It'll be the end of Nina if she's gone to the East,' I said.

I noticed that the man at the reception desk had put down the phone and was listening as he pretended to write.

'Oh, no,' said Mr Krasko kindly. 'Oh, no. You see, you do not understand. I am sorry. But I will tell you what I can.'

He started to walk towards the door and had almost reached it when I called after him.

'What about Louise?'

He turned. 'What about her?' he asked. 'She will be all right.' He smiled patiently. 'She is not going to die.'

Then he went out through the door and disappeared in the direction of République.

I walked slowly to the door and looked after Krasko. He was hurrying, but near the entrance to Oberkampf metro station he looked back and waved an arm. I didn't wave back. I turned to look in the other direction, up the rue de Malte. I supposed that I had better wait. I felt angry and a little foolish and very helpless – not that a very helpless feeling was new. Then I remembered the man at the reception and the letters that he had been reaching for. I went back into the hotel. The man had come from behind his desk and was looking towards me, holding an envelope between a thumb and forefinger.

'Mademoiselle left this for monsieur,' he

said. He smiled very faintly. As I took it, he said, 'Mademoiselle said that she wanted me not to mention it to anyone else.'

'When did mademoiselle leave the hotel?' I asked.

He looked at his watch. 'At six hours.'

'Did she take all her baggage?'

He nodded. *'Oui.'*

'You don't know where she went?'

He shook his head and looked at the envelope in my hand.

I asked him when Krasko had come to the hotel. It was very late the night before, he told me. He had come back with Nina and booked a room.

'Just before six hours, when I came out of my room' – he nodded towards the foot of the stairs – 'monsieur was waiting for me here. He told me that mademoiselle was going, and he paid her bill. Then he left with her.' He paused. I suspected that he was wondering just how long he should continue with his mild indiscretions. 'He was absent for about one hour. Mademoiselle gave me the envelope when monsieur went upstairs to get her bags.'

He went back behind his desk and asked, 'Does monsieur require a room?'

I shook my head. 'Not yet.'

I started to open the envelope, then looked up and said, 'Has Monsieur Krasko left his key?'

He smiled and gave a helpless shrug, but didn't answer. I sat down and opened the envelope.

Darling,
I know you'll be angry. I wish that you wouldn't be. I was so tired when I got to Paris, to my hotel, that I slept for hours. Then I went out for a salad and a beer to the only eating place in Paris that I had ever heard of – a café near the Gare du Nord that Peter used to talk about.

I couldn't believe it when I saw him there, sitting on the sidewalk looking anxious. He couldn't believe it, either, when he saw me. I told him everything, and he told me that I must not stay in Western Europe because Interpol would look for me. He said that I must go to Prague, and that he would arrange it straight away. He brought me back to the hotel, then went out. When he came back he said that I must leave at six in the morning.

I must trust him. He knows so much more than I do, about everything. He couldn't tell me where exactly I'm going. I will be met at the airport at Prague, where I have never been before. If you will wait in Paris, at the hotel, I will write to tell you where I am. Peter wouldn't talk about you. He did say, though, how much you had done for him – I did, too. I told him the things that he didn't know about your loyalty, but I think that he may not be sure about you. So I can't be sure that he will help us to stay in touch.

I asked him about Louise. He had phoned the hospital. He said that she would be all right. He kept telling me that there was nothing mysterious or sinister in his association with Louise – that he had known her a little in Paris, and that she had simply been a good and loyal friend to him when they had met again in London. He wouldn't say more than that.

Nina had written something after that, then scored it out heavily. I couldn't read a word of it, even though I was pretty good at deciphering this kind of thing. Then she said:

Darling – I'm so sorry. I love you so much, and I miss you so much. The time goes on and on when I don't see you. Please, if you can, wait for a letter from me. If you can't – then I don't know what. Perhaps they can send on my letter to wherever you may be.

Nina

I put the letter in my pocket and looked across at the man at the reception desk. He was watching me and smiled faintly.

'You had better book me a room for two

days,' I said.

I had been pushing my French to the limit, but this was easier.

As I stood up I said, 'I'll go out for some coffee. Tell monsieur, when he returns, that I'll be back.'

Then I remembered: no French currency. But, helpfully, the man at reception changed a couple of pounds of my sterling, and I went out and along to the café by Oberkampf, ordered a beer and a roll, and sat just inside where I could watch the street. It was going to be a hot day. When I looked out into to the boulevard, the girls in their summer dresses made me feel young again. I thought so, anyway. But it could have been the first drink of the day on an empty stomach.

XXI

When I'd finished my drink I went back to the hotel, picked up my key, and sat by the reception desk waiting for Peter Krasko. He came in at about ten o'clock. Under his arm was a leather satchel that hadn't been there when he went out. He smiled, as if he felt sorry for me. We went up to his room, where he put the satchel on the table by his bed, gingerly, as though there was something breakable inside it. Still holding his room key he turned to me. He looked tired and a little anxious.

'Sit down, my friend,' he said. 'I will try–'

The phone on the bedside table rang. He sat on the bed with his back to me, put his key on the pillow, and picked up the receiver. He said something in a language that I couldn't understand, and then, in French, 'I am sorry. I expected a call from someone else. What is it then? My passport? But I gave you the details last night. You have not got them? All right, then. All right.'

He sounded rattled and hung up.

'I will be only a moment,' he said to me. He went out, closing the door, and I could hear him going down the stairs.

I walked over to the bed and was about to pick up his satchel when I noticed, beside the phone, an airways guide and a note pad with some words and figures scribbled on it. One of the words was 'Prague', with some almost indecipherable figures below it. All this had been scored out, and underneath, heavily underlined, was the word 'Berlin', with more figures that could have been flight times, and then 'Kurt Schmidt' and an address in, of all places, Dahlem. I scribbled the address on the back of an envelope. I felt angry again. It was only a hunch, but I felt certain that that was where Nina had gone. I zipped open the satchel. Inside was a thick wad of typewritten sheets and a black notebook partly filled. Like Krasko's answer on the phone, it was all in a language that I couldn't understand.

I could hear someone coming up the stairs, and there was an impatient tap on the door as I zipped up the satchel and put it back on the table. Krasko called out, 'Will you open the door, please?' I went across and did so.

Krasko looked even more anxious than before.

'Sit down, my friend,' he said. He came round, sat on the edge of the bed, and stared out of the window. 'Nina was in great danger if she had stayed here,' he said. 'It was not Winston she had to fear so much just now as the British and their agents here in the international police. You understand what I am saying?'

I nodded.

'It was this Kolchak. Kolchak is not a man of great importance – he is just a journalist. I mean – well–' He shrugged and stared into space. 'It was what Nina did, the planted evidence and all these things, that made it dangerous for her to stay in reach of the British police.'

He talked as though it was he who had managed to get her away. He stood up.

'So I have sent her to – to Prague. I have friends there. She will be safe, quite safe.

You are interested in her, I know, but you will not want to follow her there.'

He stopped again as though that was the end of the matter.

'I might want to follow her there,' I said.

He looked at me sadly and shook his head.

'You would be very foolish to do that,' he said, looking away from me. 'It is very easy for our people to misunderstand your interest in someone like Nina. It could be very unpleasant for you, even' – he hesitated – 'even perhaps dangerous.' He looked back at me. 'You understand?'

I had decided already that there was little point in trying to pursue the matter to any kind of understanding. I just said that I supposed I did. I'd cooled down quite quickly. It was no good arguing with Krasko, but I was still worried about the forged passport. I told him so. Again he shook his head.

'I have taken care of that,' he said. 'Do not worry, my friend. There is nothing to worry *about*.'

He walked over to the bedside table, looked down at the note pad and then back at me, for the first time a little sharply. Then he tore a sheet off the pad and, as he folded it and put it in his pocket, said, 'What are you going to do now, my friend?'

I smiled feebly and shrugged. 'Oh, I guess I'll hang around Paris for a day or two and then – well, I suppose I'll go home. I'd like to see Louise again.'

He raised his eyebrows, hesitated, then said, 'She is a good girl – she *is* a good girl. I can understand your interest.' He gave a real smile. He was silent, looking at me. At last he said, 'What really, what exactly, happened at Brands Hatch?'

I told him.

When I came to André and Yvette, his lip curled a little. 'So – so!' As I finished he said, 'You are lucky, my friend. Yes, yes, of course it was Louise who saved your life, but now if I were you I would forget about Louise. If you can, keep out of England for a time – a week or two, anyway – until things cool down. Louise will be coming to Paris as soon as she is out of hospital. No matter. Forget about her – forget about everything.'

I walked over to the door. He smiled his patient smile and said, 'Thank you for helping me. If I can ever help you, I will not forget.'

I went down the stairs and picked up my key. After I had had a wash in my room I went out for a drink. I thought about Krasko and wondered whether, after all, I should have tried to pursue the matter further. Was it just possible that he would tell me more about himself – about why he had fled in such a hurry? After all, hadn't I, in a way, conspired with him on that occasion? I suppose I was a bit naïve to expect him to talk to me, but I went back to the hotel and tapped on his door. There was no answer. When I tried again that evening, and again there was no answer, I asked about him at the desk. They said that he had left the hotel.

For two days I stayed around Paris. Much of that time I lay on my bed, reading, thinking, or asleep or almost asleep, because I thought that they might be looking for me. When I went for walks I was even more jumpy late at night than during the day, because I was less anonymous when fewer people were about. That was a pity, since walking around cities at night is one of the perennial blooms in my pleasure garden.

On the morning of the third day there was no one at the desk when I got back from my morning drink and breakfast roll. I had only just returned to my room when the phone rang. It was the man at reception, whose English had turned out, to my relief, to be much better than I had expected from my phone call from London. He asked me to go down to see him. When I did he said that the police had been in to look at names of guests and had asked about me. I told him to get my bill ready. He'd already done so. I paid it and left without even going back to collect my shaving gear.

I thought of Nina but knew that I could not now leave a forwarding address for her.

If I didn't find her in Berlin – and I was not very hopeful – well, I didn't know. Perhaps I could then send back to Paris the forwarding address that she had asked me to leave.

I was very afraid now that, if the police really did want to see me about the Brands Hatch shooting, I might not get out of the country if they caught up with me. I went to Cook's at République and booked a flight to Berlin.

I felt tremendously relieved when at last I was through the passport check at Berlin's Templehof and was sitting back in a bus that sped off along Damm Mehring towards the heart of the city. With luck now I would be well clear of any police who might be looking for me until I had found Nina.

It was wonderful to go down the Kurfurstendamm again, to catch my first sight of the ruined church, and to come at last to the Zoo station. I remembered my search for a telephone there when I had just arrived on my first visit to Berlin. This time I went almost straight to the station post office and the phone boxes, with a rather silly pride in my knowledge of the local scene. I phoned my old landlady. She didn't remember me, at least not quite, but yes, she did have a room and I could have breakfast there. When would I come out? It was like old times.

I decided that I wouldn't go there until later

in the evening. I walked along to Aschinger's. There, too, it was like old times: there was still a queue for soup and bread rolls. I took my turn and got a bottle of lager, too, and stood at a table, happy and unnoticed among the locals, while I had my soup. Then I went out into the early evening sunlight and looked for a shop where I could buy a map.

With that in my pocket, I took the U-bahn from the Zoo station to Dahlem-Dorf. I remembered the little café outside the station and, although I was in something of a hurry, had a drink there for old time's sake.

I found the address of Kurt Schmidt easily enough, a quarter of a mile from the station and not far from the museum. I'd been wondering how to go about it and had not come up with one original thought. As I pressed the bell push I had an empty feeling at the bottom of my stomach that I was wasting my time. Tony and Nina finito, I thought, and that made me wonder what Jane was thinking about me just then, if she was thinking about me at all.

'*Ja?*' A woman's voice came out of the little speaker beside the bell push. My German wasn't very good, so I asked in English for Kurt Schmidt. He was not in, the voice said, in lightly-accented English. He would not be back until the morning.

Neither of us spoke, then both of us started to speak at once and both stopped.

The woman laughed.

'Proceed,' she said, and laughed again.

It was all the encouragement that I needed. 'I've just come from Paris,' I said. 'I'm a friend of Peter Krasko.'

I doubted whether I could have been clumsier if I had tried.

She told me to wait. A door opened and closed somewhere down the corridor that I could see dimly through the glass door. A light came on, and I could see her approaching. She opened the door, looked at me for a moment with a half-smile, and asked me in.

She didn't say anything as she walked along the corridor just ahead of me, but she looked friendly. Probably about forty, she was quite good-looking in a well-groomed, secretarial way, a bit heavy, but a woman who had taken care of herself.

She showed me into a big room, old-fashioned but comfortable. She went over to close a door that had been open into a bedroom, offered me a cigarette and lit one herself. What was my name? I told her. Hers was Leni. She didn't remember Kurt speaking of me. Was he expecting me? No? Well, no matter. If there was anything to talk about I could talk to her quite safely. Perhaps there wasn't anything, or I would rather not.

She smiled, eased up her skirt, and crossed her legs. It was a tempting morsel that I could feel myself nibbling. Was that a hook that I could feel with my tongue?

I took a while to consider it. No, perhaps I had better wait for Kurt, I said. She understood, of course, but I would surely have a drink before I went. She stood up and had just asked me what I would have, and I had begun to worry about whether I should risk mentioning Nina, when the phone rang.

It was Kurt Schmidt, obviously, and there seemed to be a problem. I could just make out that it was something about passports. She was upset. Unlocking a drawer, she took out a big envelope and, from the envelope, two passports. She stared at them. In disbelief? I thought so.

She picked up the phone and spoke again looking at her watch as she did so. Police headquarters?' No? The checkpoint? There was a pause. Then, looking at me, she started to speak again.

She mentioned my name and repeated it, not just once but three times. When she had put down the phone and stood up she said to me, 'I am sorry. I have to go out now.'

She went into the bedroom, taking the passports with her, and came out wearing a light overcoat.

'I am sorry,' she said again. 'I have to go to the checkpoint. Are you going in that direction?'

'Hallesches Tor U-bahnhof wouldn't be out of your way,' I said, regretting it almost before the name was out, because it was the station nearest to the checkpoint. I wondered whether I'd shown my hand. I tried to look unconcerned.

Her look was just a little questioning as she said, 'Of course. That's all right.'

She had got to the door when the phone rang again. This time she listened, then looked towards me, pursed her lips and shrugged, and held out the receiver.

It was Nina, near to hysteria. She managed to ask where I was staying, and then, confused and sure that she would forget my address, she asked if I could meet her at noon next day outside the Alexanderplatz station. I promised.

She said, 'Darling'. That was all.

Leni gave me an almost tender smile and led me out to her car. I wanted to ask about Nina but decided not to. Leni drove off with solemn concentration. I was thinking hard. Should I, as I had intended, follow Leni to the checkpoint? I was sure she was going there and that Schmidt was waiting with Nina for some passport problem to be sorted out. There was just the slightest chance that I might see Nina, though from what I remembered about the checkpoint it was very unlikely.

And even if I did? I couldn't answer that. I was just afraid that by the time tomorrow came they would have sorted me out with

Krasko, and Nina wouldn't be allowed to meet me. Finito. On the other hand, if I tried to push my way in now and did no good...

For the second time, Leni and I started to speak at the same time. Again she laughed, rested her hand briefly on my arm, and turned with a smile.

'Please go on,' I said.

'You had better come to see Kurt tomorrow afternoon,' she said. 'If you still *want* to see him.'

I had been watching for a U-bahn station, and as she spoke I spotted one a few hundred yards away.

'If you could drop me at that station,' I said, 'it'll be fine. I've changed my mind. I'll go back to my hotel.'

She pulled in to the kerb. We said *auf Wiedersehen*. In half-an-hour I was back in Dahlem, getting a warm welcome from my old landlady.

XXII

I set out early for the checkpoint next morning. I didn't expect any delays there, but it was safer to reckon that I might be delayed. Some people were nervous going east with 'journalist' on their passports, though *I'd* had no trouble last time. Perhaps I'd been lucky. There would be the usual tedious currency declaration, but so long as I was truthful, and I had no reason not to be, there should be no trouble later at the spot check on what I had in my wallet or in my pocket. It couldn't be any worse, anyway, than all that paperwork I had once gone through to get a visa to spend a couple of nights between planes in the United States.

That was how it turned out. There was, as there had been last time, that faint feeling of insecurity when I emerged from the *cordon sanitaire* and had left the West behind – but wasn't that supposed to be part of the spice of life?

Good and early – all of three-quarters-of-an-hour early – I was doing my pacing, the to and fro thing, in front of the Alexanderplatz station, feeling, and no doubt looking, as uncertain as a man already afraid that he has been stood up. My head was turning like a radar scanner.

Then I saw her across the platz, coming from the direction of Hans Beimler Strasse. I wanted to run to meet her, but I didn't. When she was still about thirty yards away she saw me and gave her most vulnerable smile. She danced the last three steps to me and gave me a very long hug.

She stood back, smiling and looking at me. Then the smile went away.

'Tony, I've been followed,' she said. 'We can talk if we're careful. But' – she gave a helpless wave – 'let's not go indoors. They're picking me up in half-an-hour. You know where we are, don't you? Let's just walk through to the river and round by the Dome. Do you know where I mean?'

I nodded.

As we passed under the line in the direction of Marx-Engels Platz she told me what had happened. She hadn't known until she got to the airport in Paris that she was going to Berlin and it was only the evening before, just before she left Dahlem, that Peter Krasko had phoned from Paris and told her that she must go back to the East.

'I trust Peter,' she said. 'I'm not sure why. He made so much of the papers that I gave to Peter Kolchak that he convinced me I was in very great danger, from both the British police and Mr Winston, if I stayed in the West. I was terribly frightened, though, when Kurt Schmidt and Leni told me to get ready right away. Then when we had the passport trouble at the checkpoint' – she put her face in her hands – 'that was terrible.'

She stood still for a few moments until she was calmer.

'That was when I spoke to you, of course. I heard your name just before Kurt Schmidt hung up. Before I could say anything, he asked if I knew anything about you. I told

270

him that you had helped Peter. What Peter says and does is terribly important to him. I wish I knew what it was all about. How often I've said that! He hardly hesitated at all when I asked him to let me speak to you. Then this morning he tried to phone Peter, but Peter wasn't there. Perhaps that was lucky. Perhaps if he'd been there he would have stopped me coming to see you.'

Then, in a sudden rush of words, she asked, 'How did you know where to find me?'

I told her about my meeting with Krasko in Paris, how he had left me alone in his room, how he had told me, too, that she must go, for safety, back to the East. I didn't tell her that what I feared more, the more I thought about it, was that she might have been brought back to help with whatever it was that Krasko and Schmidt were doing. I could believe that Krasko was fond of Nina – he was that kind of man – but I couldn't believe that he would do all that he was doing now out of a simple, kindly concern for her safety.

Nina might have been reading my thoughts, for she said, 'Strange, in a way, that I do trust Peter. I suppose it's a personal thing. I'm sure, almost sure, that he's working for the Party here in some kind of international way. But he's so kind and gentle, and that seems to make up for everything else. Silly of me, I suppose. And I *am* afraid.'

She looked down at her wrists and rubbed them.

'Will I ever again not be afraid? I so often feel that it would be better to die than to go on living as I do, waking every morning almost instantly aware that I have begun another day in the shadow of the prison cell.'

'Nina,' I said, urgently. 'Couldn't I tell what I know about Peter Kolchak, now that you can't be reached?'

'Not yet,' she said, so quickly and firmly that I was surprised. 'Not now. We must wait a day or two until I see what happens here.'

We had reached the bridge over the Spree and stopped to look downstream towards the Dome. As we started to walk on, a motor-scooter approached from the direction of Marx-Engels Platz. Nina stopped and stared at the young rider, who stared back with the look of a frightened animal. As he passed he looked back at us. Nina turned her head to follow him. A hundred yards past us he pulled in to the kerb and seemed to be examining the engine of his scooter. Nina clutched my arm.

'Oh, God,' she said. 'That's Rudi.'

Just for a moment I didn't remember who Rudi was.

We walked on and around the platz without talking. It was a painful silence. Rudi was yet another cloud that helped to blot out whatever sunlight there was that day or, for Nina, any day. He had no jailer with a bunch of keys behind him, but it seemed hardly possible, now that he knew that Nina was back in the East, that he would do nothing. He must feel that she was a threat to him.

Louise and the Brands Hatch shooting and all that had happened since we had last met didn't seem to interest Nina all that much when I talked about them. The half-hour went very quickly. When, how, should we meet again? I asked Nina, as we came back towards the station.

She didn't know her own address and had no very clear idea of where she was living. Well, I could give her my address in Dahlem. I did that and gave her my phone number. We had almost reached the underpass that led back to Alexanderplatz, and I could see in the sunlight beyond its shadow Rudi sitting on his scooter, watching us.

Nina was saying, 'Can you come back here tomorrow?'

I said that of course I could.

'Then listen. I'll try to phone you early, not later than ten. If I can't I'll try to meet you here again at twelve. And if I can't do that' – she shrugged – 'I'll write to you.'

She took my arm and said, 'Oh, darling, I wish we could be together. And I see no end to this...'

We walked on under the railway line.

'There's Kurt,' Nina said, looking towards the spot where I'd met her. A VW stood at the kerb, and a man in his mid-thirties got out as he saw us. Nina gave me a quick hug and walked to the car. Schmidt looked towards me and, unsmiling, gave a small, formal bow.

Nina had stooped to enter the car when she looked back along the street to where Rudi sat on his scooter.

She hesitated, then got into the car, which drove away. I didn't look back as I turned under the railway line again and headed towards the checkpoint.

Nina still hadn't got in touch by ten-thirty next morning, but the phone rang just as I was letting myself out of the room. Yes, she would try to meet me at noon, as we had arranged. She wasn't quite sure, though – Peter Krasko would be arriving some time during the day. She didn't know why.

Then she told me that Rudi had followed her into a bar when she had gone out for a drink. He had recognized Kurt the day before and knew him as a Party man with espionage links. When Nina had told Rudi that she knew nothing of all this, or even why she had been brought back to Berlin, he had tried to persuade her to join him again. When persuasion failed, he had tried threats.

Her forged passport was a small thing, he said, compared with what he knew, and had papers to prove, about her activities in London. If she wanted to stay alive and free, she would say nothing to anyone that would incriminate him. Distressed and confused, she had been on the point of blurting out that at least one of her new associates did know about all this – but realized in time that she daren't tell him.

Back at the apartment, where she had arrived trying to hide her distress, Kurt Schmidt had been waiting to tell her that Krasko was coming. Then he had said that they were having some problems with the authorities about her status. That was one of the things that Krasko was coming to try to sort out. What they all wanted now was her help in uncovering Winston's spy ring. What better beginning could they have than contact with the people who had given her the forged passport?

I told Nina not to worry. With a complete lack of conviction, I said that I was sure everything would be all right.

I was early again at Alexanderplatz. When Nina had not turned up by twelve-twenty, I began to think that she was not coming. Five minutes later I saw the little black Beetle come out of Hans Beimler Strasse and cross the platz. Kurt Schmidt was at the wheel with Nina beside him. When the car stopped Peter Krasko unfolded himself from the back seat and came towards me. Nina and Schmidt stayed in the car.

Krasko smiled his patient smile.

'So, my friend,' he said, 'you decided to stay with it.' He smiled again, perhaps pleased with his colloquialism. '*This* was what made it possible, of course,' he said, and he took from his pocket and unfolded the sheet of paper that he had torn from the scribbling pad in his Paris hotel room. 'Yes? Well, I can't say that I was very surprised. Only a little angry with myself that I should have been so careless – or so trusting. So!'

He held out his hands, palms upwards, pursed his lips, gazed at me sadly, sighed, and looked away, up the pavement towards where Rudi had appeared on his scooter and was watching us.

'Now that you are here,' Krasko said diffidently, 'I hope that you will help us. Well, you know it is a matter of helping Nina, really. There has been a bit of bother after all about that passport. There is nothing to be alarmed about. But now that Nina is back with us – I am sorry, but you know she does belong here – now that she is back with us it will help very much if, when she tells us everything that she knows about Winston's activities, Peter Kolchak, and all that... No, no,' he waved me to silence. 'You are going to say, perhaps, that she doesn't *know* much at all. But if our people here know all the circumstances and all the details that she can tell them, they can, shall we say, spell out very much more.

'If you, too, can tell us all that you know, it will help Nina very much. It will also make it safer for you when you go back home. You *are* going home? Well, that's *your* business. We want Nina to stay. In any case – well, let us not talk about that. Now, if you could come with us...'

He walked over and opened the car door.

I wasn't sure whether my heart missed a beat or gained one. I felt very frightened, and cowardice, I had known since my school-days, was something I was very good at.

'You're rushing things a bit,' I said.

'We are, my friend,' Krasko said, patiently but firmly.

'I must speak to Nina,' I said.

'Of course,' Krasko said. 'She knows what it is all about.'

He opened the car door where Nina sat. She looked up at me with troubled eyes.

'You've no choice, Tony,' she said. 'In any case, I think it's for the best. It's not a matter of where your sympathies are here. Mr Winston is evil...'

I nodded and followed Krasko into the back of the car. As we swung out into the traffic, I looked through the back window. A hundred yards behind us, Rudi was mobile.

We drove, so far as I could tell, almost due north into Pankow. Not too obtrusively, I hoped, I kept an eye on Rudi as he kept station like a fighter pilot flying a mission. In a rather anonymous street we stopped outside a big, new building. We all got out. As we did so, four uniformed men, armed at the waist, came out of the doorway and approached the car.

I looked for Rudi. He had passed us and pulled into the kerb just ahead. As we stood there for a moment, waiting for our escort, he looked back purposefully towards the entrance to the building, and then at Nina. His right hand was in his trouser pocket. Nina turned towards me with a look of anguish. Rudi started to smile, though his eyes were full of fear. He began to take his hand from his pocket. Nina suddenly shouted, 'No, Rudi, no!' and started to run across the street.

As I turned to watch her, I saw a gun in Rudi's hand. Nina was half-way across the street as Rudi lifted his gun hand. A big American car had come out of the turn in the street on the right, travelling very fast. Nina hadn't a chance. It threw her at least twenty feet. When she hit the pavement on the far side of the street I knew that she must be dead, killed in an instant.

I looked right and left and ran across to where she was lying. The car had skidded to a stop, half-blocking the street. A very young American got out and ran to where I was kneeling beside Nina.

Behind me I heard a clatter of footsteps and two shots. Rudi was lying on the pavement beside his scooter, and two of the uniformed men were bending over him.

Peter Krasko and Kurt Schmidt had started to cross the street, and they stood there, with the traffic stopping around them, looking back at Rudi as though at a minor street accident.

Nina had fallen on her left side, striking her head. There was a graze on her left cheek. Otherwise her face was unmarked. I felt for her pulse, but there was none.

The young American stood above me. He sounded as if he was weeping. I looked up. He had covered his face with his hands.

Krasko and Schmidt and one of the uniformed men had joined us. The uniformed man also felt for Nina's pulse. Then he stood up and spoke to the young American, who said that he didn't understand. Krasko looked down at Nina, said, 'So ... so...' gently and sadly, put his arm tentatively around my shoulder and quickly took it away.

'I am sorry, my friend,' he said. Kurt Schmidt said nothing.

Krasko spoke in German to the man in uniform, and in English to the American, telling him to park his car at the kerb until the police came. Then we all stood there, saying nothing, for about five minutes, till an ambulance and a policeman on a motorcycle arrived.

I was glad when they did come. I had always thought of myself as cool and unsqueamish, and I was trying to be like that. But I felt very weak in the legs and in the stomach, and I was trying hard not to weep. I rubbed my eyes and yawned a couple of times and looked away from Nina up the street and across to where they were waiting with Rudi, propped up in a sitting position against the legs of one of the uniformed men.

One of the ambulancemen felt for Nina's pulse, then closed her eyes. They ran across to Rudi, lay him on a stretcher, put him in the ambulance. Then they put Nina in the ambulance, on a stretcher, with a blanket over her face, closed the door, and drove away.

Krasko translated for the American and me while the policeman took our names and addresses and an account of what had happened. Then the policeman rode away, and the American drove away. The rest of us crossed the street and went into the building outside which it had all begun.

There were many more uniformed men inside, but our escort took us straight through to a big office, plain but with comfortable chairs. A big man who looked too Russian to be true sat behind a large desk. He was introduced to me by a name that I didn't catch. He stood up and extended his hand, but he didn't take mine when I held it out. Instead he used his hand to wave me to a chair.

Krasko spoke to Kurt Schmidt in German, and the man behind the desk listened and said something in German. Krasko then said to me, 'We've explained about Nina. It will be best for everyone if you tell us now all that you know.'

I opened my mouth, but he held up his hand. I was listening again to the man on the phone on my landing in Marylebone, sorting out a late-night misunderstanding with one of his women friends, as he went on gently, 'If you don't feel up to it, you know' – he turned up the palms of his hands and lifted his shoulders – 'I should understand. But my advice is: get it over with. Now, you were about to say?'

'I could do with a drink,' I said. Remembering it afterwards, I felt pleased at my understatement.

Krasko looked shocked.

'Of course, my friend,' he said. 'Of course.' He spoke in German to the man behind the desk, who reached under it and produced a bottle and a glass.

I had drunk Schnapps before, but not

Schnapps like this. It smelt like paint stripper and tasted as I had always known paint stripper must taste when it had been matured in the wood for eight years. I didn't like to think about my liver or my taste buds, but it was fine on my belly. When, presently, Krasko asked me to begin I felt able to.

What should I hold back? Everything about Walter, of course. It wasn't going to be easy to tell a smooth story. I hoped the shock that I had just had would help to explain any hesitations. Should I have felt like some kind of traitor talking like this to the secret police – I supposed it *was* the secret police – beyond the Berlin Wall? When I thought of Winston and what he had done to Nina, I didn't feel bad at all.

There were some questions here and there, and when I described how I had watched the Peter Kolchak affair from a pub across the street in Kensington and done nothing about it, I got from the man behind the desk a look that told me that my character rating was just about zero. I was there for two hours. Then, with no more ceremony than when we entered, we stood up and went out to the car.

Krasko stood beside the car and seemed to have a problem. He said at last, 'Are you on the telephone – in Berlin, I mean?'

I said that I was.

'I hope that you will not want to leave Berlin tonight,' he said, as he wrote down my number. He looked up. I shook my head. 'I would like to talk to you again tomorrow, perhaps even tonight, when we have had a look at the transcript.'

My heart sank a little, but at least he wasn't insisting that I stay in the East. As we got into the car he asked, 'Do you want to come to Nina's funeral?'

I didn't know.

Kurt Schmidt didn't speak all the way to the checkpoint. Apart from a formal greeting when we had met, he hadn't spoken to me at all. I told Krasko, although I knew that it was futile, that I wished, since I had been so co-operative, that he would now tell me what it was all about. He gave me a pitying look and shook his head.

'Unless, of course, you would like to work for us,' he said.

He kept on looking at me with his pitying, patient smile.

'I can tell you this,' he said at last. 'This Mr Winston is not just what he may seem to be. Fighting, as he says, against – against–'

'Communism,' I said.

'Fighting against Communism,' he said. 'That is – shall we say – what he is barmy about – paranoid, yes, barmy.' And holding a forefinger to his head he described several circles with it. 'No, no. His *serious* interest is industrial espionage. At least, in the end, that is more important to him than what he goes on about.'

Just before we got out of the car at the checkpoint I remembered the money – Jane's and mine – that we'd given to Nina so that she could leave the country. It seemed indelicate to mention it, but as I got out of the car I thought that I was being sentimental. So I told Krasko about it. He looked dubious, even a bit suspicious, but promised to do what he could.

XXIII

I went back through the checkpoint and decided to walk through the Tiergarten on my way to Aschinger's. It was only then that I began really to think about Nina.

All that had happened in the last hour or so seemed hardly real. I remembered how I'd felt when my mother had died, still relatively young, all those years ago. I supposed that it would be a while, and only when I was quite alone, before I would realise what had gone out of my life and how final it was.

The terrible finality of my mother's death, and my son's, and the deaths of two or three other people very dear to me, were wounds that had never healed. I found myself, every now and then, wishing desperately to talk with one of them. I supposed it would be the same with Nina.

I had a meal at Aschingner's, looking out at the crowd passing in the street with what became, after the third bottle of lager, a not unbearable melancholy. It was sad, though, to be here, where I had so much wanted to be to get away from it all, but to feel that I couldn't stay. I knew that I had to leave – to get back to London – as soon as I could, to help those who would be cleaning up the mess that I had helped to cause because I was so unwilling to act. But even Nina's death didn't make me *want* to leave Berlin.

At the department store round the corner where, I remembered, I had stocked up years ago for a long train journey to Amsterdam, I bought some cans of beer and some bread rolls and butter and cheese and tomatoes. Then I took the U-bahn to Dahlem.

I badly wanted to go to sleep, but before I could be seduced by the bed and the empty room I put through a call to Walter. I was sorry to find him there – this wasn't a conversation I was looking forward to – and more sorry when I found him, unbelievably, so angry. Yet, could I blame him? When he stopped sounding off at my irresponsibility, I told him all that had happened and said that unless anything delayed me I would be back in London next day.

'I'm sorry, Tony,' Walter said. 'I'm also glad – glad, I mean, that you're coming back. Kolchak is still locked up. Am I free now to use as I think best what you've told me about the girl's part – about Nina's part – and your part in this affair?'

I said that he was free, and that of course I also meant free to publish.

'You're already in the papers,' he said. 'This woman – Louise – has told all she knows. She's home – out of hospital – by the way, but under police guard. She's made it clear that the bullet was meant for you, though she protests that she didn't know about it beforehand. Strange, isn't it,' he said after a short silence, 'to find ourselves almost on the side of the Russians in all this, the Communists – so far, anyway – against Winston's crowd, who must get their comeuppance before we can wrap it up. Indeed, as you'll know well enough – *too* well – *you're* in greater danger than ever.'

'I know,' I said. 'I know.'

There was another silence.

'Don't feel bad about saying your piece today, to the Ruskies, or whoever they are,' Walter said at last. 'There's no disloyalty that I can see. None at all.'

I told him that I'd let him know when I was arriving back in London. We left it at that. Then I took off my shoes, lay down on the bed, and went to sleep. When I woke it was past midnight, and I undressed and got into bed. Now I couldn't sleep. I lay there looking back over the past week or two, wondering where I'd gone wrong, if I had gone wrong.

When Krasko hadn't phoned by eleven o'clock the next morning, I counted my money and decided that I'd fly back anyway – I was beginning to think again of what was safest – and rang through a reservation. I phoned Walter at home, and he promised that someone would meet me at Heathrow.

I knew that if Krasko wanted to reach me in London he would have the number of that phone out on the landing that he knew so well. I was thinking more of the money Jane and I had given to Nina than of any help that I might be able to give him. Then, at noon, I set out for the final ritual of a meal at Aschinger's. No James Bond, me, I thought, remembering the food he used to eat, as I stirred the thick, nourishing soup, and, remembering Nina, pouched in my cheeks a mouthful of lager.

It was a fine day, and sitting in the sun on the plane in a window seat I went to sleep. The seat beside me had been empty, but I woke to find someone patting me gently on the arm. An air hostess had sat down beside me.

'Mr Fredericks?' she said.

I nodded sleepily, yawned, smiled, and apologized.

'There's a message from the captain,' she said. 'You're to go to the VIP lounge when you arrive. I gather you'll know what it's about.'

I nodded and thanked her. She asked if I'd like anything. I ordered a lager. When I looked out of the window not all that much later the clouds had parted, and the Essex coast was ahead.

The man from whatever branch it was that was dealing with me recognised me as soon as I came through the door of the lounge. He introduced himself as plain Mr Scott. We sat in the back of the car as we drove into town. He told me that Peter Kolchak had appeared briefly in court that morning. Simply on the strength of what I had told Walter on the phone the night before, they had let him out for what, considering the kind of charge he faced, was nominal bail.

'We're keeping an eye on him, of course,' plain Mr Scott said. 'For his own good. Just as we're keeping an eye on this woman Louise, and will have to keep an eye on you.'

I felt, as we drove through the rush-hour traffic into town, that I had been away a long time. At his office I told Mr Scott all that I had told Walter. He asked me a lot of questions, a good half of which I couldn't answer. He told me that they had searched

Nina's flat but found nothing helpful. They had even questioned Jane, whose account of my last day in London and of Nina's departure was the same as mine.

I asked him if Kolchak's missing files on Winston had turned up. He looked at me very sharply, as if I was a suspect, and said that they hadn't.

When we had finished talking, he called on the intercom for someone to join him. While we waited, he opened a file and produced a sheet of paper with a press cutting pasted on it that he passed across to me to read. It was a report of Louise's statement about the Brands Hatch shooting.

A young man came into the room and was introduced as plain Mr Roberts. Plain was the right word: he looked as anonymous as Mr Scott did. Mr Roberts was apparently to be my personal bodyguard.

'He'll take you home now. We won't stop you going out if you want to. I don't think it's a very good idea, but if you do go out at least you won't be on your own.'

Then he said that he would want to see me again next morning. As I was going out the door he called out, 'There's someone in Krasko's old room, by the way.' He laughed. 'Another foreign – ah, gentleman. Don't let it make you nervous. We've checked on him. He's quite harmless.'

When plain Mr Roberts dropped me at

my door, he asked me if I would be going out. When I said that I wouldn't, he gave me a number where I could reach him if I changed my mind or wanted anything. He told me to call him, anyway, in the morning, and said that uniformed men would be keeping an eye on the place.

'But don't answer the door,' he said, 'and keep away from the windows. You're a very important witness.'

It was good to be in my room again. Even so, I felt depressed as I sat on the edge of the bed and untied my shoes. I lay back, stared at the patches of damp or mould or whatever it was on the ceiling, and wondered whether I should phone Jane's office on the off-chance that she had worked late. I smiled at the lecture that I was sure she'd give me and decided that I couldn't face it just yet.

As I began to feel drowsy, I did get up and phone Walter. When they told me that he was busy, I left a message to say that I was back, in case he wanted to speak to me.

I didn't go to bed, though. That would have been far too sensible and taken far too much effort. Instead I went through the old, so familiar routine of falling asleep with my street clothes on and waking, hours later, rather cold even on this midsummer night, and very miserable.

I went over to pull the curtains, remembered Mr Roberts' warning, turned off the light, and quickly covered the windows. I did take a small peep between the curtains, but the only thing that I saw moving in the still, early morning street was a policeman. I had a quick wash and then went to bed.

Once I got to sleep it was the real thing. I felt drugged by it when a heavy knocking on the door woke me after daylight. It was the lady from the room next door, calling me to the phone. The call was from Roberts. He said that Scott wanted to see me as soon as possible – it was already nine o'clock – and could I be ready in half-an-hour?

I had barely had time to shave and wash and dress when Roberts rang the downstairs bell. Twenty minutes later I was back in Scott's office. There had been developments in the night, he said. They had talked with Kolchak again.

'Winston seems to be a more dangerous man than we supposed,' he said.

He must have seen that my eyes opened rather wide.

'Oh, no, no. I'm not making light of your little encounter at Brands Hatch,' he said. 'But this is different: an arsenal, ideas about a private army, that kind of nonsense. Must have been reading *Billion Dollar Brain*. We knew where his headquarters were – did I tell you that? – but he's gone from there. We've a feeling that he may try to leave the country. Anyway, I want *you* to disappear for a bit. No, not abroad. Just go to live somewhere else. We'll set it up. And – well, I've someone here that I'd like you to meet. If you don't mind I'd like him to take over your room for a bit.'

He spoke into the intercom. A door behind him, just to the left of his desk, opened. I looked through the doorway and wondered whether my drinking had at last caught up with me. I seemed to be looking at a mirror image, but it wasn't the mirror image of me sitting there that I saw but me walking towards me. The image smiled, and my hallucination seemed to be fading. It wasn't *my* smile at all. Then the rest of me came through the doorway and sat down at the end of Scott's desk.

'Not bad,' Scott said, grinning at me. 'Not bad, surely?'

'For Christ's sake,' I said. 'A joke's a joke…'

He waved his hand in an introductory way.

'Mr Robson,' he said. 'Mr Fredericks.'

My mirror image got up. As I stood up, still, I was sure, looking rather angry, he came round the desk and shook my hand. I could hardly say that I shook his.

Scott seemed to assume that I would know, in a flash, what it was all about. He was going on to the next item. He was picking up a piece of paper from his desk and putting on his spectacles.

'Your new digs,' he said. 'St John's Wood. I hope you don't mind.'

'Oh, no,' I said. 'I don't seem to have much say, anyway.'

Scott took no notice.

'The general idea,' he said, 'is that Robson' – he waved at my double – 'looking like you but trying not to smile too much' – he gave a grimace that was probably meant to be a smile – 'should wander around Marylebone fairly freely from your old Mareylebone flat – ah, bedsitter – and hope to be – ah, picked up. By Winston's heavies, of course. We think, though we may be wrong, that he may still try to kill you if he has the chance. He's that kind of nut. Robson's used to taking risks.' He gave Robson the same grimace. 'You're not.'

He gave me a sort of smile. I had a feeling that no one was putting much on me in the bravery stakes. *I* wasn't putting anything on me.

'Now, could you give Robson a bit of a run-down on life in the, ah, seedier parts of Marylebone, West One,' Scott said.

Something, I decided, had happened overnight to make me even more contemptible than I'd been yesterday and the day before. Something, perhaps, that Kolchak had said, though I couldn't guess what it might have been. Possibly Walter had been putting in a

293

kind word or two.

'Do you think,' Scott said, 'that you could lie completely low for, say, a week? For a start. Just not go out at all. It's a nice flat,' he hurried on, before I had time to answer. 'Better than your, ah, bedsitter.' Again there was that sort of smile. 'Colour TV and all that. We'll see you're taken good care of. Even lay on some company, if you want it. You're quite fond of women, I gather.' His mouth twitched. 'Well, I can understand that. All this is for your own good. You can see that, I'm sure. For your own safety.'

'I haven't much choice, I guess,' I said. I was beginning to dislike plain Mr Scott.

'You haven't really,' Scott said. 'Not unless you want to do Robson's, ah, risky job.'

He looked at Robson. Robson smiled back at him and at me. I was glad *I* didn't smile like that.

'Okay, then,' Scott said, with the satisfied tone of a man who had wrapped everything up. 'I think we won't move you till tonight, till it's dark. If you want to take a last walk' – he seemed to enjoy the phrase – 'this afternoon, there's no reason why you shouldn't. Do you think so, Robbie?'

He turned to Roberts, who'd been sitting silent through all this. Roberts nodded.

'Robbie will stay with you,' Scott said. 'It's not just another pot-shot we're afraid of. There's also, ah, abduction. Then tonight

294

you can get your things together and Robbie will take you to St John's Wood.'

He took a look at some notes in front of him.

'Okay, then,' he said. 'You and Robson had better get together. Robbie might as well be in on it, too. There's nothing more I need you for – not now, anyway.'

With Robson going before and Roberts after, I went into Robson's room. I hoped that the fore and aft escort thing wasn't significant. I was feeling rather needled. 'Robson and Roberts,' I thought. It sounded like a comedy double act, but I knew it was early to be feeling smart. There was going to be a lot more of this, I was sure, before it was all over.

Robson started to ask me about my habits: the kind of places where I ate and drank, whether I walked or took a bus or a cab, where I was most likely to be looked for and when. He showed that he didn't like my eating habits – the rolls and cheese and all – though what the hell it had to do with him was a question I asked myself.

Every now and then something, though generally it seemed more like nothing, seemed to amuse Robson, and he would give this infuriating smile. I thought what a laugh it would be if he ran into Jane and she stared at him and, with that smile of his, he gave her the come-on.

When we came out into the street Roberts said, 'Look, I know how you're feeling. Let me take you somewhere that you'd like to go. I'll stick around, but I won't get in the way.'

I shrugged, and we got into the car. He sat back and closed his eyes.

'Take your time,' he said.

I, too, closed my eyes and almost went to sleep. Was it five or ten minutes I sat there? I don't know. Then the voice of Roberts came out of what should have been darkness but was technicolour playing on my eyeballs. 'Snap out of it, fella. It's not the end of the world.' In front of me the car's engine suddenly started.

'Where to?' Roberts said.

'Hammersmith Bridge,' I said, and with not another word between us we went there.

Roberts followed me as I walked up the river to The Dove, and he sat with a drink in the cosy inner bar while I went out on to the terrace with mine and looked enviously at the Dutchman moored at Hammersmith pier. If only, I thought, I were on that Dutchman, if only it were mine, with Nina or Jane or Louise or even my poor bloody wife – there was a quick flashback to our flat at Warrington Crescent – going downstream to the Channel, or upstream from the Channel to Paris, or wherever.

It clouded over. I went inside and bought

Roberts a drink, and he bought me one, before we went out and drove across London to Marylebone. On the way we stopped while I bought some sandwiches and a bottle of Scotch that Roberts suggested and insisted on paying for. It was something new, and I wasn't sure that it was a good idea. But what the hell? I thought. I had to be practical, and I really didn't know how I was going to keep the tide in during the long, dry summer of incarceration that lay ahead.

At my door Roberts said, 'I'll call for you about ten. Okay, fella?' He gave a thumbs-up sign and drove away.

XXIV

I still had the late afternoon and the whole evening in front of me, and I opened the Scotch and made a modest start. I hoped they were going to find Winston very quickly. Too much of this and I could find myself, at the very least, doing something incredibly silly.

After an hour I phoned Walter. Like Scott, he didn't sound very friendly and said that he had no news for me. Would he like to see me? Not really, he said. Supposing that I wasn't meant to talk about my part in police plans, I just said that I'd probably be out of circulation for a bit. He already knew that.

I was beginning to feel a bit friendless. It occurred to me that Jane would be leaving the office soon, so I went out to the landing and phoned her.

She was icy at first, but after I had rambled on, rather incoherently I supposed, for a while, she said yes, okay, she did understand, a little bit, why I had done what I had done. I said something about being charitable. She gave a bitter laugh and said that charity wasn't something she cultivated with men who made a fool of her as often as I had. Would she like to see me that evening? I reminded her of the money that I owed her. As it happened, she said, she couldn't see me, so – she laughed again – she was spared the problem, if it was a problem, of making up her mind whether she wanted to see me.

At the end of a silence I said, 'I'm having to lie low for a bit. Can I come to see you later?'

'Of course you *can*,' she said. 'Whether you *may* is another matter.' She laughed, then sighed. 'Phone me if you want to, Tony,' she said. 'We'll see. But I don't see the point, really.'

I went back to my Scotch, ate my sandwiches dutifully but with little enjoyment, and, true to form, went to sleep. But I was awake, feeling really dreadful, and getting my things together yet again, when the doorbell rang.

I opened the door to a young woman who said that she'd been told to collect me. She stood just inside the door as she produced an identity card, then came upstairs to help me down with my baggage. There was a man on each corner of the street. She noticed that I noticed and said as we drove away, 'Not to worry. They're our men. Just keeping an eye on things till we elope.'

She turned to me and laughed. I wondered if this was the kind of company to relieve my loneliness that plain Mr Scott had in mind.

I was a bit startled when we turned into Acacia Road and stopped only a few doors from where Nina had lived. But why not? It was a strange coincidence, but Nina was gone and dead.

It was a nice room, rather like Nina's, with its own kitchen and bathroom. There was a lot of food in the kitchen: bread and butter and eggs and cheese and ham and tinned stuff, a lot of tinned beer, and a bottle of Scotch. There was the colour television set that Scott had mentioned, the evening paper, a few paperbacks – thrillers, mostly – and some girlie magazines.

The young policewoman stood just inside the door while I looked round. I picked up the girlie magazines, glared at her, and said,

'You can take these back to your boss.'

She took them but looked hurt.

'Oh, sorry,' I said. 'I'm sure you're not to blame. I just don't like the, ah, assumption.'

Good God, I thought, I hoped this 'ah' business wasn't something that you caught from Mr Scott.

The young policewoman gave me a phone number that she said would reach someone at any time. Would I, she asked, please phone at least once each day, anyway, to say if I wanted anything? Then she went out.

I'm easily bored, but I've never been more bored than I quickly became and stayed, steadily, all the time I was in that flat. Television quickly bores me, anyway, and after the first day I didn't switch the set on. And who wants to read thrillers when he's a character in one that's still being written? Starting to drink early each day, I almost got bored with alcohol.

The same policewoman came with a sort of meals-on-wheels service every day. If I didn't order, she brought something that someone apparently thought I should have. Most of it went, eventually, into the tidy-all, which I greatly regretted but in the circumstances couldn't avoid.

She was the only desirable thing around, and she would sit and talk for half-an-hour, showing once or twice a provocative bit of leg. I could never decide whether she was

trying to tempt me. I could see no professional reason why she should. Playing safe, I
didn't react. I hoped that she didn't think I
wasn't interested.

Around five o'clock on the third day,
bored and despairing, I phoned Jane. Yes,
she'd be home, she said. Yes, I could call if I
felt I really must. She gave the longest and
loudest sigh that I'd ever heard.

So at seven o'clock I closed the door and
stepped out into the street. Why hadn't I
ordered a taxi? I wondered, as soon as I was
outside. Well, who orders a taxi in London?
I looked back but couldn't bring myself to
face the long walk up those stairs again to
the telephone.

Well aware that I might be setting out on a
suicide journey, but hardly caring, I walked
down to the tube station and looked right
up Finchley Road and left down Wellington
Road. There wasn't a cab in sight, and there
still wasn't when I reached Abbey Road.
Now I was starting to feel anxious.

I had just crossed Abbey Road when a car
pulled into the pavement beside me. It was
all too familiar. The back door opened, and
before I had time to yell I was pulled inside.
We got going like a plane at the start of its
take-off run. There beside me sat the gorilla,
smiling for the first time, if what he was
doing *was* smiling, because I had never seen
a smile like it before and hoped that I never

would again.

I looked at my watch with some foolish idea that if I knew how long the journey took and estimated the car's speed I would know at the journey's end how far from London we had travelled. It was one of those inconsequential things you think about to avoid the unpleasant facts. And the unpleasant fact, I knew when I got around to it, was that I probably had only about half-an-hour to live. I felt very scared, but I managed to ask, in a voice that unexpectedly seemed relatively steady, 'Why don't you get it over?'

The gorilla smiled again, a quite fantastic Dracula-cum-Frankenstein performance.

'I wish I could,' he said, with a voice that matched his smile. 'But we have to save you for the boss. The boss likes to do some jobs himself.' He laughed.

It wasn't much of a conversation piece for a journey that went on for about an hour. I sat back and tried to relax. For a while we seemed to be among traffic. Then there was just the occasional car, and after a while what sounded like the beat of a helicopter that stayed with us.

Suddenly the car, still travelling very fast, swung sharply to the left. I was thrown against the gorilla. He must have thought that I was trying something, because by the time I had recovered he was holding a gun at my stomach. We were going over a very bumpy surface, and I was glad when he took the gun away and just held it across his knees.

We slowed, and the car stopped with a jerk. The gorilla opened the door on his side, got out, and, still holding the gun, told me to follow him. It was a bit like one of those iris-outs that they used to have in the movies, but in reverse. I had never felt more curious, or apprehensive, about what the complete frame would show.

First, there was the car doorway, the gorilla almost filling it, then a helicopter on the ground, its rotor turning, as the gorilla stepped aside to let me out, after that a cottage in the middle of a small woodland clearing.

I could hear the beat of a second helicopter above, getting louder every moment. The gorilla held his gun in my back, looked up, as I did, and then across at the cottage. The front door opened. A man stood there for a few seconds, looking up before he went inside again and closed the door. Just then the car jerked away from us a few yards and stopped in the middle of the small open area where the helicopter was about to land.

As the helicopter seemed about to lift again, the gorilla grabbed my shoulder with his gun hand and gave me a push in the direction of the house. I managed to stumble and fall. As I did so, I kicked out viciously at the gorilla's legs. It was a lucky kick that brought him down. I jumped to my feet and started to run towards the nearest trees, close to where a rough driveway emerged from among them. I could hear a car approaching from ahead of me as two pistol shots sounded from behind. Then from the driveway a police car raced into view and swung round behind me. It almost hit me as I threw myself on the ground. Then it stopped beside me. I looked up as Roberts and the driver got out of the car and, with guns drawn, crouched beside it. The helicopter still hovered.

'Are you all right?' Roberts asked, without turning round.

I said that I was.

'You don't bloody well deserve to be,' he said. 'Now stay where you are. Don't move a bloody inch.'

I peered under the car. The door of the house was opening again. The man who had come out earlier was standing there with a sub-machine gun in his hand. Roberts had dropped beside me. He fired one shot under the car. The man stumbled forward and fell. Behind him, now exposed in the doorway, was Mr Winston, a suitcase in one hand, a sub-machine gun in the other. He started to fire, indiscriminately, as he ran towards the helicopter on the ground. Roberts and his driver were firing, Roberts under the car, the driver across its bonnet. I don't know who got Winston, but he had covered only a few yards, still firing, when he crumpled and fell. His suitcase pitched forward, and as it hit the ground it came open and papers were scattered around.

I couldn't see either the gorilla or his driver, but I told Roberts about them. Not far above us, the helicopter that had shadowed Winston's car still hovered, as the car occupied the only place where it could touch down. Roberts looked up and gave it a reassuring wave. Then he reached into his car for a loud hailer and, looking towards the cottage, began a 'give yourselves up' appeal. There was no response. After about half-a-minute Roberts looked up again. One of the crew was pointing towards the helicopter on the ground. Its rotor had stopped turning, and its pilot was walking away from it with his hands in the air.

Still holding his gun, Roberts walked towards him. The police car driver put his gun in its holster and went over to Winston's car. I stayed where I was, but I could see that he was looking down at something in front of the car. By this time Roberts had put handcuffs on Winston's helicopter pilot and was leading him to where his driver was standing. He left him there and went into the house. In two or three minutes he came out and shouted in my direction.

'Okay. It's safe to show yourself.'

I walked over to Winston's car. The gorilla and his driver were slumped in front of it, both obviously dead from Winston's wild fusillade.

Roberts had gone to where Winston himself and his man lay. Then he made a call from his car radio. Winston, he told his driver as he came back to us, was still alive but obviously in a very bad way. His gun-man was dead.

We all helped to push Winston's car out of the way so that the police helicopter could touch down. There were five armed police-men in it, but they had nothing to do.

We waited around until two ambulances arrived to take Winston and the bodies away. Then, with the handcuffed helicopter pilot sitting in the back with Roberts, and me sitting up front with the driver, we set off for town. It was almost dark now. I didn't ask questions, but I could tell from the signs that we were driving south-east from some-where in the Chilterns. I knew my stocks were low, so I kept quiet and waited for Roberts to make the running, if there was going to be any running to make.

Half way to town, after a long silence from everyone, he said, 'You didn't surprise us. We had your phone tapped, of course. We were tailing you when you were, ah, ab-ducted, though we didn't quite expect that.

Your girlfriend Jane couldn't have tipped them off?'

'Oh, no,' I said.

'We'll see,' said Roberts. 'We'll see.'

The idea seemed so idiotic that out of a feeling of sheer superiority I began to feel better. But I just said, 'Oh, Jesus!'

We'd gone quite a long way when the driver picked up his phone, and when he put it down told Roberts over his shoulder that Winston was dead. Otherwise the journey back to town was almost as silent as the one out had been, and we were well down the Edgware Road before Roberts asked me, 'Where to?'

'St Mary's Terrace,' I said.

XXV

I might just as well have gone straight home. Jane answered her bell promptly enough. She listened to everything that I had to tell her about all that had happened in Paris and Berlin and wherever as if it was a story that she had heard before. After a few minutes of shock, she even lost interest in the shoot-up in the Chilterns. I gave her a cheque for the money that I had borrowed, hoping that I wasn't in the red – not that it really mattered. I said I'd phone again.

'Do,' she said, with what I felt was unnecessary acidity, as she let me out.

I walked back to Acacia Road.

It was the next afternoon when the young policewoman came out and picked me up. *She* was as friendly as ever, which was a welcome change. When I asked as she drove south if I might perhaps buy her a drink some time to show my gratitude, she smiled and said 'Maybe.' We left it at that. I had a pretty good idea that I'd do nothing about it.

Scott was just as unpleasant as he had been when I had last seen him. I was glad when I'd signed the last statement and was on my way back to St John's Wood, though sorry that this time I had a quite anonymous police driver. As I got out of the car, he said, 'I'm told you'll be ready with your baggage at eight tonight. Is that all right?'

'I do as I'm told,' I said, and slammed the car door harder than I really needed to.

In the event, I kept him waiting – first for me to arrive from the pub, and then for me to pack. By ten o'clock I was back in my seedy old bedsitter.

I woke next morning much too early – it couldn't have been a minute past ten – to a quiet tapping on the door. I lay there and listened. Who could possibly be so discreet? Then, with a dressing gown round my shoulders, I tottered across and opened the door.

It was Peter Krasko and Louise, and I wasn't at all surprised by his first words.

'I am so sorry, my friend.'

I asked them in, and they sat down. Krasko opened the same battered old briefcase and produced a bottle of vodka. What he'd really come for, he said, after I'd produced something to drink out of and he had poured for us, was to ask me to come to lunch with him and Louise. Yes, that very day. They were leaving for Paris in the afternoon. No, no, he smiled, nothing as definite as marriage, but, yes, yes, it was true they were very fond of each other. She wouldn't be going on to Berlin? Perhaps to help him with his work? Hm? He almost laughed at that before he gave the palms up, lifted shoulders routine.

Yes, I said, of course I'd be pleased to go to lunch with them.

He finished his vodka, looked at my glass, raised his eyebrows, and leaned forward to pour me another.

Was it just Louise, then, that had brought him back to London?

Not quite. Not really. Not exactly. You see, young Rudi – of course I remembered young Rudi – had been, well, persuaded to talk a bit about the things Winston was doing. Yes, indeed, there was a lot of industrial espionage. Who could blame him for that? But Winston had this anti-Communist bee in his bonnet, and what with one thing and another – his private arsenal, his private army, the kind of megalomaniac thing he had done with Kolchak – he was doing a lot of harm and likely to do a very great deal more. So he – Peter Krasko – had come back to help to sort things out. Unfortunately he had arrived too late.

How did he know that, when it had all happened so recently? Of course I hadn't seen the papers yet, but I'd gathered that it was being kept out of them. Was Mr Krasko perhaps working for British as well as East German intelligence?

Krasko smiled and looked out of the window into the morning sunlight.

Well, anyway, he said, he was sorry that I had been bothered. He had taken his wallet from his pocket and was starting to count out some notes.

It was strange, he said, without looking up or interrupting his counting, the little things that bothered people like Winston. Or perhaps not so little? For a start there had been this coincidence that I had had a room in the same block as he, Peter Krasko. Then, did I know that Peter Kolchak had been seen with Walter Marshall, at the BBC Club of course, only about a week before Kolchak was arrested? And that they'd been overheard talking about Eastern Europe, where, coincidentally, Marshall was at that time about to go.

Krasko looked at Louise. She gave an almost imperceptible nod.

If I hadn't known about this, Winston had, Peter Krasko said, and from then on he'd had Walter Marshall followed. And that meant – he looked at Louise – that I had been seen talking to Walter at the Television Centre club. So our talk hadn't been quite as private as perhaps we'd supposed.

Krasko looked at Louise again. And again she nodded.

'So what with this and that, one thing and another,' Krasko said, 'all roads led to Brands Hatch, and – and all points north.'

He really was getting quite good with the colloquial.

Now – Krasko looked at his watch – he, we, really must go. In familiar territory, he led the way down the stairs. Just as he reached the door he felt in his pocket and put on a pair of dark glasses.

It was a small surprise. There was a bigger one outside in the little dark-windowed Mini that stood at the kerb. This time it was one of those cars that you couldn't see *into*. Krasko quickly got into a back seat. Louise opened a front door for me and then got into the driver's seat.

'Louise did more for me than I can say,' Krasko said over my shoulder as we drove off. 'She knew what Nina was doing. We just hoped that Nina would find out enough to help us more than she did before we got her out of the country.'

'We?' I said, as I glared at him over my shoulder.

He gave me that gentle look and said, 'I am sorry, my friend.'

We drove in silence till Krasko said, 'And Kolchak. He was more important than I'd supposed. There were these papers – I'm sure you know about them – that were recovered when Winston was shot. A whole file on Winston. Kolchak's file.'

I looked over my shoulder again. He'd taken some papers from his battered briefcase and was holding them up for me to see. I wondered where the hell he had got them, but I didn't say anything. He *must* be a double agent, I decided.

'*You're* even mentioned in this file,' Krasko said, as he put it back into his briefcase. 'You and Marshall.'

The lunch was a surprise. We didn't have it in a restaurant but in a little flat in West London. Louise prepared it for us. It was a nice lunch. She was charming. I envied Krasko. She was going out of my life, if she had ever been in it. Nina was dead. Jane was, to say the least, discouraging. Just now there seemed to be only my wife.

On an impulse, I went out to Heathrow with Krasko and Louise, to say goodbye. We went in the same dark-glazed Mini, and Krasko wore the same dark glasses whenever he was outside it. It was still a bit puzzling, but I'd got past caring.

After they had gone, I went to the bar. I'd been drinking far too much under all the recent stress, but with the pressure off at last I felt I deserved just a couple of celebratory drinks. As I called for the second I had a nostalgic memory of a now-dead colleague who at this very bar, about to fly out to New Zealand, had justified *his* second round with the reflection that you can't fly on one wing.

I counted the money that Krasko had given me and did a little sum on the counterfoil of my cheque book. If I wasn't extravagant there was still enough left for a holiday in Amsterdam.

Back in town, I was still overcome by a feeling of relief that it was all over. I turned the corner a few yards from my room, then stopped. A police car stood outside my door. Robson was at the wheel. The engine was running. A plain clothes man got out of the car and came towards me. Without apology or explanation, he took me by the arm.

'Where the *hell* have you been?' Robson asked, as the car took off. I got the impression that I should have known I was just on a kind of parole. 'The boss wants to see you,' he said. 'It's bloody urgent.'

It was an unpleasant interview. All about

Kolchak's file on Winston. The file was missing. As I was one of the few people who knew that there was such a file – and by the way, how *did* I know? – plain Mr Scott thought that perhaps I could help them with their, ah, inquiries.

I looked at my watch. Krasko, I thought, would be well on his way now to wherever eventually he was going. Did it matter a damn where he was, anyway, how far away or how near? I mentioned his name. Perhaps *he* could help with their inquiries, I said. I'd supposed, anyway, that he was one of them.

If Scott had been the kind of man who might jump up and down in his seat, I'm sure he would have done it then. But he just went a pale shade of purple and said that Krasko was not only *not* one of them – they didn't even know that he had been back in Britain.

In the end, as ungraciously as possible, they let me go. They didn't even offer me a ride back home. Well, it didn't matter: the pubs were open again by now, so I got back to Marylebone the slow, easy way.

I woke next morning far too late to go to Amsterdam, even if I'd wanted to go. Perhaps I'd go tomorrow. It was a possibility I was beginning to feel at home with. After two leisurely hours in The Old Rising Sun I sat in the little cemetery garden where I could see the sad little sculpture of the sad little boy, and with no effort at all I thought myself into a mood of the deepest melancholy. Then, still taking my time, I set out through the park and St John's Wood for my old home territory.

The way I was feeling it should have been autumn, but in the gardens along the canal and down the gentle slope of Warwick Avenue, from the pool at Little Venice to the tube station, the trees in their summer dresses were still a vivid green in the strong summer sunlight.

I remembered suddenly the plump old lady who had once sold flowers below the grey tower or St Saviour's Church. She had been there when I'd first surfaced from the underground all those years ago, looking for a flat to take my bride home to. And, the flat found, I had bought a single red rose from the old lady and taken it back to Jill.

It was red rose weather, and I was again going to see Jill, but there was no old lady selling flowers beneath the church tower – there hadn't been for years. I went on, past the hotels at the start of the crescent, and turned into Formosa Street. Outside the greengrocer's shop, just as I had expected, among the courgettes and peppers and mushrooms, I found what I wanted.

Straight away, holding the red rose in my hand as I turned back into the crescent, I felt a little foolish. And nervous, too. Silly to feel nervous when you were going to see your wife. Well, here was the flat. Jill must be at home: it was her kind of music, the new kind, that was coming out of the open windows.

I looked at the rose that I had bought for her, but it was Nina lying dead in a Berlin street I was thinking of. I put the rose in my buttonhole and looked at my watch. Ten minutes to opening time. Why rush things? I asked myself. I would just take a turn around the block. And I walked on.

This Large Print Book, for people
who cannot read normal print,
is published under the auspices of

THE ULVERSCROFT FOUNDATION